THE DARKEST
VALLEY

Rick Dewhurst

quotidian

Quotidian Books

Published by Quotidian Books
Duncan, BC

ISBN: 0-9867457-6-6
ISBN-13: 978-0-9867457-6-8

For the people of
Cowichan

*"Even though I walk
through the darkest valley
I will fear no evil
for you are with me..."*

Psalm 23

CHAPTER ONE

Qu'wut'sun. Warming your back in the sun. For thousands of years the first people lived in their warm land. The salmon river gave its life to them, and the forest supplied them with berries, plants, deer, and elk. But then the disease came. The Europeans came to Cowichan. They had a gunboat. And the illness came with them. The illness had many heads, white foreign heads, and they talked a different language and had strange ways. The *hwunitum* moved in and lived on the land, and then they took it for themselves. And then their church and government moved the children away to live in the residential schools, and the people remaining were given some land to live on, reserved for them. And the sickness spread. The sun still warmed the valley, but the first people's hearts grew cold. If only they could get back to being the people they were, then they would be a real people again. But how was that going to happen? There was too much confusion in the land, and too many white people, and too many of the first people had learned the ways of the *hwunitum*. They had learned their ways so well that the enemy was now within, and the damage to the first people's lives had been done. From the top of the mountain looking down at the valley you could not see the hatred that lived among the people. There were no banners that announced *Racism Simmering Here*. From the top of the mountain, you could see the ocean, and the river, and the forest, and the many houses with people living in them. From the top of the mountain, the valley looked peaceful, but greed and misery flourished down there, nurtured by the racism growing on both sides. And the question lingered. Whose land was it? From the top of the mountain it was easy to see that all the people down there lived in the valley together. But would they ever come together in their hearts? Was forgiveness and healing possible? And where was the Creator in all this? There had to be answers.

Jesse Thornton, editor of The Cowichan Leader, was parked on Boys Road, visualizing that clown up there again, the one who was hiding behind the dark clouds. He was the one who was responsible for keeping the spotlight burning in the sky. At least Jesse thought he was the one responsible. The clown that he imagined up there was the standard circus variety, with slap-happy feet, white face, polka dot suit, big red smile, and orange yarn for hair. Real funny. The kind who scared toddlers. But Jesse had yet to decide if that clown was the devil in disguise, or if he was the God he had known as a child, who later developed a twisted sense of humor. Either way, so far in this life the clown had not been a friend of his.

Jesse came down to earth and looked over at the tall maples that grew on the Cowichan Indian Reserve. They were tossing their spinners into the autumn breeze, a few of the higher flyers twirling above the cracked pavement and sailing over the high cedar fence to find their destiny in the White Man's trailer-park. Jesse was stalling. He'd been there for at least twenty minutes, and the heat the spotlight up there had generated through his windshield was beginning to cause beads of sweat to surface on his forehead. But he wasn't going to roll down the window. Not this time of year. The cool fall air might give him a chill, and then the itch would begin in the back of his throat, to be followed by a stubborn head cold that would stay there for two weeks. A cold was an excuse to drink rum, but she wasn't there anymore to offer the excuse to. He squinted up at the battle the dark clouds and the spotlight were waging. It looked like a draw.

Sure, the story had been his idea, but sitting there now, considering the barriers, he lacked the motivation to get out of his car. He knew that his wary publisher was opposed to stirring up the White Man-Indian controversy again, and he knew that the newspaper's advertisers wouldn't see any profit in it either. But what about his readers? Why not do it for them? Why not tell the truth for a change? The story had the potential to make a difference in the community, not to mention give him the opportunity to showcase his talent for investigative journalism. Maybe he would win an award. The setup was perfect. They lived in two separate worlds on opposite sides of Boys Road. On one side a collection of white, ordinary citizens, most of them retired, passing their time in their mobile homes, secure behind their tall cedar fence. On the other side, the Cowichan Indians suffering through their Reserve lives, having no use for White Man's time and waiting for those demanding clocks to stop, a nuclear war maybe. And after the White Man's world fell apart, they would have their valley back. But a war wasn't going to happen any time soon, not since that other barrier came down last year in Berlin. He also knew that in some ways this Boys Road fence between the races was more impenetrable than the Berlin Wall, that symbol of the Cold War that was now committed to history. Race was harder to breach than ideology, and in the Cowichan Valley most of the citizens wanted the race barrier to be reinforced, not taken down, and the war between the races to remain cold.

And what about those insightful questions he would have to ask? *How do you get along with the Indians across the road?* The retired folks would have an evasive answer of course: *"Why, they're Indians, aren't they, not like the ones we're used to though. We've been out here on the Coast nearly ten years now, since we left our farm on the prairies. Yep, that's right, nearly ten years now. You're from the newspaper, you say, well, you know you're*

3

spoiled out here. Why I remember back on the prairies it got so cold some winters your spit froze before it hit the ground, yes sir...."

And so on, an hour shot and nothing more said about the Indians across the road. No, there was nothing more to do on Boys Road today, because small-town newspaper people were expected to be polite and not get pushy. He had to live here, didn't he? In this valley people were acquainted with other people's business, so Jesse had to maintain respectability, have a good reputation. This wasn't Watergate. It was small-town, West Coast, Canada.

And what about the Indians? He knew he wouldn't get a straight answer from them, either. *How do you get along with your neighbors in the trailer park?* Or maybe load the question. *How do you get along with those retired white folks behind that tall fence, you know, the fence that blocks access to your river?* And they say, W*e have to go to town, have you got the time, sir?* And then they would wait for him, the editor of The Cowichan Leader, to go on his haughty way, having been addressed with respect and told to go to meet his ancestors both in the same breath, since to be called *sir* by the Indians around here was a secret insult.

There, it was decided. He had reached the logical conclusion. The proposed combatants were not going to cooperate with him, so he was justified in not doing the story. Why waste the time? Besides, the races here in the valley had frozen each other out for years. So why bother? There was nothing useful to dig up on Boys Road. What did four years of university and journalism courses and twenty years of experience have to do with fixing the world's problems? He was here to report the news, not make it. If he wrote the story, he would be the one to suffer, and for a bonus none of it would change. There would be a tiny ripple, maybe, and then calm. Racism liked to stay out of the public eye. It was happier that way.

No, there was nothing to be done. His liberal education came back to haunt. It wanted peace among the nations, one world united, justice for all, food for the hungry, and computers in every room. Spend quality time. But idealism was just part of the clown's comedy routine. And here he had been, the crusading editor, the peacemaker, about to fall for the practical joke, trying to do his part in bringing understanding between the races. There was no winning for him with that clown up there. Still, if it wasn't for his delusions of grandeur to get him motivated, he might never leave his apartment.

The dark clouds got pushy and covered the spotlight, but Jesse figured that the clown was still up there. He lit a cigarette, tossed the package onto the dash, and returned his lighter to share his shirt pocket with his walnut pen. The pen was a gift from his fiancé. She wasn't anymore, but she was five months ago. It was a good pen though. She bought him the pen to write poetry for her. Jesse couldn't make it do that. To him the idea had been terrifying. After the sixties revolution died, the poetry in him died too. Becky had tried to resurrect it, the two of them living together for two years and all those laughs. And then came the abortion. Defiant Becky, she had to have her way. But she couldn't make him write poetry. He had drawn the line there.

Jesse slumped behind the wheel and began to review his failed career again. Should he have taken that job on the city paper years ago and gone to the big time? That was what you were supposed to do after five or ten years of sucking on the small-town pump, after you learned something about the world and how to look busy and how to ask those insightful questions on the telephone. If you were any good, you moved up. You were expected to step up to better things. But he had been cautious. He had compared lifestyles and the cost of living in the city, and then there was that most important of all commodities, fear. There was no question that the thought of failure had something to do with it. So why not take the editor's job in Duncan in the beautiful Cowichan Valley? There was nothing the matter with that. A lot easier, too. Ambition was for believers, or for Yuppies. Too bad about that stock market crash though; too bad about the way those ambitious believers in prosperity lost their designer shirts in '87.

But now it was middle-age time, and he was still here in Duncan, and prickly hair was growing out of his ears, and his nose ran when he ate, but what was worse he seldom noticed or cared now. He lowered the rear-view mirror to take a look at his 44-year-old face. There were lines in the forehead, and the once dark brown hair had lines in it too, gray ones that each morning swirled down the shower drain with their younger looking companions. His short trimmed beard had a few stray gray ones, too. And what about the glasses? They had silver wire frames and were round, a tribute to the revolution that happened a long time ago, so long ago in fact that students now didn't know what a liberal education was, and what's more they didn't want to know. They had no frame of reference in which to put the concept of a liberal education. And he couldn't tell them about the glory days of a liberal university education for the masses, because he wasn't a frame of reference for them either. He was history, literally; the history department at the university now taught a course on the Counter Culture. He knew it did, because Becky had introduced him around to her young friends that first year when she went back to take her Master's degree. One party-night, he was humored as a curiosity when he delivered his rap about a liberal education for everyone, *you know, like they had back in the sixties!* Blank stares all around. Who would have thought obsolescence could have happened to him? After all, he was a special individual, he was unique. He was the center of it all, he had a destiny, or did everyone think that? Did everyone believe they were the center of it all, the one who would make a difference? Probably, which meant everyone was in for a big disappointment. But the way he figured it, the longer special individuals were able to put off realizing their insignificance the better. It only took Becky a little less than two years to discover Jesse wasn't that special. Then she ran away with her intellect, her new special man, a philosophy professor. Jesse had learned his lesson. He now hoped to find someone simpler, not an airhead, but maybe a kind person with fewer active brain cells to complicate the issue, maybe a small-town girl who liked it that way. He needed to find someone soon. His heart was shielded by his hard-nosed reporter's attitude and pacified by alcohol, but inside he was aching. He was middle-aged and lonely.

Outside the wind had stirred up a few discarded fast-food wrappers to blow against the fence. There was nothing else for him to do here. He turned the key in the ignition of his '75 Valiant, listened to the slant-six engine kick to life, and then leaning over the steering wheel he peered at the sky for a sign. The gathering dark clouds began to spit at him, speckling the windshield. Just what he needed, a sign from the clown upstairs confirming his decision to abandon the story. Jesse butted his cigarette in the ashtray. It was beginning to rain now, and he turned on the wipers before pulling off the shoulder and onto the road. He was not going to write the story about the good neighbors of the Cowichan Valley who lived on Boys Road. No, not today. He had a better idea. He would go down to Maple Bay, have a few beer, and watch the ocean get rained on. Yes, he had to cheer up; things weren't that bad. He would escape to the comfort of the pub for a few cold-ones. And, as for work, he would have to stretch the new, young, energetic reporter for more copy. Send her after the Boys Road racial scoop. That was the answer. Let her have the Pulitzer Prize. The younger ones were accustomed to abuse. They were competing for their share of the ever-dwindling North American pie. And to hell with them, too.

CHAPTER TWO

Pastor Tom Pollard liked his office dark. It made for a better praying environment. The only light in the room was sneaking in through the slits in the Venetian blinds, casting thin parallel lines onto the office wall and the framed print that hung there of the tribes of Israel encamped around the Ark of the Covenant. He often wondered, seated behind his desk, if his faith would have survived back then, or would he have been one of those who succumbed to worshipping idols?

An automobile horn sounded outside the window. Tom turned in his chair and parted the blinds to look out on the small-town streets of Duncan. The peaceful procession of vehicles, taking their turns at the four-way stop, had been broken by a cheating pickup.

It was beginning to rain.

Will Joseph sat in front of the pastor's desk, his hand propped under his chin. He was the first to break the silence.

"It seems like it's too far to go," Will said, his eyes focused on the floor. "It seems like it's another person who will be going and not me at all."

"Don't worry, you'll be fine," Tom said. "You won't be the only native there."

Will was about to continue expressing his doubts when the office door opened and Ruby Pollard leaned her head in.

"Busy?" she said, her thin figure following her head into the room.

"You know I'm never too busy for my better half," Tom said, standing to meet her with a kiss on the cheek. "Will and I were just talking about his plan to go to Bible College next year. But if you really want to know, I *was* busy earlier, busy feeling sorry for myself."

"Now you do know pastors shouldn't behave that way," Ruby said.

She mustered a laugh and eased herself into one of the donated worn wicker chairs. Tom turned and again found safety behind his desk. He looked over at Will who was preparing to make a break for it.

"I'll go downstairs and see if the furnace needs more wood," Will said.

"Don't go, Will," Ruby said. "We don't see you that often."

Will shrugged his broad shoulders and collapsed his wiry, six-foot frame into the other frayed wicker chair in the corner. He bowed his head, his dark brown eyes staring at the floor, his shoulder-length, straight black hair cowling his face. He waited for them not to need him anymore.

Tom noticed Ruby's complexion, and that persistent fear began to rise in his stomach. Before the cancer verdict her face had been creamy. Now it was pasty. And the few streaks of grey in her black hair had ceased being stylish highlights and were now marks of age.

"How was your appointment today?" Tom said.

He felt guilty. He had spent the morning at his Freedom Center instead of going with her to the clinic.

She nodded an understanding forgiveness to him and said, "Same as usual, you know, bottom line, there's nothing we can do, rah-rah and away you go."

"Please don't joke about it," Tom said.

Ruby sighed, and then glared at the floor. She looked tired, and angry, and disgusted with him. But Tom was thankful he had been spared the clinic. There was nothing for him to do there but suffer, like the kind of suffering he was compelled to preach about now. He was never much help to her at the clinic anyway. Besides, she was stronger than he was. She could handle it there by herself; he was hopeless there. Death was a different matter when it was part of his job. Burying people was impersonal. And besides, he buried Christians, and they were going to heaven, weren't they, so what was the problem? Sure, they would be missed by their families, and sure, a few of his close friends had made the final journey. But none of them had been Ruby.

"So then, it was quiet here today?" Ruby said.

"As busy as usual," Tom said.

Since Ruby insisted on forcing the issue of his underemployment, Tom decided to ridicule himself and his life's work, and save her the trouble.

"Old Phil was in," he said. "He's on the wagon again. He was here first thing, and by eleven he'd drained the coffee urn, and downed most of the sugar and coffee-creamer. Then he bounced off the walls for a while, wouldn't do any of the work around here I suggested he might do, and then he ran out to get the free Wednesday lunch at the psych ward."

Tom smiled at Will, looking for approval of his summary. Will was looking the other way.

"The church is really making an impact on his life," Ruby said.

Tom noticed a guilty smirk invade Ruby's face. He could see she now regretted kicking him, since he had already agreed to administer the punishment himself.

"I'm sorry," she said, staring at the pale blue wall, and then she looked over at Will. "So, anything else exciting?"

"You bet," Tom said. "A few of the regulars came at twelve sharp, slurped down their soup, pretended to listen to the sermon, and then left, except for little Fred, who hung around long enough to empty his bladder in the armchair beside the bathroom. He's probably back in front of the liquor store by now, holding up a wall and holding out his hat until he collects enough money for another bottle."

"It did smell a little more earthy than usual when I came in."

She looked again at Will. He refused to smile for her.

"I did the job with Mr. Clean," Tom said, continuing his theme of self-derision.

"Always the sacrificial servant, isn't he?" she said to Will.

Will squirmed.

Leaning forward, his elbows on his desk, Tom said, "So what *did* they say at the clinic, anything?"

"No, you know as well as I do they're not there to tell you anything. They don't specialize in information, you know that."

Glancing over at Will's bowed head, Tom said, "No, I didn't know I knew that."

Ruby said, "Well, I guess I should go home and do something. I only dropped in for sympathy. After all, this is a drop-in center, isn't it?"

Ruby looked to Will to verify her point. He managed to emit a condescending grunt.

"You're a good pastor, Tom," she said, smoothing the waters. "You've just taken a lousy assignment."

She looked at Will.

"I made my choices," Tom said.

"Now don't start telling me at this point that you think they were the wrong ones," Ruby said. "That would really disappoint me."

She stood and turned to leave.

"I only meant...."

"Never mind, I know. See you tonight at dinner. I'll burn some lamb chops for you."

"Don't be nasty," Tom said, rising from his chair to see her out.

Ruby stood and turned to look again at Will, to see if he would acknowledge her joke. Instead he got up with his head down and walked out the door.

"I'm sorry," she said to Tom, "I lied. You're getting stew again."

Resentment for dinner again tonight, Tom thought, as he opened the door for her. She touched his arm and then walked toward the Center's exit. Tom trailed behind her and again noticed the absence of the taut athletic strength that once graced her legs. A weak tentative step had displaced her vitality and threatened him with its suggestion of her impermanence.

From the main window of the Center, Tom waved and smiled to her as she got into her Tercel, and then he returned to his office and his chair, where he tried to convince himself that he should be comfortable with death by now. After all, death was coronation day, the day when Christians began their real life with God, when they were finally saved from this world. But what about him? Ruby was going to leave him here on this alien planet to fend for himself, and he had never been effective in his solitary fending. Of course God was here to help him. But God was more difficult to see and touch than Ruby. No, he wouldn't allow Ruby to die. He was not able to face life that way.

To halt his descent into the abyss, he let his mind begin to think its cold, detached thoughts. Of course he could get along without Ruby. And he would remarry. God would send him a second wife, and he and his new wife would have children. She would be young and attractive, but she would not have to be that attractive. He would not be that fussy in his middle-age. He would have a new wife, a pleasant one. They would have children, the ones he and Ruby never could have, after their first one.... Tom's eyes began to fill now, because he knew he could not start again. His shallow imagining of how his world might be after Ruby left for heaven was a flat, pretty picture that he knew God would not bother to paint for him. And now that his church was getting rid of him he would have nowhere to hang the forgery anyway. No. It was all too much. Even the thought of her death was too much for him to take. So would his faith be strong enough to pull him through after the actual loss of her? And if it was not, then who would he be when she died? Would he revert to what he had been before his conversion? No, he knew he would not fall back that far. And he knew who he would not be. He would not be a middle-aged man marrying a young wife and having children and carrying on the battle. He would never be that. He was too weak for that. His strength would be going with Ruby. She was the one who had always carried him. Life was impossible to face without her. And that is why he laid his head on his desk and cried like a little boy who was lost in a department store, and who had never had anything so frightening happen to him before in his whole life.

Will had made a successful escape to the basement where he was pretending to look after the fire in the furnace, and where he would not have to answer any of Pastor Tom's questions about how she looked today. They had been performing for him again. They did it every time. Put on an act for the Indian. They were good people, but he didn't like to be part of their phony scene. *We* needed him to stay. Will knew who *we* were. *We* were the two of them together, the pastor and his wife, using him as an audience for their *fighting cancer together* act. He avoided *we* as much as he could. Everyone knew she hated his drop-in Center. But the pastor was safe from criticism with the Indian in the room, because she wouldn't embarrass him in front of his convert and would pretend to overlook her husband's failing dream. He was disgusted with their polite game. He guessed they had too much time on their hands together at home.

Will poked at the fire through the door of the old furnace and stuffed in more alder to feed the glowing coals. He was tired of his role as the background person. And what was the good of trying to say something to ease their pain. He'd tried that before. They wouldn't hear him, and they wouldn't let him go either. He stared into the flames and wondered if there was really any place for a Christian Indian like him to go. He was the pastor's token Indian convert. He wasn't fooled. He tried to think better of himself and the pastor, but thinking that way didn't change anything much. He was still the pastor's token Indian convert. There was no way around that. Christian Indians were a hard breed to find in this valley, and he didn't take any comfort in being unique. He opened the door and threw in a few more lengths of alder. Lunch time was over. He had to get back to school.

CHAPTER THREE

Jesse parked in a stall beside the entrance to the Maple Bay Pub and leaned forward on the steering wheel. He looked out at the ocean and the rain, and paused to review the highlights of his life on the Mainland, where he had paid his dues in the newspaper business. There was that first job in Merritt, eager and energetic he was, and then there was Hope, where visions of the crusader faded, and then there was the one in Port Moody, when he began to drink too much. And then he balked when he had a chance at a big city job on the Vancouver Sun, and then away he ran to Vancouver Island. It was safer here, one of the better places to live because of the westerly wind. Any radiation would blow inland. But that survival advantage was insignificant now, since the threat of nuclear war had been reduced to near zero.

Inside the pub, Jesse grabbed a stool at the bar and ordered a draft. Slick black haired Benny poured, nodded at Jesse and then at the weather and then shook his head. Jesse didn't care about Benny's silent weather observations or for his bar-side manner. Jesse paid for the beer and remembered when you could get five of them for a dollar. He took a big swallow, and then looked into the bar mirror. He saw one of the local Maple Bay wives reflected in it. She was perched at the end of the bar, sipping. He ignored the furtive nod she sent in his direction, since it was intended for the man in a wet duffle coat sitting to Jesse's left. The man twitched, lowered his head, and began to poke at his ice cubes with his swizzle stick. Hanky-panky in Maple Bay.

Jesse lit a cigarette, blew the smoke toward the mirror, and analyzed the face staring back at him. It was the face of a

Teddy Bear type. Women loved Teddy Bears, and they knew Jesse was one of those, no matter how hard he tried to project his tough reporter image. But there was more to Cowichan Leader editor Jesse Thornton than being a cuddly bed companion. He took a big gulp, looked deeper into his reflection and confirmed to himself that behind the counter culture glasses stared the sharp, blue eyes of survival.

Jesse nodded to slick Benny for another beer. Benny returned the nod, put his cigarette in the ashtray, and tapped the draft. Jesse watched the foaming head rise and slop over the rim. He tossed more money onto the bar, and then the man in the duffle coat, a local accountant and one of the town's respectable citizens, slid off his stool, head down, and exited. The wife of the Bay's garage owner hopped down and left through the other door, her wrinkled, pink raincoat rustling and her brunette fluffy hair showing its age. With the two of them now off to seek their mutual fortune, the only other customers in the pub were Sig and Wilma, sitting at a table near the window. Jesse decided to pay them a visit. He took his change and his glass, and on his way over to say hello he smirked at the decor. On the walls were blown-up historical photographs of the Cowichan Valley and its early settlers. Editor Jesse sneered at the one picturing horses pulling buggies on Duncan's main drag. The caption read, "Station Street in the late 1900s." He had told Benny six months ago to tell the owner that the world was just now entering the late 1900s, but nothing had been done. Nobody cared about editing anymore.

The man in the red blazer saw Jesse coming and said, "Come on, Jesse, sit down, take a load off your feet."

Wilma, the platinum beside Sig, forced a half-smile and tucked her bare arms farther down under the synthetic fur draped on her shoulders, and then she poked one hand out to grasp her Margarita.

"Why aren't you back at the dealership pushing the new models, Sig?" Jesse said to the ocean outside, before sitting to face the car salesman and his sweetheart.

"Don't you think it's about time you gave me some business," Sig said, flashing his caps. "Your Valiant's a death trap."

"A classic, you mean," Jesse said, turning to Wilma to receive her appreciation of his glib response, and wondering if she saw him through her blue tinted contacts as a John Wayne type or as a Teddy Bear wearing a ten-gallon hat. No. She wasn't fooled. He took a few healthy swallows of draft. What was he doing here? And who were these people? And why was he sitting down with them? Who were they to him? He didn't really know them. And what was there to talk about? Sig talked a lot because that was his job. And Wilma did not talk a lot because that was her job.

"Ooh, look," Wilma said, losing her cool and shooting her hand out to point at a fifty-foot, white yacht leaving the marina, her fur sliding down to reveal a bare white seductive shoulder.

"Another drink?" Sig asked Wilma, knowing he couldn't sell enough cars in twenty years to buy a big white boat, and continue to meet his alimony and child support payments, not to mention what he had to shell out every month to pay the mortgage on his condominium, which Wilma had decorated in late-twentieth century vacation souvenirs grabbed and brought home at least twice a year from every trendy resort on the globe that honoured Visa. Jesse studied Wilma and Sig and realized he was witnessing the emancipation of the small-town citizen. They were cosmopolitan tour junkies now, their innocence swapped for credit cards. He wouldn't be surprised if they smoked dope in the privacy of their hot tub. Come to think of it, he did know them after all.

"Thanks, Hon," Wilma said, recovering from her outburst and shifting her attention back from the yacht's wake to her life source.

"How about you, another beer?" Sig said to Jesse.

Salesman Sig's voice and smile were offering Jesse a beer, but the other Sig, the one who had no use for intellectual types, no matter how low they were on the totem pole, was in control of Sig's eyes and forehead, which were screaming at Jesse to go away and let his inner-man forget for a while that he had to flap his tongue and flash his caps every day at a furious rate to keep the whole show going. Sig loved his Wilma, but if she were to become too expensive to operate, Jesse suspected Sig would find himself an economy model.

"I've got to get back to the office," Jesse said, letting Sig off the hook.

Sig smiled, "Come in real soon and we'll get you into something that's at least dependable."

"Sure," Jesse said, standing and downing the dregs, "and have a nice day."

It was a nice day in the pub all right, a couple of sexual adventurers cheating on their spouses, and Sig and Wilma, fulfilling each other's needs in their mutually beneficial business deal. Jesse wanted something better. He still hoped there was such a thing.

Walking toward the door, he ignored the Cowichan Valley pictorial history on the walls of the Maple Bay Pub. He was out of sneers for the day. Instead, he was conscious of how he felt in his clothes. Why was he wearing blue jeans and a tweed sports jacket? Why did he always wear that? Who was he trying to be? His hair was too long for a middle-aged man, wasn't it? But what was a middle-aged male Baby Boomer supposed to look like? Jesse was too young to be as old as he was now. When he went to the movies he identified with the hero, but that just wasn't so anymore. He could be the father of the Top Gun now. And why was he wearing these tight blue jeans? And his jacket tugged under his arms, and his sagging gut strained his lower shirt buttons and drooped over his belt. Did women notice his lard now? And did his ancient notion of *cool* now look foolish to the younger ones? But what if he did look foolish? So what, why get into shape? Jesse exited the pub, grunted at the rain, and climbed into his car. He wouldn't take up jogging for anyone. What was so sexy about sweat? No pain, no brains. Man, was he ever in a mood today.

He turned the ignition key and looked over at Saltspring Island across the bay. A nice place to retire some day, but would he make it that far? He shook his head. What had gone wrong? How could middle-age have happened to him? Where had the years gone? He remembered that first black and white television in his family's living room, and all that moral, homey programming and then later there were those American leaders being shot, and then there was the man on the moon, and then students being shot, and helicopters flying from the roof of the US Embassy, and then a car salesman giving the peace sign with both arms raised before getting into a helicopter, and then there was a Me Generation malaise and hostages and then pride again and cowboy boots for eight years. But that was just American time. Why did he have to keep time by them? Canadian time wasn't that boring, was it?

Time. That was the problem. Jesse shifted his Valiant into drive and pointed the nose toward Duncan. The rain had stopped. Clocks. That was it; clocks were the problem with time. They were round and deceptive. Time was never intended to go in circles. Unless, of course, you looked at the year as a cycle, like a race track, where spring was at the starting gate and winter was at the finish line, and then you went around again. But that was too tiring. What you needed was a straight stretch, so you could see the total distance of the decades. Calendars were no good either. You had to get a new one every year. What the world needed was one whole stretch of time, so you could look at it and get a better idea of the whole thing. Stretch it out around the globe. Put it on the news every night. If it was the year 2000, for instance, the linear hand would be ticking through Chicago. That was what was needed, Jesse thought, his Valiant's tires swishing through the periodic puddles on Maple Bay Road, a linear clock. And have a deadline. A real deadline. The human race either smartened up by 2050 or the clock said Bombay, and bang it was all over. That would give people something to think about, something to shoot for. Once the clock hit the coast of India the whole globe would send its sweaty odor through the known universe. A doomsday bomb at the end of time. Hot stuff.

Yes, time was an excellent topic for an editorial. Time. Time the troublemaker. Centuries were a problem too. In order to convert from centuries to the right year you always had to go back one hundred. The correct years were always a hundred behind the number of the century. No matter who you were you had to stop and figure it out. But he had the solution. In the year 2000, instead of calling it the beginning of the twenty-first century, you would call it the twentieth century. Then it would be all square. From then on the hundreds would line up with their centuries. And for previous years, move all the centuries back one. Then they would all come in line. You could dump the first twentieth century in its entirety into a black hole. If it had to be referred to at all, you could call it the first twentieth century that no longer had a slot in time. It would be a black hole that sucked in all the evil. Gone and forgotten. Jesse would write an editorial and circulate petitions. He knew that if people were anything like him they hated having to think of the century and then move back a hundred in their mind. Tedious and annoying, and a waste of time. Yes, people just hated it. He would be famous. He would be the man who eliminated all those future headaches that, without his genius, would have been suffered by students, teachers, and professors – not to mention the agony of the common man who got his occasional fill of history on TV. Jesse's destiny was now clear in his mind. He would be one of the few remembered from the nonexistent first twentieth century. And he would be a shoo-in for the Nobel Prize in Mathematics. And for good measure he would be knighted by the Queen.

The beer had hit the spot. He lit a cigarette, opened the air vents and contemplated nurturing a new image for himself. He would buy a hat. That was what he needed now, a man of his age. A hat would give him a feeling of completion. His father had worn a flat cap and had informed him one winter that wearing a hat kept your feet warm because it stopped the heat from escaping out of the top of your head. Scientific stuff.

Jesse pulled into his reserved parking place in front of The Cowichan Leader. He opened the glove box and removed the flask. Pretending to search the floor of the car for something, he took a swig, and then another, before sliding it into his inside jacket pocket. Then up his head came, reading his watch. It was three o'clock. Just enough time before dinner to write a few town council briefs, growl at the help, and start on his incisive editorial. And, on second thought, he would forget about the Nobel Prize for this week. Maybe he would write something moral and just on the environment. You could always do that these days. He opened his car door, climbed out and surveyed the facade of The Cowichan Leader. Its external motif was washed-out pink. No wonder he couldn't think in sharp, black-and-white type anymore. He climbed the stairs, grasping the railing. Yes, he would give them hell in his editorial this week, he thought, pushing the swinging door open. Acerbic, that's what he would be. And he would throw that word into it for good measure.

CHAPTER FOUR

Will had stopped at the Center on his way home from school and had made himself useful by feeding the furnace. He liked to sit in the basement because it was a quiet place to study scripture. He was reading the Book of Daniel, where Daniel translated for King Belshazzar the meaning of the handwriting on the wall. The second line of the inscription stood out. *You have been weighed on the scales and found wanting.* Will resisted the temptation to feel guilty. Why should he feel guilty? That scripture had nothing to do with him. He wasn't King Belshazzar. And as far as he could tell so far, everyone was found wanting. The church, the Indians, the government, all fell short. Being found wanting was a big club. Everyone was a member. You paid your dues by being a human. He was in that club for sure, but where did he belong here in the Cowichan Valley. His people called him an apple. Red skin but white inside. But how was that his fault? He'd been brought up off the Reserve. His mother was white, and his dad, Big Doug Joseph, was a rebel, an Indian who didn't take any nonsense from anyone. He worked in logging as a faller his whole life and had made good money. They'd lived in a nice house in a middle-class subdivision. But these days, since his mother died, his dad was going back to the old ways. He was going to the Longhouse more. And Will knew that the changes in his dad were going to spell trouble for him, an apple Indian. His dad was moody now at home. And after their mother died, his older sister hadn't liked the way his dad was behaving and had left and gone to the mainland. Their mother had made sure his sister had gotten a good education, and now she was over in Vancouver working as a nurse. And now he was supposed to go there too. But something told him that the trip wasn't going to be so easy. Sure, he was going to enroll in the Bible College, but did he belong there? Did he belong here? And what about the church? Did he belong in it? Pastor Tom said he did, but he was pretty sure not everyone was so happy having him there. He felt like he was wandering around on the outside, still found wanting, and lost.

Will heard the basement door open, and he saw Pastor Tom's legs at the top of the stairs.

"Are you down there, Will?" Tom called.

"Yeah, I'm down here."

"How's the fire doing?"

"About as good as usual," Will said.

"That bad, eh? You know you don't have to think it's your duty to keep it going."

"I like it down here," Will said. "It keeps me humble. Just the way us good Indians should be."

"We don't deserve you, Will."

Pastor Tom's legs left and the door closed.

What did he mean, *we don't deserve you*? Will wondered if that was one of those Freudian slips psychologists liked to talk about. Not that Christians believed anything that Freud had to say about anything. But Will knew that his dad didn't think he deserved him; he was pretty sure of that. His dad had done a lot for him, and now Will had become a Christian. His dad had provided everything he needed growing up, except a sense of who he was and where he belonged. But maybe everyone was like that, no matter what color they were. He was an Indian as far as the white people were concerned, and as for the Indians, they weren't sure he was one of them. His mother, who was Catholic, had sent him to the private Catholic elementary school so he could get a good start on his education. His young life had been good. He was treated well by the teachers there, some of them nuns. And then in the higher grades, when he went to public school, he told his mother he didn't want to go to the Catholic Church anymore. He wasn't one of them, either. That made his mother sad. And then later when he was struggling with everything in his life he met Pastor Tom at the Center. Now he was a born-again Christian and still didn't seem to fit in. And to make matters worse, just lately he could feel the pull of his Indian blood calling him to come home where he belonged. That reminded him that he had to start heading home now because he wanted to take his favorite route along the river to do some thinking and praying, out in the open air.

He stood, closed his Bible, opened the furnace door, looked at his Bible, set it down, and then threw in a few rounds of alder. The fire in there wasn't burning as hot as it would be burning in hell. And then he had a comforting thought. At least he knew he didn't belong down there.

CHAPTER FIVE

Ruby Pollard sat at the table in her California-style kitchen, staring out the window at the gray day. The kitchen was one of the main reasons they had bought the house. Its windows faced the large sundeck built on the cliff overlooking the Cowichan River and their half-acre of maple, fir, and hemlock trees. She loved this room, and she loved to go down to the river on sunny days and absorb the shades of green and lose herself in the light that sparkled on the water. This past summer Tom had twice gone with her and helped her down the steep shale bank. The walks had been a great concession on his part, for he had never warmed up to nature, even though she had encouraged its appreciation many times during the last twenty years. But would she be taking walks by the river next year, even if Tom were agreeable? She doubted that. She doubted whether next year would be coming for her at all, since her body had decided to create evil cells that were crowding out the good ones and whose goal was to crowd her out of an existence.

But what was the cause? There were theories. She knew all the theories. Was it her emotions that had ordered her body to pervert the growth of its cells? Or had it been her body's exclusive idea? Her mother had experienced a cancer scare, and then after her father died, the cancer came back and took her away. Was the disease programmed into Ruby's genes? If that was true, then her emotions and her memory and her mind had nothing to do with the fact that her body was preparing her for a middle-aged departure from the land of the living. But it was more amusing to think that her emotions were the cause. This diagnosis gave her mind more to play with. And

Ruby's mind liked to play. Such playful thoughts floated her above the discomfort and provided entertainment.

It was wonderful fun to speculate on the tangled relationships shared by her spirit, soul and body. She believed the Bible, and the Bible said people had three parts. And she loved to pick herself apart and play one part off against the other. It was a way to objectify her terminal condition. What else was there to do at times like this? To begin with, her spirit had been renewed when she was converted, but her soul and body were less eager to follow along. Her mind, will and emotions, which comprised her soul, resisted her spirit, and they found a willing ally in her body. But sometimes her will would join her spirit, and she would will herself to stay in the Kingdom of God, but her emotions would drag on that will. They were angry for what God had done to her only child years ago. He was born but never took a breath. According to her emotions, that was not the way her God was to behave. And despite her mind's understanding of the Bible, most of the time her mind agreed with her emotions. No, that was no way for her God to behave. Jesus healed people. He did not kill them. Of course her spirit was above all this mundane nonsense her soul peddled. Her spirit's desire was to be with God. Her spirit knew that her son was with God, and that they would be reunited in eternity, but that was not yet good enough for the rest of her. She was tied to the earth in this body. So her body was taking the punishment. Her spirit and soul were having an internal disagreement, so her body got sick and punished her whole miserable self. That was one way to look at it. But on the other hand, she thought, her cancer might just be the result of heredity.

He would have been nineteen now. And of course there would have been others, a brother or sister. A daughter would have been a challenge. But after her son was born dead there were no others. Barrenness. It was a punishment. And she was bitter. Her bitterness was a big black ball that she brought into the light for occasional examination, like it was someone else's pain. Her objectivity could understand how bitterness might make a person sick, but that was not the case with her, because she understood her bitterness so well, since her bitterness could be seen and examined. But she did know that she should have gotten rid of the burden years ago, instead of dropping it back into that compartment it shared with her growing resentment over an unfulfilled life, soon to end, playing second fiddle to her husband's ministry. Of course she knew she shouldn't think that way; she should be gracious and forgiving and supportive despite her suffering. But why couldn't he understand? But no. It was useless finding fault with him; what was the use? His flock had always come first. She had many times in the past wished they would be stricken with anthrax.

So why had God allowed Satan to kill her child? That is if there was such a person as Satan; the Bible said there was, so Ruby knew there just had to be. Maybe it was Satan that was killing her now too. But she was educated, and sophisticated; how could she believe there was a being called Satan? Nonsense. But the Bible said there was. So Satan had killed her child and now he was killing her too. But why was God allowing him to do that? No, that could not be right. That way of looking at it was all too complicated. It was her emotions; they were making her body sick. Or maybe it was just heredity. Yes, heredity was the safest. Why blame herself or God -- or Satan for that matter? Her sickness was the result of her having been given a loaded chamber in genetic, Russian roulette.

She looked again at the newspaper in front of her. She had to look at it again. Then she began to sob, because the headline said a three-year-old girl in Vancouver had been missing from her home for two days. The worst was feared. It was always the worst they feared. She tried to imagine what the child's mother must be feeling, and then she tried to form an image in her mind of her own mother and then cried some more because she couldn't see her mother at all. She often tried to bring her mother back, the way she had been when Ruby was a girl. But she couldn't. When had those times been, the ones she was supposed to remember that would bring her mother back into sharp focus? She had to do that. If she couldn't, who would, and then what would her mother have been? There was no one else to remember her. Her father was gone. She an only child, and now no children, and then what? She had to remember those good times she had with her mother in order to bring her back, to give her substance, otherwise where would her mother be? Her spirit would be in heaven, of course, wouldn't it? But where would the flesh and blood mother she knew as a child here in this world be, if she couldn't remember her and see her image or give them a good time together in her mind. But she couldn't. There had been good times, ones they had shared together; there had to have been. She knew they had to exist somewhere. But instead there was a blank space in her mind where those good times and her mother should have been. And now Ruby had cancer, and most of the time that was all she could think of, no matter how much she tried to become a child in her mind again and make her mother come alive.

At the kitchen table with the newspaper in front of her, Ruby cried for her missing mother, and the sobs and choking and groaning coming from her little girl inside were bringing on more pain from the growing cells that were programmed to replace her life, and push her outside to where her mother had gone, and leave her corpse choking on the black blood and bile that she knew would come tearing up from her wrenching body when the end came. She feared that's what would happen, because a few years ago one of the women in the church had died that way. She knew that was what happened because Tom came home the morning after he had helped the woman die all night, and he told her that was what the woman's body had done. Ruby stopped sobbing and went over to the counter, where she pulled some tissues from the box to mop up the mess she had made of her face. She saw her reflection in the glass of the microwave oven and wondered how long it would take for her head to cook in there. Suicide by agitation. She knew it had been done though, because everything had been done. *Twice as absorbent,* she said, holding up the box of tissues and giving the product her endorsement to her reflection on her microwave glass television. *They soak up your life twice as fast, and at a fraction of the price of your old tissues. Yes, if you have to go, you should drain your lives with this new improved brand.*

She returned to the table and fell into the chair. What a mess it all was.

CHAPTER SIX

Tom sat at his desk in his office of his Freedom Center, skimming through the material that had been handed around at last Thursday's meeting of the Duncan Ministerial. He had stuffed the pain of Ruby's visit in that numb place he had created to care for it during his quest for daily survival. The evangelist, Chester Thomas, was coming December 4th. The biographical notes described a man who had been around for many years and seen it all. The ministers of the Cowichan Valley had agreed two months ago to bring Thomas in for a mid-week crusade, to stir the hearts of the saved and the unsaved alike. Nobody at the ministerial meeting had been talking revival, but that was the motive of the Pentecostal ministers, although they were stifling their enthusiasm in deference to both the conservatives and the liberals, who had only agreed to the crusade in order to be conciliatory. Besides, for them it would be a minor event. After all, nothing apocalyptic ever happened at an evangelistic crusade. Sure, a few people would get themselves *saved*, and there would be rumours of healings, but overall the event would not generate too much instability. The wave of zealousness would surge, hang over the heads of the Cowichan Valley's church leaders and then be dashed on the wall of religious tradition and everyday Christianity, letting everyone off the hook.

Tom tossed the evangelist's life into the out-basket and turned in his swivel chair to look out through the slats of the dusty Venetian blinds. There was a lot of activity on the street in the cool autumn wind. He did not consider himself much of a prophet, but he could predict what the majority of Duncan's citizens would say when they heard that an evangelist was coming to the Cowichan Valley: *Another con artist, they're all in it for the money.* The secular world had enough ammunition stockpiled to fire for eternity. But there was too much pain growing in Tom now for him to worry about the predictable noises that would come from the townsfolk. And Tom was even less concerned about the sniping going on inside the Cowichan Valley church among the different divisions of what was supposed to be the same army. He knew that the members of the ministerial had agreed in public that Chester Thomas should come, but he also knew that dissenting opinions circulated each Sunday among the Cowichan Valley's individual congregations. But what was that to him anymore?

Politics. That was what the church was all about, and power and prestige, and preaching a message affluent North America could accept. But if he were to preach the kind of message he wanted to preach, which for the last few months he had been attempting to do, no one would want to join. Preaching the true gospel would be suicidal, which for him it had been. Suffering and sacrifice took a back seat to success and riches. Come join the church and suffer and make sacrifices. Sure. Preach that part of the gospel and your career was finished, which for him it was, here in Duncan anyway. To be successful you had to advertise the church as just a little different from the world but in general the same. Come and join, it's like a club, don't you worry about reading the Bible or doing what it says, there are so many interpretations anyway. *Jesus Please Us*, was the new slogan. The popular church specialized in picnics and pot-lucks and building bigger, fancier sheep sheds to attract more goats. That was the church that was being merchandised today. Watering down the gospel was required to suit the spiritual tastes of those who lacked passion, those who desired to play safe but wanted to look righteous in the eyes of the community because they managed to get out of bed on Sunday morning. A lukewarm attitude toward the church made Tom gag. If people were going to sin then why didn't they just fly at it full bore, but if they were going to choose the way of the Cross why didn't they do that with the same intensity? Most in the church chose to straddle the fence. But that wasn't supposed to matter to him. His job description said that he had to be the caring, understanding pastor of the flock, no matter what level of commitment they were willing to make. But the pain that was growing inside him was causing resentment in his pastor's heart, even though he knew that it was his duty to nurture the sheep, not resent their weaknesses.

He had realized part of his dream though. He was operating a street mission that ministered to the lost souls of the Cowichan Valley and to the poor and to the transients. But now here he was, his future uncertain, sitting behind his desk in the sergeant's office of the dilapidated former RCMP building, which the church had leased for his street ministry after the RCMP vacated and moved to their new modern headquarters. Yes, here he was all right. But what was he waiting for? Armageddon? All things considered, he thought, the end might come as a welcome relief.

He glanced around at his dingy pale blue office, and then stared out at his fellow citizens again. There weren't as many problems out there wandering the streets as there were in the big city. The police enforced town council's policy of keeping the transients moving on. There would be no youth hostels established here; keep those young derelicts moving on to the larger urban centers. After all, Duncan was a small town, there wasn't enough space here to allow vagrants to spoil the view. *Keep the tramps and bums from burdening the church.* That was how one eloquent local cleric had put it during a recent ministerial meeting. One would have thought the church was some kind of charity organization, instead of the pleasant middle-class club God intended it to be. Tom was now positive that the essential thing wrong with the church was the people. And since the church was the people, then there wasn't much right with it except for the Gospel message, which was being spread somehow by its unholy messengers. Why would anyone want to join a group of people who most often treated their brothers and sisters in the faith worse than the people in the world treated one another? It was obvious to him that God had to be the one who was drawing people into His Kingdom – right under the noses of the Pharisees.

And now he had been at it five years in this town and the elders in his church were tossing him out. He had built the church, and now they were going to replace him with one of their own, one who would fall more into line with their way of thinking. He had given spiritual birth to many of them, nurtured and fed them, and now when they thought they were grown-up, they were going to disown him and lock him out of his own house, the one he had struggled to build, the one he had held together by giving himself at the expense of everything else - including Ruby. She was the one who had suffered the most. His failed ministry had been the hardest on her.

Through the blinds, Tom saw the mayor, Mike Stout, exiting the hardware store across the street. The mayor was stout all right, and tall. In his red plaid shirt and logger's boots he was playing the role of the mountain-man mayor. Stout knew what appealed to the voters in a mill town. But the mayor didn't believe there was any overriding force governing the universe. Tom knew this because one evening the good mayor had let Tom in on the secret. When he and Ruby first arrived in the Valley five years before, they were invited to the mayor's house for a small dinner gathering. They had just returned from California, back to the Cowichan Valley, the scene of his rebellion, where he had been a bartender and a hippie when he and Ruby first met in 1970. And Ruby had been a school teacher then, and a devil for punishment, until she got converted by the Jesus Freaks on a visit home to Anaheim, and then she returned to Duncan and tugged him into the Kingdom too. But the dinner at the mayor's house was not intended to be a welcoming dinner for them. The mayor had summoned them to his house and to his table to tell them his major revelation: *There was no overriding force governing the universe.* But Tom was to learn later that the mayor, despite his superior understanding of the cosmos, served his political interests nonetheless by rising early every Sunday morning, so that he and his charitable-causes wife could attend the meeting of the largest denomination in the Valley. Of course, to the mayor, it was just another meeting. And meetings were the mayor's best thing.

Tom closed the blinds and turned back to his desk. He should pray. That was the thing a pastor should do when trials came along. But he couldn't. He couldn't talk to Him. His congregation was going to replace him with one of their own, Elder John Baker, until they could find a new pastor, and he still couldn't talk to Him. And he wouldn't fight them either. If they wanted him gone, he didn't want to stay. The eldership had been against his street ministry from the start, although they pretended to agree in the beginning because he was the pastor and they were yet unsure of their power. But now that they had been successful in their rebellion, the Center would soon be remembered as the foolish indulgence of the former pastor. And in the meantime they were not going to tolerate any more of his messages on *taking up the cross* either. He hadn't even got warmed up yet, and already he had become too salty for their religious tastes. There he had been, the proverbial hypocrite, preaching the true gospel to them, when he couldn't even speak to its Author. No, he couldn't pray to Him. Why should he? Look what He was allowing. Ruby was dying of cancer. No, that wasn't the way God should behave. He leaned his elbows on his desk, pressed his chin into his fists, closed his eyes, and tried to think of nothing.

CHAPTER SEVEN

Will stood near the White Bridge on the Reserve side of the Cowichan River, tossing rocks into the fast flowing current. He found one that was the perfect size and threw it all the way across to the other side. It clacked on a boulder beside the small sandy area where some of the white folks came in the summer to cool off in the river when it was low. But the river was pretty high right now and the cold wind blew in his face. He had a pretty good throwing arm but not as accurate as some of his Indian brothers who fished with spears. They were skilled at spearing the salmon that came up the river to spawn. In fishing season they would have plenty of salmon to eat, or to smoke, or to sell in town. Will had tried spearing them when he was younger, but he wasn't much interested. His life didn't depend on spearing fish. There had always been lots of food at home.

Will looked over at the White Bridge and saw again the same white sedan driving over it with the three men inside pretending not to look his way. Will was pretty sure they were sizing him up in order to find the best time, and the best way, to grab him. It wasn't his imagination either, unless the three men in the white car just liked to drive around pretending not to look at people. But there was nothing he could do about them spoiling his time to be alone by the river. He had come to find some peace so he could think clearly about the choices he had to make about his future, and now all he could think about was being *grabbed*.

"Hey, Will. You're not thinking about jumpin' in, are ya?"

The voice was coming from a pack of five of his schoolmates walking across the bridge, heading for their homes in Eagle Heights. He sure didn't need them around right now, either.

The same voice said, "If you need some help, let us know. You know how much we like to throw Indians in the river."

The voice was coming from Larry Wright. Larry liked to hear himself talk. His friends liked to hear him, too.

Will's first thought was to ignore Larry, but on second thought he decided he would play along and pretend to be a good Indian, the kind who danced for the white man. He looked up at the sky and began to chant in deep guttural sounds and then he began to move in the Coast Salish way, hunched over, his head down, and his feet hopping from one to the other to the beat of his people. He closed his eyes and hoped Larry and his buddies would go away. He also hoped that he would not fall into the river and make their day.

"Hey, look, the Indian's dancin'," Larry yelled. "Did you know, guys, that Will's a Christian Indian now, one of those born agains? Why don't we go down there and see if he can walk on water?"

Will didn't like the sound of that. It put him off his dance. He stopped and looked up and over, and there they were, coming down to see him. If his dad had been there now he would be fine, but his dad wasn't there, so he would have to deal with the situation himself. This kind of thing wasn't new, though. The Indian kids and the white kids had a quiet dislike for one another, mostly inherited from their parents. And sometimes, like right now, it would come out into the open, and the Indians usually ended up on the wrong end of the stick. But at the moment he had no time to analyze the racial situation any further because the five of them were nearly in his face.

"You think you're smart, eh, Will," Larry said, "dancin' around like that, makin' fun of us?"

The five of them were now surrounding him, and it looked

like Larry was about to use his six-foot, 220 pound frame to do something stupid. But doing stupid things came natural to Larry. He was just that kind of white guy.

As senseless as the idea was, Will decided he would try to change the subject.

Will said, "You guys ever do any fishing in the river?"

"Listen to him," Larry said. "Do we do any fishin' in the river?"

Will's question had confused Larry, and passing the question along to his buddies failed to get a response. They looked to one another and then back to Larry for guidance.

"Yeah, you know," Will said, "with a fishing rod and bait."

"You don't have to explain to us how to fish," Larry said. Larry's face was beginning to redden. "You're a smart Indian, aren't ya." And to his buddies Larry said, "Will's on the honor roll. He thinks he's better than us, don't ya."

"You're starting to turn red," Will said. "Pretty soon you'll be looking like one of us."

Larry's right-hand bully, Ned Jones, said, "Punch him out, Larry. What are you waiting for?"

"I'm goin' to let him squirm a bit first."

"He's not doing any squirming," Ned said.

"That's 'cause he's a half breed, and his white half ain't as chicken as his Indian half."

Will was now tired of the situation he was in. There was nothing new or unique about it. It was just life for him around here.

Will said, "I didn't know you could figure things out so good, Larry. You're the one who should be on the honor roll."

"Come on, we're wasting time," Ned said. "Punch his face in."

Will could see that Larry was about to do just that when he saw the three men who had been cruising in the white sedan appear above them on the top of the river bank. They just stood there. They were big, and they didn't look happy. Will's five attackers saw them too and started to nudge each other and shuffle their feet.

"I guess we'll be seeing you guys later," Will said. "It was nice of you to come by and encourage me in my time of need."

Larry and Ned and the other three decided to save their fight for another day.

"This isn't over," Larry said.

"I don't think it will ever be over," Will said. "Not for me at least."

Larry shook his head and sputtered, "You people never make any sense." To his gang, he said, "Let's go."

The five of them hurried along the riverbank and then climbed up and over as far away from the three men as they could get without having to go under the bridge. Back on the bridge and now safe, Larry yelled, "Dirty Indian." The sound of their laughter continued as they disappeared out of sight, recounting to one another the great victory they had just achieved, baiting the Christian Indian.

Will turned and looked up at the top of the river bank and saw only space where his rescuers had been standing. He thought it was kind of them to keep him from getting beaten up. They had saved him from the white bullies, but only so they could do the job right and save him from his white Christian blood. He knew that no matter what he did, he was in for a lot of trouble. Both sides were competing for a piece of him, but in no way did that make him feel special.

CHAPTER EIGHT

Ruby fingered the raw stewing beef on the butcher block and began to slice off the fat. Tom liked his meat lean. Bored with the chore, her mind decided to pass the time by observing a scene from last April. She was on a gurney, waiting for the operating room orderly to wheel her in for one of those clever colonoscopies. That's when it happened. God flooded her with his power as if to reassure her that everything would be all right, which it did not turn out to be, at least from a human perspective, since the discovery of a growth in her colon wasn't to her a positive outcome, but then God looked at such matters from another perspective, she knew. And there she was in the operating room and the power of God was flowing through her so that she couldn't separate her fingers or toes and the operating room nurse was alone with her and she wanted to share with her what was happening and maybe touch her so she could feel the power too, but all she managed to gush was *Wow, the power of God*. The puzzled nurse looked at her, but then realized it was the Demerol and Valium beginning to work, and then the puzzled nurse looked at her again knowing that she hadn't had any yet.

Ruby mused over the hospital scene and laughed to herself about the nurse's stunned response and seeing herself there on the gurney, careless and glowing, under the operating room's bright lights. She dropped the beef into the pot and shot two squirts of Worcestershire Sauce at it. The surgeon told her beforehand that they liked to keep the patient semi-conscious when they went for their little look-sees. They preferred that the patient was able to cooperate with them during their cozy time together. And then she remembered the surgeon telling her to hold on, and then a distant sharp pain. Snip. And she saw herself stupefied by the effects of the Valium and the Demerol, trying to make sense of the round spongy growth in the jar. It turned out to be benign. She dodged the bullet that time. The next time she didn't, not the next time, when they found it in her lymph nodes and lungs, and God knows where else.

Ruby reviewed her recent thoughts, and her mind flashed back twenty years to the picture of a hot smouldering joint sucking back to her lips. She realized she had been tripping along just the same as if her mind had been stoned on marijuana. And she a pastor's wife too. She sighed, and then looking outside she laughed for no reason at the thick trunk of the nearest hemlock tree. Perhaps the cancer had spread to her brain. She added the onions, the spices, the celery and the stock, and left the pot to simmer. She would add and boil the vegetables later.

"Oh, boy, stew again," she said to no one.

Her imagination fell short now when it came to life's little particulars, such as eating.

She collapsed into her kitchen chair and glanced out to see a gust of wind blow through the trees and loose a few leaves from the short maples that grew like weeds among the large trunks of the fir and hemlock. The maples had to be cut back each spring or they would block the view of the river. Now their dry falling leaves, a mix of orange, yellow, and brown, were flying up in the wind and over the deck's railing where in about a week they would collect into a large enough heap to make it worthwhile for her to sweep them up and throw them back over and down the steep cliff. It was a small job. But Ruby decided she would not do it this year. Tom could do it. Let him discover there was such a job to do around the house, one that he didn't know about, or didn't care to know about.

Then, glancing at the clock, she washed and folded what she considered her nasty mood, which was becoming more prevalent these days, and returned it clean and fresh smelling to her mind. She would sweep up the dead leaves herself. Yes, she was just like that.

And then she remembered the days when she and Tom first met, when they were young, and how their relationship had been, and how Tom had made such a show of being the tormented outsider, who took pride in rebelling against the system. She had thought his inability to face life was a temporary condition and that after he was converted he would begin to grow up. Then they went back to Anaheim, back to where she was born, where life was more familiar. Tom joined her father in his real estate business, and she began to realize that she had been more attracted to the cynical rebellious Tom than to the reformed Tom. She had gotten her man converted, and then she was stuck with him. Tom, she discovered, was an introvert. And then no child. And guilt. And then life carried on by itself, as if it had a life of its own. Teaching school again. That was what they urged her to do for the grief over her baby's death, and that seemed tolerable. And she would be able to support Tom, who had decided he would quit the real estate business, so he could finish university and go to Fuller Seminary because he believed God was calling him into the ministry. The whole time she pretended to have recovered from the loss of her child, and when Tom matured in seminary she thought there was some hope for them together. But their first church was nothing but trouble.

Ruby pushed herself up from her chair, turned the ceiling lights off and found the bag of potatoes in the cupboard. She took five of them out and began to slice their skins into the sink. She would get to the carrots next.

Tom climbed the stairs leading from the carport, knowing he forgot to get the litre of oil his engine needed, and looked out at the Cowichan River, which was beginning to rise enough to allow the Coho salmon to come up to spawn late again this year. He turned and kicked a few of the leaves accumulating on the deck and promised himself that he would cut down those maples that grew like weeds and spoiled the view. He looked through the kitchen window and saw Ruby peeling at the sink. Stew again. Thin and gray and black in the shadows, she was trying to disappear on him. But he wouldn't let her get away with it without a fight. He turned and looked down at a patch of the river visible through the maples and wondered again why he had never enjoyed fishing as a hobby. After all, the river was right there. Sure it was a steep bank, but it was right there, and the fish were there. But the fish had never encouraged him the few times he had tried. Fishing was an annoying pastime anyway, the lures always catching on the bottom and the line tangling every chance it got. It was all stacked against him, and besides, fishing was too symbolic for a person in his line of work. His fishing guilt dealt with, he opened the back door and greeted Ruby, whose head and one shoulder turned to acknowledge his arrival and then returned to face the peeler and the sink.

Ruby's courage had deserted her. She was too tired now to put on a brave show for his benefit. Besides, they were at home, and there was nobody else here to impress. There was no point in putting on an act when they both knew the truth about each other. Not that there was any devastating truth to be revealed about either of them. They just had knowledge of each other as human beings, and that was enough. Of course there was that other matter that happened years ago, but what was the point of her confessing to that? He didn't have to know everything.

Tom leaned on the kitchen table and began to read the story under the headline.

"Hmm," he said, "haven't found that lost kid yet?"

Ruby dropped her peeler, pressed her pelvis against the sink and sighed. Tom put aside the daily paper, opened the local weekly to the church page, and read the Ministerial's ad for the crusade.

"Duncan Ministerial's bringing that evangelist in," he said. "Seen the ad?"

"They all agreed? What a miracle," Ruby said.

"Oh, come on, they're not that bad," Tom said.

Ruby didn't bother to reply. They both knew the Ministerial was much worse.

Tom folded the newspaper and advanced to lean his elbows on the butcher block.

"They're going nowhere, especially together, and you know it," Ruby said.

She turned her flashing dark-brown eyes to face him for the first time this evening in the kitchen of their three-bedroom house that they knew was too big for them when they bought it, the three-bedroom house she had adored when the real estate agent showed them through it, the three-bedroom house with the large living room that was the perfect size for church home-meetings on week nights. But now, when the two of them were there alone, life in their house overlooking the Cowichan River could be frightening.

"Well?" Ruby said, hands on hips, waiting to hear another one of his weak excuses for his colleagues.

Tom knew this mood, and he didn't need another argument. The Ministerial was a bad conversation topic, and so was a discussion about their church. Since the elders on his board were going to replace him with someone who would tow their party line, Ruby was often challenging him now to make a declaration to *those cowards*. She wanted him to stand up to them. She was always insisting that he stand up to life, as if it could be lived any better that way. His quest was for peace. Confrontation originated in pride and arrogance and resulted in more strife. If his flock desired another shepherd, then it was also his duty to help them find one – not that they had asked.

"Don't upset yourself," he said. "The Ministerial can't change the world."

"You would think they might be able to change the church, though," Ruby said, dropping the vegetables into the pot.

They both watched the slopping water hit the burner and explode into hissing steam.

"But first they're the ones who need to change," Tom said. "That is if they want to. God will change them, if they'll listen. But I'm no one to talk. I haven't been listening to Him lately, either."

Ruby slipped past him, retrieved and unfolded her newspaper, resumed her chair at her end of the table, and felt a rare headache coming on. Tom was so passive it made her head hurt. Her father had at least remained loyal to his calling. Despite his few attempts at sobriety he had maintained his integrity as an alcoholic to the end. He had been a man. He had been the commander of his real estate company. He had been a success. His blood alcohol reading was .24 when later they took it, after they found him in his wrecked pink Eldorado at the bottom of a 50-foot cliff on the coast road. A sense of humor to the end, he had broken through the guard rail and must have soared like a pink elephant, before hitting the rocks. She saw her father in poetic terms. She kept him in her mind always in mid-air, flying in his pink Cadillac, the rocks below out of her picture – since the rocks were only hard reality. But she was unable to form an image of her mother at all.

Tom, who had been staring at the sink she had vacated, lifted himself off his elbows, and turned to offer his excuse to her for his failure in his faith and in life.

"It's just not my fault," Tom said, "I can't take the blame for everything."

"No one is blaming you," she said, wondering why he couldn't see that it was all his fault.

He went over and sat in the chair across from her, and then they both looked up to gaze at more leaves blowing over the railing.

She said, "Do you think you could sweep up those leaves sometime?"

"I know," he said, "I've got to get those maples cut down one of these days."

"Uh, huh."

She watched him poke at the crumbs on the harvest-gold place mat and then begin to gather them into a pile.

"It is my fault," he said.

"No, it really isn't," Ruby said, knowing she had made her own choices, and she had to take responsibility for the consequences. But why did he have to be so weak? She moaned and again read the headline on the front page.

Tom said, "Yes, I know, it's too bad about that kid, but don't let it upset you."

"It's a sad world," she said, going along with his interpretation of her moan, sparing him her anger, as the simmering stew rattled its lid in short bursts of steam. She noticed the stillness around Tom's bowed head. He was probably praying. Praying for her? Or praying to watch the football game with the minimum of fuss from her? Or maybe he was pretending to pray. She would never know. She studied the thin form of her husband, whose hair was turning gray in just the right places to give him that middle-aged distinguished look that would still play well with the gals in the church. He had kept his looks; that was one thing you could say for him, despite the weak chin. Slim, six-feet-tall, a minor paunch. Some of the women in the church weren't eager for Tom to go, she knew. But that line of thought was fantasy. He had remained devoted to her, and there was something to be said for that.

"Would you like to have your dinner watching the game?"

"No. It's all right," Tom said.

She saw his weak smile that wanted to expand into a thank you for what he hoped was her understanding and approval of his game plan.

"I'll eat in here with you," he added.

"A noble sacrifice," she said, responding with her best rendering of her part in preserving domestic peace. "But we can both eat watching the game, if you like."

Tom tried to keep the smile on his face, but it wilted away. He would accept her offer to compromise. It was gracious of her, although he preferred to watch it alone. Once he had believed that two could become one flesh, and he continued in faith to believe that, even though Ruby's flesh had rejected him and was making a serious attempt to leave him. Unity had been difficult before; now it was impossible. He didn't know how to drag her body back from its chosen direction downward to the grave. In his profession he had seen many go that way; he had thrown the dirt on a lot of them. And Ruby emanated death, the same way the rest of them had before they died. But maybe he could still drag her back, even though he felt so weak. But there was one other hope. The healing evangelist who was coming might pray for her and they would have a miracle. Their marriage would be reborn, and somehow their relationship would be healed and his ministry renewed and they would go forward together. He believed in miracles. But he had never experienced one, except for his initial salvation. That had been a miracle. And now he hoped for another one, and then at other times the whole idea of miracles vanished; at those times, signs and wonders and miracles seemed fantastic, and he was without hope.

Ruby saw that Tom was sinking into himself.

"Oh, no, wait," she said, "you'll have to watch it by yourself. I just remembered I have to go out and finish some shopping, get a few things, you know, at the drug store before it closes. I'll get my list together here while I'm eating."

Not that she ate much of anything anymore.

"Oh, well, whatever you think. I'll go if you want...don't forget, you shouldn't overdo it. I mean don't go for too long. Are you sure you don't want me to go for you?"

Ruby leaned her bowed head forward, her hands clasped against her diaphragm, pressing hard into the table's edge. And she held onto her anger.

In control, she said, "No, don't be silly, it won't take any time at all." She stood to get the plates from the cupboard. "And anyway," she said, offering Tom a bold face, "I'll have lots of time in eternity."

"There is no time in eternity," Tom said, smiling at her.

Smiling back at him and setting the plates on the butcher block, she said, "Don't confuse me, Tom, I don't want to lose my mind and then have to launch my journey to heaven from the psych ward."

CHAPTER NINE

Jesse Thornton manned his desk in his office at The Cowichan Leader, eating a ham sandwich and scanning the various big city papers for an idea that would develop well for this week's editorial. He had been experiencing a rare sense of well being this morning, which had begun to disrupt his diligence and stimulate his enthusiasm for the latest scheme he had conceived to escape a monotonous future in the newspaper business. It would be easy, he thought, popping in the last bite of ham-on-white, except for some wear and tear on his middle-aged body. Yes, it would be a cinch. He would begin in Newfoundland, invite the press to the eastern shore, and there he would dip his big toe in. To begin with, he would relate a few clever anecdotes about his life and goals. He would tell them he was doing it for them all. All the middle-aged people who shunned exercise in favor of a life of ease on the couch. There would be an immediate swelling of support. But the run would have to be managed just right. He would need a small bank roll to start out with, and a camper, and lots of tape to bind the shin splints. And a trainer. Perhaps a woman jock, a young woman jock. And of course he wouldn't have to run the whole way. After all he was at a disadvantage. He was out of shape; he would emphasize that aspect to increase the public's identification with him. He had been a sedentary member of society since Little League. He was an out of shape Baby Boomer who would be doing it for all the others. The money would pour in. At each major center along the way he would provide the press with a few more anecdotes about the thrill of it all, get the public behind him, that sort of thing. No sweat. There would be plenty of time to create entertaining insights during those long lonesome miles of walking and trotting. By Manitoba he would be laughing. The Early Retirement Run he would call it. Come one, come all and donate to Jesse Thornton's Early Retirement Run. The press would eat it up, keep them amused all the way across Canada. Canadians needed such events to bind them together. It would be a public service, a good cause. Begin in Newfoundland and run for the West Coast and retirement. It would take two years tops. Raise a couple of million at least. He might even get into shape. Buy a few acres on Saltspring Island with the proceeds, brew his own beer, become a sage. Maybe buy the local newspaper, to keep a finger in, that sort of thing. A two-year investment and set for life. Yes, it was a glorious morning and Jesse felt hope rising to greet him. Canada was a land of opportunity all right.

Jesse reflected on his joyous mood this morning. He was excited; he almost felt like he was in love. But how could that bring joy, given his previous experience in the realm of pairing? Such an emotion, he thought, should instead inspire in him a great deal of dread. Jesse opened his door to sneak a peek at Isabel, the new clerk in the ad department across the hall. She was poised behind the counter with the eraser of her pencil pursed between her luscious lips, and her hazel eyes were reading an ad just placed by an elderly woman who was now driving a walker with short slow measured steps toward the main door of The Cowichan Leader. Jesse rushed out to open the door for the departing Mrs. Long, who grinned back at him, craning a stiff neck. Jesse thought he must have gone mad to be so thoughtful, until he turned and saw those lips come to a full smile beneath the chestnut hair that fell over the shoulders and down the back of Isabel. And Jesse felt good. But was she too young? How old could she be? Maybe twenty-three at the most, and that was close to half his age; he was old enough to be her father. But why did he feel so good?

Jesse attempted to project a pleasant smile in Isabel's direction but instead produced a Teddy-Bear smirk, not knowing whether he should be a father type to her or what? And how did she see him? Confused, he looked at Isabel and then gestured with his head toward the woman departing down the ramp, and by way of explanation said the most inane thing that he could think of: "Poor woman, she ought to be dead."

Isabel returned her pencil to her lips and her eyes to the ad form, and then she lifted her head again, the light from the window haloing her hair, her eyes asking him for some hidden meaning in his words, which to him had fallen to the floor like lumps of oatmeal from the mouth of an ape.

"She's old, you see," he said to Isabel, offering her an explanation for his ill-considered remark, an explanation that was intended to fix everything, and then he strutted back to his office door as if he had been clowning all along. To reinforce the light-hearted image he was now projecting, he glanced back before entering his office, and asked, "Say, isn't Isabel a Catholic name?" Then we went in.

He stood leaning his back on the door, while his blood pounded in his ears. He was too old for this. He wasn't supposed to be floating around his office with love in his head, feeling good. It was bad for him; he knew that much. Recapture his youth, what a joke! Staring straight ahead he could see without looking down, his gut protruding. Lifting his chin higher to put his fat out of mind, while visions of barbells and jogging shoes danced in his head, he released the air that had been inflating his courting chest. No, he couldn't do it. He hadn't exercised since Little League. Still, Isabel might go for the older type, the mature man with a few years of living under his belt. But no, that was impossible, so why bother making the effort? No doubt she had one of those narrow-hipped monsters for a pet with a V-shaped back and springy stumps for legs, who got his kicks grunting and sweating in union with inanimate objects.

Jesse found his swivel-back chair and fell into it. He was feeling more depressed now. That was better. Depression was easier to live with. Anyway, her type would have him dining out and going to movies and having him enjoying himself in no time. Wooing her would be expensive and too destructive to his self-image. It was an editor's duty to project a sour, care-worn attitude, and she had already inspired him to attempt chivalry in the hall. But at least nobody else had seen him, except Mrs. Long. And who would she tell? Jesse turned his attention back to the city newspapers and then to his word processor. Forget controversy this week, he thought, approaching the keys; how about an editorial the majority would agree with, like another clever piece on the environment.

Jesse made his way through his measured commentary with ease, wondering if anyone had noticed that his editorials had been the same for two months now. His thrust remained the same, even though he changed the identities of the culprits and victims. Everything was harmful, dangerous, or both. He pitted parklands versus logging, clean air and water versus their pollution by the mills, and then there were fast-food containers and the ozone, and garbage and the incinerators, and PCBs, and on he went. For his own self-satisfaction he liked to imagine that when his few dedicated readers would read another one of his incisive editorials they would nod their heads and say to the spouse, *Did you read this, dear? Clever man*.

He leaned back in his swivel chair, a job well done, and nodding his head at the screen, resolved that one week he would, for variation, take the side of the capitalist, fascist pigs. For in the nineties, the sixties revolution didn't matter much anymore. Besides, his readership, like everyone else, had short memories.

He stood and stretched. It was lunchtime, and he was thirsty. He reached for his coat and opened the door, keeping his head down in case Isabel was there waiting for him to embarrass himself again, and then he turned down the hall for a stop at the washroom before he made his escape to the Maple Bay pub. He got there without incident, accomplished his task, washed his hands, dabbed his face, pressed the hot-air blower, and then wiped his hands on his pants as he made his way out through the Men's door and back down the hall. His head down again and beer on his mind he bumped shoulders with a man whose familiar face said, "Excuse me," which brought Jesse up short. He then realized the man was the Reverend Tom Pollard, who ran a Christian drop-in center in town. The reverend stood there wearing one of those TV evangelist grins, and then Jesse remembered seeing an ad in his own newspaper. It was for a crusade the local ministerial was putting on. His nose for beer took second place to his nose for news. He decided he wanted to talk to the reverend about the upcoming sordid event.

"Say, Reverend Pollard," Jesse said. "It is Pollard, isn't it?"

Jesse pasted on his face his best impersonation of goodness, his eyes widening with his smile, his body bending at the waist, his damp hand extending to steer the shoulder of the misguided man of the cloth to his office, where he would interrogate him about the fiasco soon to take place in Cowichan Theatre.

"Have you got a minute," Jesse said, "in my office, if you don't mind? I've got a question for you."

This was a fortunate meeting, Jesse thought. The church, as everyone knew, was fair game. Some of the older folks cared about it, but Christians were a minority, about four per cent of the Valley's population. He remembered reading that statistic last week in one of the press handouts he received from the provincial government. He escorted a compliant Tom into his office and offered him a chair. Church corruption would make good copy. Jesse hoped his glee wasn't showing.

"First of all, can I help you in any way?" Jesse said. He noticed the pastor's silly grin was gone.

"I came about our ad on the church page," Tom said. "There's a mistake."

"These things do happen," Jesse said. "So tell me the bone of contention, and I'll look into it for you."

Reverend Tom removed a clipping from his breast shirt pocket, and then held it up for Jesse.

"Duncan Christian *Fallowship*," Tom said, pointing at the typo.

Typesetter Bernie upstairs had a sense of humour, Jesse thought, but who could ever catch him at it for certain. He was the shop steward, and if he was unhappy with management for any reason at all—such as too much overtime or perhaps not enough overtime—copy errors would begin to appear, and each one would communicate a veiled message. Jesse suspected that Bernie stayed awake nights searching his dark intelligence for his next creation. But this one, Jesse guessed, was not the result of a tiff with management. This one was a direct shot at the church, both barrels fired, one shot coming from Bernie's socialist leanings and the other from his narrow-minded delight.

"Yes, I see," said Jesse. He tapped his lips with his left index finger, projecting deep concern. "Well, we'll have to fix that up for you right away."

"Fine, thank you."

Reverend Tom pushed himself up from the chair and got ready to make his escape. Jesse wasn't going to make it that easy.

"Oh, wait, if you've got another few minutes, Reverend. That question I mentioned. Do you have any more information on that meeting you're going to have at Cowichan Theatre? There's an ad for it in our paper this week."

"It's not my meeting," Tom said, lowering himself back down into the chair. "It's being put on by the Duncan Ministerial."

"Yes, I see, Reverend, but I thought you could answer a few questions anyway. You're a member of the Ministerial, aren't you? Is this evangelist reputable? I mean, as you know, there's been so much fraud going on lately, er...."

Seeming to be flattered by the attention, Tom smiled and crossed one leg over the other, his eyes studying the blue and white stripes on his Adidas.

"You know, Jesse...may I call you Jesse?"

"Yes, absolutely," Jesse said, amused to be on a first name basis with a dinosaur.

"And you may call me Tom," he said, a surge of anger escaping. "You know, Jesse, I've been working at our drop-in center two blocks from here for about five years now, and you haven't taken any interest in doing a story about what goes on there. But now that you see a chance to stir up some mud, you ask me to help you out."

Jesse winced and thought of Maple Bay and beer. Nothing was easy anymore.

"You mean there is some mud to stir up, Rev?" Jesse said, no longer nice.

"I wouldn't know," Tom said. "If you want any more information on the meetings, call the Baptist minister, John Derry, he's the one in charge."

"Oh, come on, you're here now, what's the harm? Let me find the ad. Is this Evangelist, what's his name...?

"Chester Thomas," Tom said.

"That's it, what's his game, anyway?"

Jesse looked at Tom's Adidas. What was a reverend doing wearing sneakers to town? Wasn't a man of the cloth supposed to wear those expensive brown brogues, or those shiny black dress shoes? The man had no pride in the job by the look of it.

"Do you know what an evangelist is?" Tom said.

"Yes, I know what an evangelist is," Jesse said, taking up the challenge. "He's one of those double-chinned, pompadour-haired, capped-teeth Bible junkies who say "Amen" every second word. And as for what they do, well that's easy. They promise a lot, deliver little, and abscond with as much money as they can swindle from gullible people who are afraid to die."

That ought to settle the matter, Jesse thought, waiting for the reverend's reaction and being very much in love with his glib tongue, his girth now seeming of less importance for such a great one as himself. Maybe Isabel would fall for muscular brains, he thought, his mind improving his odds with her until he remembered his recent humbling in the hall, which jerked his brief fantasy right out of his head and flung him back to Tom and their conflict.

Jesse straightened himself in his chair and faced Tom, intent on rebuffing the reverend's response.

"That's a nice convenient stereotype," Tom said, "but you're throwing out the spiritual baby with the bath water."

"What's that, some kind of Christian code you're talking, Rev?"

"No, it's not code. You can't understand it because you don't want to understand it."

Jesse leaned back in his chair, took a deep breath and then blew the air out toward Tom.

"I'm as open as anybody, Rev. Why don't you back up and try again? Who knows what I might understand?"

Jesse challenged Tom with a grimace, removed his glasses and then nibbled on one of the arms.

"Are you sure?" Tom said. "I wouldn't want to be accused of forcing religion down your throat."

Jesse heard the good reverend's petty anger escape again. Where was the man's humility? Behavior like that gave God a bad name.

"Sure, let's hear it, Rev," Jesse said. He was now impatient with the whole scene. The beer was waiting at the Maple Bay Pub, and Reverend Tom was beginning to bore him.

Reverend Tom said, "An evangelist has a gift for communicating the mercy and grace of God, the God who sent his Son to die for us, and that includes you, whether you like it or not."

"Is that so, Rev?"

Jesse paused and leaned forward over his desk. He was annoyed at Tom's piercing stare and Tom's thin face and his trim body, and who did he think he was coming in here to preach?

He said, "If you insist on talking about those who are lost, from what I hear around town, you're the one who's lost. I'm not lost, I'm in Duncan, and this is my office, and if you've finished peddling your propaganda I'll be calling it a day."

He didn't have to be nice. Who was this guy anyway? Besides, who cared about him and the rest of the four per cent like him who were clinging to their illusions in the Cowichan Valley?

"Fine with me," Tom said and got up, looking defeated. He opened the door and for something to say added, "I'll pray for you."

"Do that, Rev," Jesse said, smiling at Tom's back, "if you can find the time."

Reverend Tom then closed the door.

Jesse waited for him to leave the building and start down the street before he followed him out. The coast clear, Jesse made his way down the hall and out the door. Unlocking his car, he glanced at the ad office window for another peek at Isabel, who caught him at it. Embarrassed, he mumbled to his Valiant's door, *the nerve, preaching to me in my own office.* Then he climbed into his car, his mind anticipating the soothing comfort of a few, or perhaps many, glasses of luncheon beer at the Maple Bay Pub.

CHAPTER TEN

Tom's eyes studied the sidewalk in front of each footstep that he put forward in the direction of his center, where he would find as much peace now as he ever did. He could see and feel the gray dome above; it was about to release white flakes that would fall on the Cowichan Valley, beginning first with cold salt-grain sized specks floating down and then increasing until they covered the frozen ground, and then coming thicker, blowing down, the flakes medium-sized and stacking up until it had to be shovelled. But if the warm air from the Pacific cooperated the snow would turn to rain by nightfall and then the shovelling would have been done for nothing. He remembered one night last winter when the snow blew at 10 knots across the face of a bright full moon. But Ruby hadn't been interested. He'd walked out onto the deck to see, and then he came back in and told her that the weather was out of joint. In response she mumbled to him from the limbo before sleep that it was The Black Death. The following day the wind blew the snow like liquid nitrogen on the roads, as if the weather thought the West Coast was Siberia in deep winter.

Tom stopped at the door of his Center to see two of his flock coming toward him, looking up and around at the white specks beginning to fall. Tom knew that Taylor and Dobbs had slowed their pace enough to allow him to enter the Center and avoid conversation. But Tom had decided he would not let them get away with that. He waited. And they, seeing his strategy, began to yell toward him about the rotten snow and how bad it was to drive in, and how much work it was when you had to shovel it. But they were offering their complaints in little-boys' voices, their wide little boys' eyes sparkling, and their smiling mouths cracking their age-hardened masks.

"Yes, it's beautiful, isn't it," Tom said to their little boys, but their middle-aged men rose up, became confused and with side-glances and now frowning mouths questioned each other, as if Tom were mad. Tom smiled at them, opened the door, went in, and left them like that.

The prayer-room door was closed. Distorted human shadows rippled on its thick marbled glass window. He considered knocking but then turned and saw Will sitting on one of the couches next to the coffee urn.

"Who's in the prayer room?" Tom asked.

Will lifted his brown eyes from his study Bible, shook himself free from his meditation, focussed on the question and then said, "Hmmm. Geoff's trying to lead some guy to the Lord."

"You don't seem too enthusiastic about it," Tom said. "What's the problem?"

"No problem," Will said, and returned his eyes to his reading.

"Checked the furnace lately?" Tom said.

He knew Will hadn't. The temperature inside the building had dropped about five degrees since he'd left for The Cowichan Leader about a half-hour before.

"Mmm, I'll do that now," Will said, pulling himself away from his reading.

Will had his priorities, Tom knew, and tossing another log on the fire on a day like today was low on the list. Will's good sense knew better than to feed a dead horse, and that's what the furnace downstairs was when the temperature fell below freezing.

"Never mind, I'll do it," Tom said. "Keep reading."

On his way down the shaky stairs Tom wondered whether he had just now been sarcastic or just fatherly. Either way he knew that Will would resume his reading unconcerned about Tom's self-image.

Tom opened the furnace's door and frowned at the red coals in the four-foot long box. His hot idea to convert the inefficient oil furnace to burn wood and save on oil bills was not hot now. He came up with the idea to appease those in the church who were against funding the Center. He thought he would sacrifice himself in winter by hauling and stacking wood to keep costs down, so that there would be enough money to keep the place going. But his decision had resulted in misery all around. The furnace was a full-time job in winter, and except for Will his motivational techniques had failed to inspire the young men of the church to come and tend the monster.

He threw a few two-foot lengths of semi-seasoned red alder onto the coals. In a few seconds, flames wobbled up between the firewood and then began to stiffen. He threw in six more pieces of the split alder, shut the door, opened the draft and the damper, and then sat on the splitting block.

Why is it so hard to keep this fire going? Tom asked the stacked cord of alder and the few sticks of knotted fir left from a previous load. He got no answer, and then he wondered where the next cord would come from. There was enough space left in the half-basement to store a few more cords and still leave plenty of room to swing a splitting maul. Tom looked at the bare cement wall and then up through the sooty street-level window to see the passing shadows of cars that matched the sounds of muffled rubber rolling by the building. He was a prisoner down here. He had been sentenced to keep the fire alive. The previous tenants, the RCMP, had a new headquarters down on Canada Avenue with electric baseboard heating. The oil bills must have been in the thousands each month by the time they ended their stay. What a great notion it had been for the church to lease the old RCMP jailhouse, which no one else wanted, to serve as an outreach to the community. Ministering salvation from a former jailhouse. What a clever idea! What potential! But not in winter. No wonder no one else had wanted to lease the place.

Tom stood and opened the top grate to see how much creosote had accumulated on the pipes. There was at least an inch, and that was enough to ensure that no matter how hot the fire got in the firebox, the circulating water would be lukewarm on its way up to the radiators and be near freezing on its return down. The pipes were strung through the crawl space under the other half of the building, and many of the pipe sections were left exposed where the gnawing rats had left the insulation hanging. Even when it was burning oil, the odds had been against the worn-out oil furnace in the winter months, but now with wood in its belly and layers of creosote fused to its cast-iron boiler, there was not much left for Tom to do in the cold but laugh in his mind like a mad man.

But no, he wouldn't give up. There was one tiring job that might help. He grabbed his five-foot long reinforcing rod with the wire brush attached to its end. It was homemade. He'd wired the wire brush onto the end of the rod so that he could reach into the narrow four-foot long cubbyholes with it and try to scrub a few layers of the creosote off the pipes. But after a few minutes the wires holding the brush would expand in the heat and the brush would begin to loosen. Then he would have to tighten the hot wire on the hot brush on the hot rod. He used the same gloves for the job as he wore when splitting the wood. The gloves had been transformed into clumps of furnace grime and were useless when agility was required. Another troubling feature of his homemade tool was that the wooden part of the brush eventually turned to charcoal. But if the weather turned mild, his brush might last a few more months. He hoped to save the church the price of a new one for as long as he could. And since he was leaving in February, they might be spared the expense of ever buying another.

He decided to discontinue his bitter thoughts and slid the rod with its brush into the first opening, knocking off the loose accumulation of soot. He then began to scrub the black scales from the pipes. The first time he had cleaned them, almost five years ago now, when he had been a naive furnace man, anxious to bring the gospel to the streets, he had the pipes shining like the bumpers of a new '58 Buick.

The black grit flew, and a sooty haze engulfed his head, and he wondered if the South American mission field was any worse than this. He again eyed the insulation on the top of the furnace. He suspected the gray fabric was asbestos. What else would they have used in the '50s when they built the place? He should have asked someone who knew about those things whether it was asbestos or not, but since he was stuck with the job he had decided to remain ignorant concerning the identification of asbestos in the workplace. He knew the particles were bad for the lungs, and that asbestos was no longer the insulation of choice. But most of the people in this town would be crying for the stuff when they got to where they were going. He laughed and then felt guilty for the joy he had just experienced, imagining the naughty Duncan citizenry hot-footing-it on scorching coals for eternity. Forgiving himself for his lapse in judgment, he wiped his sweaty forehead with the sleeve of his tan duffle coat and then frowned at the black streak left there. Another lapse in judgment.

It was no use. In this weather no matter how hard he scoured the boiler the wood would not burn hot enough to heat the building. He leaned the rod against the cement wall and returned to his seat on the splitting block. He stared at his black gloves and remembered last winter's experiment with coal. Norman, an accountant and one of the church elders, had suggested the coal. He said coal was cheap and would burn longer, and keep the fire going overnight, so the building would be warm in the morning, and the furnace wouldn't need to be restarted cold every day. Mix the wood and the coal, heating problem solved. Norman should have stuck to his books. The coal was cheap and burned a long time all right, but it also lowered the fire's temperature. He would get the fire roaring and then throw in Norman's coal to extend the life of the fire, and then the coal would lower the temperature of the roaring wood so that it would burn like coal too. Norman was a good accountant. In his office he had cozy forced-air, heated by a furnace that burned oil. He remembered visiting him there. He was pretty sure it was forced-air from an oil furnace, but it might have been electric heat. Either way, he knew Norman was comfortable sitting in his warm office, with a thermostat on the wall that he could set to as comfortable a temperature as he wanted. If you were cold you just turned the heat up. But here he was, staring at a converted oil furnace that now burned wood at a temperature just high enough to prevent the air in the building from freezing his face. Why hadn't he stayed in Real Estate? Working for the Lord was brutal.

He shook his head at the left forearm of his soiled duffle coat and then wiggled his toes in his Adidas. He was reflecting on which was worse, wearing running shoes with a duffle coat or owning a duffle coat, when his thoughts were interrupted by Will's boots and jeans coming down the creaking gray stairs. They descended out of sight behind the partition that formed one wall of the RCMP's former storeroom for lost and confiscated items, and then all of Will appeared, coming around the corner.

"Need any help?" Will said.

"No thanks," Tom said. "Unless you can do something

about the weather."

Will moved a round of alder closer to the furnace and sat down on it.

"You know I'm not supposed to do that anymore," he said.

"Sorry," Tom said, a burst of laughter rising from his stomach and snorting out his nose, "I forgot about your roots for a second."

"You have a black face, pastor," Will said, as he noticed the soot on the forearm of Tom's duffle coat.

"It goes with the territory," Tom said. "Life in God's Kingdom can be a struggle. We make a good pair."

"My face is red," Will said to his boots. He raised his eyebrows and looked at Tom, his mouth producing a grin that lit his entire face. Then he lowered his head to stare at his boots again, his light extinguished.

"So is there anything I can I do for you, Will?"

"I have to get back to school, but I just came down for a minute to mention something I've been concerned about."

"What's that?" Tom said.

"It's the dances this year."

"What about the dances?"

"Well, I've been thinking a bit, and what if they grab me?"

"Grab you? They can't grab you if you don't want to go. You're a Christian now."

"Who's going to stop them?" Will said. He stood and tossed his log chair onto the wood pile. "I think my dad would pay for them to grab me. He believes in the old ways now. And he doesn't like the way I'm going. They could grab me and think they're doing me a favor."

He turned to leave.

"Don't worry," Tom said, and then added for assurance, "fear is the real enemy. They can't grab you."

"They could grab me easy," Will said. "And I'm feeling the

sickness coming on too."

"Sickness? That's nonsense."

"They don't think it's nonsense," Will said. "You don't know what they can do. See you later, pastor. I have to go back now."

Before Tom could think of what he might say next, Will turned away, his shoulders hunched, and walked around the corner. The stairs and railing creaked under Will's weight, and then his jeans and boots reappeared at the top of the stairs before they were gone again.

Tom shifted his weight forward on the chopping block and stretched his legs. Why had Will come down to tell him that? The sickness! He had to be imagining it. Will was a Christian now; he didn't have to bother with all that superstition. Or was it? Could they really grab him? Who would stop them if they did? Could he stop them? The Longhouse was a different universe. And his knowledge of Will's culture was second hand. He would never experience it. So how was he supposed to be Will's spiritual father, how could he raise him to spiritual maturity? And where did Will belong? And would he ever be allowed to succeed? When Tom was young he had to work at destroying his own life. Failure wasn't just handed to him. He had to reject opportunities that would have led to success. No, for him failure hadn't been easy. He had to work at it. But for Will, who was standing up against his own culture, was failure guaranteed? He didn't want to think so. But at least he and Will had one thing in common; they were miracles. God had intervened and plucked them both from the fire. But could they ever be united? Sure he'd led Will to the Lord, and he could teach him Scripture, but how was he supposed to become a father to him and have a genuine relationship with him when the gap between them was so wide? And to make an impossible task absurd, he also lacked fathering experience. He had never done the real thing. So how was he expected to be a father? Was he supposed to just play the part? He shook his head at the furnace. It didn't matter. Will was going to the Mainland. He was going, and that was just a fact. Soon he wouldn't be his responsibility. And there wouldn't be any others. He wouldn't be continuing the street ministry without financial support from the church. The board wasn't going to keep funding the place after they removed him from the pulpit. The Center was one of the main reasons they wanted him gone. And there would be no help coming from the community. Why would they support a renegade minister, preaching the gospel no less? Yes, the end was right here, in front of his perverted furnace. Maybe Ruby had the right idea. Death was the noble way out. She knew where their lives had been headed. The faith they'd shared when they started the ministry was long since spent. The big question now was how did he lead Will to the Lord in the first place? The answer was simple. It must have been the Lord's doing. And would that be his legacy, one convert out of the seven Cowichan Tribes, not to mention the rest of the Valley's citizens? But why was he thinking about a legacy at forty-four years old? And as for his vision of a street ministry, the whole thing must have been his own creation. If God had been the one who had given him the vision, then the result would have been steady growth, not a dried-up ministry that continued to shrivel until he was crouched in the basement fearful of life. At the beginning it had seemed right. Even Ruby thought so. He even had the background for it. In the sixties he had survived the corruption that destroys youth. He would be able to identify and show the young people the way to the Lord. Now the whole thing sounded as naive and superficial as the Care Bears winning the day. His faith was gone.

He stood and looked up at the sooty window. Through the

inch-wide clear glass that bordered the wooden frame, some daylight filtered into the basement. There he was, alone in his own prison, and then he saw himself in that department store, lost again, and his mother gone away. His tears began to trickle down and streak his blackened face. He hoped they would stop and spare his duffle coat any more stains. Then he heard it. There was a change in the sound of the passing cars. The muted sound of the tires had become the swishing of spraying slush. That meant the falling snow had turned to rain. He knew the pattern. First the small flakes had become giant cotton flakes, and then the cotton had mixed with large rain drops, and now the large rain drops were falling, and now with some more scrubbing and some more alder, the water in the boiler might be heated enough to cooperate with the warming air to restore the building temperature to a livable level.

He grabbed his makeshift brush and began to work. He wasn't defeated yet. The Creator of the elements had smiled upon him, and he hadn't even asked him for rain. Sure, there was hope yet; if he were to re-establish contact with God, then his mission would be saved. But he didn't really want to talk to Him. He was too angry at Him and too bitter for words. How could He be so uncaring? He had sacrificed his life to serve Him, and now Ruby was dying. And this was how he had ended up, feeding a dying furnace. Then an unwelcome thought surfaced. He imagined that sometime in the future he might look back at himself, labouring here over this furnace, and he would be embarrassed to remember that he once thought he had been performing a useful work for the Lord.

Finished with the boiler, he closed its door and leaned his brush against the wall. He threw a few more lengths of alder into the firebox and then went upstairs to clean himself up. Inside the bathroom he leaned on the sink and told the streaked, sooty face in the mirror things weren't that bad; he wasn't defeated yet. The fire was burning, and Ruby might have a miracle. Cancer didn't have to win. Faith, that was the key; all he needed to do was resume talking to the author of it. But how could he forgive God, when it was God who should be asking him for forgiveness? That was a stupid thought. He knew the relationship was never to work that way. God was always right; errors were alien to his nature. That made talking to him always challenging. How could you talk to someone who knew everything? But Tom knew at least that his present misery was his own awful creation. He washed and dried his face and then used a damp paper towel to rub the soot mark deeper into the fabric of his coat sleeve. So, he might start talking to Him again and he might not, even though he knew that such an attitude was the exact opposite to wisdom.

CHAPTER ELEVEN

Tom knocked on the door of the prayer room and then entered. Sitting there was a chunky citizen about forty years old, who grinned at Tom with yellow, brown, and black front teeth. Seeing Tom, the man turned to Geoff, whose bright eyes were heralding a miracle in their midst.

"Jimmy here just gave his life to the Lord," Geoff said.

Jimmy nodded in agreement, his compliant face marred by coagulated blood from recent shaving gashes. Geoff was gushing pride.

"I see," Tom said.

He could see very well what had happened. Jimmy manifested the air of a professional, a professional convert.

"He has repented," Geoff said.

Geoff nodded to reinforce the victory. Jimmy nodded, too, and smiled at Tom.

Geoff, a tall sandy-haired nineteen-year-old university student on a mission, looked confident he'd won his first convert since he had begun volunteering a few hours a week at the Center.

"Why doesn't Jimmy talk?" Tom said. He looked to Jimmy and then to Geoff.

"Well, I don't know the exact reason," Geoff said. "But I don't think he can."

"What do you say, Jimmy?" Tom said,

Tom hoped for Geoff's sake that the silent man would find his voice and confirm that he was no longer one of the lost. But Jimmy's response was to nod at them some more, his bloody angelic visage inviting charity and understanding.

"Want a cup of coffee, Jimmy?" Tom said. "Yes? You do?

Okay, you go on out and we'll join you in a few minutes."

The prayer room door closed on Jimmy's rolling gait.

Tom said, "What did he use on his face?"

"I lent him that razor that's kept in the bathroom cabinet."

"You mean my razor?" Tom said.

"Oh, was that your razor, pastor?"

"Never mind. Sit down a minute, let's talk about Jimmy and his confession of faith. Do you think it was genuine?"

Geoff's joy began to escape into the doubting air of reason, as he realized he had failed in his discernment of Jimmy's spiritual condition.

"Come to think of it, there was something funny about the way that guy responded to the Lord, like he knew all about it, like he'd done it all before."

"Funny, huh?" Tom said. "So what happened when you asked him about Jesus?"

"He just smiled the whole time, and when he said the sinner's prayer he was giggling. He seemed to be filled with the joy of the Lord."

"So how did he say the sinner's prayer when he doesn't talk?"

"Oh, he mostly grunted, while I said it." Geoff managed a self-conscious chuckle. "Now what?" he said.

"See what he wants. And remember we don't want him to become a permanent fixture around here."

"How do you save a guy like that?" Geoff said.

"Good question. Jimmy's got things to do, people to see, places to go. He's a travelling man. He's not from around here. He's touring the country on people like us. See Canada on two Christians a day. He's an artist. And who knows what he might be addicted to."

"I guess I blew it," Geoff said.

"Forget it. It's all a learning experience. You'll know the

next time."

Geoff then hesitated before leaving the prayer room. He had something else on his mind.

"I've been wanting to ask you," he said. "I've heard you know a lot about the Indian people here, and their customs and rituals."

"A little bit. What do you want to know?"

"Well, for instance, what do they do in the Longhouse?"

"And why do you want to know?" Tom said.

"I'm curious, that's all. I've heard about the demonic stuff and the witchcraft and I've wondered if it's all true."

Tom had a suspicion that Geoff was on some kind of mission. Of what kind he wasn't sure. He weighed up whether or not a little knowledge would be a dangerous thing. He decided a few facts might not hurt him.

"It might be helpful for you first to understand some background. The Cowichan elders believe preserving their culture is the answer to the challenges facing their people. And the Longhouse and the winter ceremonials are central to what they want to preserve. And they think that getting their young people involved in preserving their culture will give them a firm foundation so they can survive in the world today. But as you might have heard, some have died during the Longhouse spirit dancing initiations."

"Yeah, I've heard that. So what's this spirit dancing all about? How do people die from dancing?"

"Spirit dancing is about spirit possession, and that kind of activity sometimes has a bad result."

Tom could see Geoff's interest growing.

"So you mean the dances they do are for real," Geoff said. "I mean when they dance, they really are worshipping spirits?"

"They're not worshipping the spirits. They're inviting them to come and be their spirit companions, like guardian angels.

But remember that even though spiritually we don't agree with what they are doing, it's not up to us to judge them. We are the ones who came into their territory and in God's name devastated their families with the residential schools. It's a wonder they've survived at all. And they continue to face many chronic problems on the Reserve today. Many of the young people are lost, and kids are having kids. That's why Will is so important. He has the potential to bring light and hope to the Cowichan people."

"How do you know so much about it?" Geoff said. "Have you ever seen spirit dancing?"

"As a matter of fact I have," Tom said. "Years ago when I was a hippie, high on drugs."

His confession accomplished the desired effect. He enjoyed watching Geoff's eyes widen.

Tom said, "An Indian hippie friend of mine took me to the Longhouse one night. I grooved on the whole scene. I didn't understand then what was going on. I do now. The dancers were dancing to the beat of evil spirits, and considering the drugs I was on at the time, so was I."

Geoff tried to find words, but his self-righteous disgust silenced him.

Tom said, "But even though I know all this now, there's not much I can do, except pray. As a minister of the gospel there's no way I can start telling them what I think about spirit dancing, given the church's early history here. They'd just call me a racist, and the media would too, if I quoted what the Bible says about the demonic forces at work in the world and how the spirit dancing rituals are one manifestation of those forces. It would just sound like hate to them. And as for the rest of the valley's population, including the majority of Christians, if I made an issue of the Longhouse ritual abuse, I'd be laughed out of town. Most of the people here, who care about it at all, think spirit dancing is harmless, just Indian tradition."

"But I still don't get it," Geoff said, shaking his intelligent head. "What goes on during these rituals that's so bad?"

Tom had talked enough, and he'd had enough. The subject was too depressing. And no wonder. In the last few months his heart had been troubled by a crucial question. What were his motives? Did he really have a genuine love for the native people and want to have a relationship with them, or had he been fooling himself? And were they just potential converts that he hoped to enter on his eternal scorecard?

"We'll talk again some other time," he said. "Why don't you go and see if you can find out what Jimmy wants and then come back and tell me?"

Geoff shrugged. He wasn't satisfied, but he knew he wasn't going to get any more information today.

Geoff said, "Yeah, he won't fool me this time."

"Go easy on him. We're not here to condemn him."

Geoff nodded, got up, and then left the prayer room. Tom leaned back on the green cracked vinyl of his favorite donated recliner, a perfect fit for him in the extended position. He closed his eyes and listened to the rain that pelted the windows in periodic light gusts. He became drowsy, the expanding radiators crackling and popping in his melting consciousness as the temperature of the water coming from his furnace rose. And he thought about the people he had nurtured in the church and the coming loss of them, or were they the ones who were losing him? Either way, there would be a wall built now between him and them. The bricks were already knee-high and rising. On his side he was using resentment for mortar. But he had to wonder if they ever had been a church family to begin with. How could they have been? A real church family was supposed to look after its members, the same way natural families did, but that was wrong too, natural families were often dysfunctional, and at Christmas time sometimes vicious. The annual celebration was coming soon. He and Ruby would do what they always did, feed turkey to the homeless, token stuff, make everybody feel good, and then later when January arrived the poor would resume their stare in his mind: Gaunt faces and hollow eyes, frayed tweed sport coats and flared polyester pants, out for a night on the town. But before the New Year was rung in, and before the Christmas season came into full bloom, the Ministerial was having the evangelist, Chester Thomas, come to town. And who would get saved? What were the odds? Then he remembered *odds* weren't supposed to be part of a Christian's belief system. But odds or no odds, there was always hope. Maybe there would be a revival this time. Such a thing was possible.

But there was no sense wasting time thinking about it. Praying was a better use of his time, although there was a minor detail to be worked out. He wasn't on speaking terms with the Boss. He knew, of course, the first move was up to him, and that his pride was the obstacle. It was always pride. He knew all he had to do to have the burden lift was to get on his face and ask for forgiveness and let go of his bitterness. So why didn't he? Maybe he liked to suffer. Or maybe he thought he deserved the pain. No, that was all too psychological. How could the Center's failure and Ruby's illness be his fault? He had dedicated himself to establishing the Center and building the church. He had sacrificed himself, his whole life. And there was nothing he could do about Ruby's cancer. He didn't know why God was allowing the enemy to kill his wife and destroy his work. But the game wasn't over yet. There was still hope, for Ruby anyway, but not for the church. He knew his church was determined to dump him and his Center, not to mention ridding themselves of his radical preaching.

He made his move and slid the recliner into the upright position. Then he fell to his knees, and then he lay on the prayer-room carpet. Face in hands he asked the Lord if He had time to hear what he had to say. And He did. After a few minutes the burdens of the last few months lifted, and he felt the peace and joy a merciful God can impart to one of his own. And he felt faith begin to rise. And the wall, the one he had been erecting around himself to keep out more of the pain and sorrow, crumbled, and his self-pity was transformed into prayer for Ruby. And he knew his season of selfishness had been blown away by the Spirit of God.

Geoff opened the door, and saw Tom on the floor.

"Uh, sorry, pastor," he said, "but I figured out what Jimmy wants. Twenty dollars for ferry fare to the Mainland. When I arrived at that amount he grunted and grinned. Uh, sorry again for interrupting."

Tom squinted and then smiled at Geoff.

"That's all right," he said. "You know we don't usually hand out cash, but we'll make an exception this time. Take it out of the coffee money. And tell him we'll pray for him. And stand back when you give it to him. He'll be in a hurry to leave."

"Right, thanks pastor."

Tom lifted himself to his hands and knees and then stood. He took a Bible from the bookshelf and lay back again in the chair. He opened to the book of Joshua and began to read chapter three, where Joshua meets the Commander of the Lord's army. And he imagined himself in the presence of the Commander. Tom knew he had a lot to answer for, but still the battle was ahead; the good times in the Spirit were yet to come; he would never have to look back and say, *those were the good times,* because in the Lord there was always something new ahead, something greater than the former moves of the

Spirit. And the movement was always toward that final revelation of Jesus, when he would return the second time for his Bride, the Church. But if he were to tell his fellow citizens that the Lion of the Tribe of Judah would be returning soon, they would laugh and scoff. But if he were to tell them that Lord Konan of Pluto was coming in a flying saucer to liberate the earth, many would at least consider it as a possibility. That was the way the world was these days.

But as for him he knew that he had been loosed now from the bitterness he had been nurturing. The Spirit had broken through, and his heart had been relieved of its burden. He had remembered the truth. His life was in eternity, not here on earth. He was a sojourner here, a temporary resident, waiting for the Eternal Truth to be revealed in His fullness. And now he had to go home and reassure Ruby of the truth. He had to encourage her in her faith, whatever the outcome of her illness might be. They had been on a downhill slide long enough. They had eternal victory on their side. This life on earth was a wisp of smoke in light of their future glory with their Lord. And even if he had to continue here for a while longer before he joined her there, what was that but a flicker compared to forever? And then Tom felt the warm glow of God's Spirit and the peace of His presence increase until he could see himself cupped in the Lord's hand, a precious vessel to be used for His glory. And then he put a healthy, young Ruby there too, and they were content, holding each other in the palm of the Lord's hand, the Spirit of God enlivening them forever. Then, secure, he nodded off, holding that beautiful golden image in his mind.

CHAPTER TWELVE

Jesse Thornton sat at a window table overlooking Maple Bay. The pub was half empty. The nerve of the guy preaching to him in his own office. And criticizing him for being delinquent in not covering his joke of a Center. They were all the same. Hypocrites. He probably beat his wife besides.

Jesse gulped down the last of his glass of beer and waved to Benny for another. Bloody fanatics. They were all the same. None of that nonsense for him. He was Catholic of course. He was done as a baby. He had been sprinkled with the water. His parents had told him about it. But was that the only thing that made him Catholic, some water sprinkled on him when he was a baby? That couldn't have been the only thing. He remembered going to church a few times. He was certainly never an altar boy. They were finding out now that many of them had been abused. He had never been abused by a priest. But there were those times when his parents sent him to visit his pedophile grandfather. He didn't like to think about those times. Why bother dredging that up? His parents must have known though, but why be bitter?

Benny brought Jesse his next beer, took the money, and went back to the bar. Jesse drained half the glass in a few gulps.

His parents, they never went to church, except to Mass at Christmas, and sometimes Easter, but they claimed to be Catholic. Maybe a person only had to be born a Catholic to be one, like being born into a certain race. When he was forced to give an answer about his religion, he always said he was Catholic. They asked him his religion at the hospital when he had his gall bladder out, and he said, "Roman Catholic," just as if he went to Mass twice a week. You could stay away from the church and feel guilty all your life if you wanted to, and then you could be buried a Catholic if the priest got to you in time and gave you last rites. Or could you? He wasn't sure about that. Either way, there was something civilized about being allowed to belong and also being allowed to be a reprobate.

Besides, here in North America there was more acceptance of life's pleasures, more tolerance of the human condition. Not like in other places, Northern Ireland for instance, the Protestants and Catholics shooting and bombing each other to kingdom come. And you only had to look at those crazy religious fanatics in the Middle East. None of them got along. The Arabs and the Jews at each other's throats over a few square miles of land. Killing each other. You would have thought they had nothing else to do. And those young Palestinians throwing rocks, and the Jewish soldiers firing tear gas and bullets, rubber and otherwise. Crazy. Inflamed over who was right. The Americans had the solution though, they just couldn't see it yet. But it was right there in front of them. Every major American city had one. And those young Palestinians would be perfect. Their arms had to be in great shape, throwing those rocks day after day. Their energy needed channeling, that's all that was needed. Get them some uniforms. Teach them a few of the fundamentals, they were good at fundamentals. Yes, that's what was needed, some organization. Release hostilities in a harmless way. Sure, the spikes might fly a little high at second base, but once they learned the rules they'd settle down. They would be real *Bush* leaguers. Build a few stadiums. Sell tickets. There would be plenty of money to be made too; that would keep the interest up. The West Bank Rebels vs. Arafat's Angels, check your guns at the stadium door. Ah, sport! And then there was football in winter for the hard-core. And for the brutal at heart, there was hockey. Yes, hockey was the answer. He would propose the solution in one of his upcoming editorials. Peace through sport, what an ingenious concept it was. And as for him, he of course would be guaranteed the Nobel Peace Prize.

His deepening meditation on religion was interrupted by the appearance of a frail, middle-aged woman, her black hair streaked with gray. She had entered the pub and was taking cautious steps toward a window table three over from his. Her dark eyes were transfixed on the seascape outside. Jesse looked out at the coming winter night, the rain and the shadows of dusk dimming his view of the ocean, the day's snowfall now melting in the rain. He wondered what the woman was staring at out there. She seemed to be gazing through the scene in the same way she gazed through the window. He suspected she was holding it all in her mind, as she ignored the process of finding the chair and of sitting down. She performed the routine actions nevertheless, her eyes wide and glistening, perhaps a tear there escaping but wiped away by her passing hand, which, with the other, then removed her gray scarf and black cloth coat. She made him nervous the way she was, the way she was there, three tables away locked in her trance. But snap, she looked his way. Face to face. She was middle-aged lovely despite her drawn features. And there was something else that radiated from her, an aura that attracted him like a flame draws moths. He remembered his editor in Port Moody who had taken a month to fade away. He visited him that one last token time. There in the hospital bed, where his editor used to be, were orphaned Ethiopian child's eyes engulfed in black hollows. He saw death on the woman three tables down, and he desired to know when it got there and why it was there and who she was, and so on, the five Ws of death, a newspaper editor's bread and butter. Death was always news, but was she an even bigger story? He'd seen her somewhere. He tried to remember. In his mind he molded more flesh on her face and body and made her smile. She was becoming someone he had met, but he couldn't be sure. If it was her, then the day wasn't wasted. He watched her turn her head toward the bar, and he could see that she would have been a knockout twenty years ago. Knockout? No, a groovy chick, that's what she would have been twenty years ago. A beautiful woman, that's what she still was. He would wait a few minutes and then go over and find out her story.

Ruby ordered a cider, a dry one like she used to have, and she would enjoy peaceful, happy thoughts the way she used to have when.... But why should she fool herself? There was no *when*, unless she went back to high school, but that was too far to go right now, and there was not much joy to remember when she got there. Why not stay in the here and now? This was the first time she had been back. What a mess they had made of the place. She shouldn't be here, of course. Everyone knew that a respectable pastor's wife shouldn't be found dead in a place like this. But what did appearances matter now? God, she knew, didn't object. Jesus had broken bread with the sinners of His day. So what did her being here matter to anyone? And Tom could make his own stew; he knew by now the ingredients. And he would find her note.

Benny plunked down the bottle of cider and a glass, collected the money, nodded his taciturn thanks, and slithered back the way he came. Ruby's memories were not of this. The old Maple Bay Inn she carried in her mind was younger and more romantic, even though she'd hated the place twenty years before when Tom had spent his life here. Still, you had to cherish memories of your blossoming womanhood, and sometimes it was necessary to store a bad memory in your mind with a white lace border, since it had to be there anyway. But what about that picture of young hippies on the back cover of the Whole Earth Cookbook. She had discovered it yesterday, hiding in the basement under a stack of National Geographic magazines. And what about those other pictures, the ones she felt she had to dig out of her old album? What about those? They couldn't have been that young. She and Tom and the rest of them must have been older than that; she had felt older than that at the time. They couldn't have been children; could they have been children, those long-haired children in the photographs, in their early twenties, hiding their collective fear behind their smiles?

Still, the view was the same. Out the window was the Bay and Saltspring Island, ignore the rest, including that ogling monster of a newspaper editor three tables down, trying to appear the intellectual in his tweed and jeans, suede elbow patches, too. She had seen him there too late. She would have to stay now. Besides, what harm was there in her being here alone, in a bar, a pastor's wife in a small town, drinking cider, three tables down from the town's chief news gatherer? Forget about possible damage to her husband's reputation; what more could the Cowichan Valley do to them? Look at him, trying to be warm and fuzzy in that beard, but dangerous underneath. *The pen is mightier than the sword* and all that. But not so mighty in his case, considering the editorials he seemed fond of writing. That's right, she was safe, she wasn't fouling the environment in any way. Ecology seemed to be all he could write about. She guzzled a mouthful of cider straight from the bottle for effect. It tasted the same, sweet and tart. Then she glared over toward the editor. Why not toss the bottle into the Bay and get a mention on page one? Carousing pastor's wife causes mayhem in Maple Bay: Throws in her empties, maims two seagulls and stuns a frolicking porpoise. Christians, a mortal threat to Mother Earth. Hell to pay.

Was he getting up? He must be leaving? No, was he

bringing his glass over here? No, he couldn't be. Dear God. Picked-up first time out, and by an intellectual too. Oh, what would he say? Was he saying it now? His lips were moving beneath the moustache, and yes, sounds were coming out.

"Forgive me for interrupting. I'm Jesse Thornton, editor of The Cowichan Leader, and…er, do you mind if I sit?"

Ruby shook her head and poured her cider into the glass. No, she didn't mind. Why should she mind being given an opportunity to discuss the environment?

"You see," he said, sitting, "I thought I recognized you. Aren't you Mrs. Pollard, the wife of Pastor Tom Pollard?"

Ruby furrowed her brow in thought and raised her pondering fingers to her chin. He responded with a polite smile.

"I cannot tell a lie," she said. "Yes, I am that very same person of whom you speak."

She sipped her cider and awaited interrogation.

"Come here often?" she added.

"Yes, often," he said. He leaned toward her, his hands clasped on his stomach, his elbows resting on the arms of his chair. "This is quite a coincidence, but I talked to your husband this afternoon, and he seemed a little upset…er…is he feeling well?"

"Only back wounds," Ruby said.

She felt her flippant mood beginning to harden into hostility.

"As a result of?" he said.

"Retreating."

"You lost me there."

"Thank God, I thought you were here for the evening."

Oh, oh, she was as bad as her husband, Jesse thought. Trouble, more trouble.

"That's not a Christian attitude, Mrs. Pollard."

"I'm backsliding, so I don't have to be nice."

He leaned back in his chair, digesting his beer and her last remark.

Ruby managed a weary smile, her sudden fatigue and the cider beginning to clash.

"May I buy you another cider?" he said.

He didn't wait for her answer and motioned to Benny.

"You people of the press are a forceful bunch," she said.

Ruby had come to the Inn to be alone and indulge her self-pity, but here he was, the newspaperman, insisting on disturbing her, so why not give the poor man a scoop?

In a firm, loud voice, she said, "I've got cancer. You know, six months to live, you know how it is."

Jesse looked around to see who heard, and then he turned back to her in time to hear her continue in a quieter voice, "But I'm a Christian, so I'm not too worried about it."

That took a lot of energy, Ruby thought, exhausted, and she wondered if she would make it out of the place alive.

Christians were all alike, Jesse moaned in his mind. And this one was extra special.

"But you look well," he said.

Jesse's hand brought his beer to his lips for a sip to hide his face's embarrassment over distorting the facts.

"You mean I'm pale, emaciated, wan and gaunt, don't you, Mr. Editor?"

Ruby had more fight left in her than she realized. He had asked for the interview, let him try to finish it. Her conscience tried to find herself guilty for her behavior, but she overruled with another sip of cider.

She said, "Were you a Yale man, Mr. Thornton?"

Jesse looked toward the window for consolation. Journalism was a lonely life. First the husband sits in his office and preaches at him, and now his better-half bludgeons him in his own pub, and all he wanted to do was provide a service for the public by exposing corruption in the church.

"Okay, you win, Mrs. Pollard, I'll go back where I came from."

Jesse leaned forward, grabbed his glass, and began to propel himself upward.

She said, "It wasn't Yale then?"

She realized she had won, and she began to feel sorry for the man. He seemed humane enough. She had been too nasty no matter what his motives were. She touched his tweedy forearm with her left hand.

"Stay," she said. "I apologize. It's the cider's fault. I'm sorry."

Jesse teetered and fell back into his chair. He paused a moment to consider his options and then decided to confess.

"Your husband and I had an uncomfortable time this afternoon," he said.

Jesse noticed his voice had taken on an intimate tone, which surprised him. He had, in that instant, between standing and sitting, entered into a relationship with this woman.

"You were at the Center?" she asked.

Ruby was now concerned for her husband. Had Jesse been taking advantage of him?

Jesse reached for the package of cigarettes in his shirt pocket and then stopped.

Ruby said, "Go ahead and smoke, the air in here is already blue, what's the harm?"

Jesse snorted a laugh and left his cigarettes where they were.

"Your husband came to the Leader to correct an ad, and I asked him for some information about the evangelist who's coming to town next week and...."

She smiled at his disclosure, and said, "Going to get the goods on those crooked preachers, are you Mr. Thornton?"

He then saw himself through her eyes, and feeling self-conscious he realized that from her viewpoint his motives and methods were amusing, and then they were to him also. He tapped the side of his glass with a fidgety finger, snickered at the glass and himself and then looked up into her eyes. He was tempted to immerse himself there until he saw the specter of impending death luring him with its mystery. A sudden shiver jerked his eyes from hers, and he turned his head toward the bar. His rising discomfort was compounded by the mental image surfacing again of his dying Port Moody editor. On a dreary day like today, he thought, who needed to be reminded of death? This chance run-in with Mrs. Pollard was upsetting his pub life. He lit a cigarette, took a deep drag and then placed it in the ashtray.

"What is it with you people anyway?" he said.

"You people? Do you mean dying people, or do you mean women, or do you mean just dying women...?"

"Okay, fine, I get the point. I mean Christians, you Christians."

"Oh, I see. You came over to visit me so that you might become more informed about the religious life. In that case, I'd be happy to help you understand. For one thing, the ultimate question has been answered for us. Death no longer threatens us with extinction. And even though we often falter along the way, in the end we know we will arrive at our destination."

Ruby was proud of herself now. She had managed to give a sturdy witness to her faith despite her current lack of it.

"You're brainwashed, all of you," Jesse said. "When you're dead you're dead, end of question, end of answer, the end period, there is no more, amen."

He crossed his right leg over his left, in the process tipping the table up with his knee but not spilling a drop, and then he crossed his arms, steadfast in his position, as his knee let the table down and his upraised chin challenged her. He then saw himself in the window's reflection and realized that his indignant posture was a ridiculous one. Nevertheless he was stuck with it.

"None of it matters," he added.

His parody of a stern manner was undermined further by his inability to stifle in its entirety an exploding belch.

Ruby was about to challenge his professed atheism, when she was distracted by the view through the town-side window. A green Volvo, with some stubborn white slush clinging to the roof, jerked to a halt under a parking-lot light, and a handsome middle-aged man jumped out into the rain. It must have been the note, she thought, perhaps the part about the Maple Bay Pub and the cider. And what would he say about Mr. Thornton? But how was she to have known he would be here? What a blessing!

"Is that your husband coming?" Jesse said.

Jesse's emotions were sloshing between the hope of a newsworthy event and his reluctance to witness a domestic scene.

"Maybe he'll shoot you, Mr. Thornton: Yale man murdered in local pub by crazed pastor. How would that sound? But then who would write the editorial condemning the dangerous use of a firearm in this delicate waterfront habitat teeming with endangered shellfish?"

Ruby could see that Jesse didn't think that was funny.

The second cider was making her giddy, but it was also fortifying her enough to face any unpleasantness Tom might incite. He was now poised inside the door, searching for her, a bundle of turmoil and anger.

"Oh, good, he sees us," she said.

Jesse began to drum his fingers on the table and to hum a subdued and unstructured tune. How did Christians handle these kinds of situations, he wondered? Perhaps the pastor would drop his annoying self-righteous attitude and rant and swear. But hold on, what about that fundamentalist couple on the Mainland a few years ago? He shot her, didn't he? Damned violent fanatics, all of them were. He began to hum a different tune, *The Man Who Shot Liberty Valence*, a little softer and an octave higher.

"Over here, Tom," she called.

Ruby's heart was overjoyed to see him and her cider tongue was eager to do battle.

Tom stalked toward the table that harbored Ruby and the pagan. Why this, he thought? There had to be a reason. He had just gotten right with God, and now he was sinning in his mind again. Strangle lard gut and harangue Ruby; they both deserved punishment for tormenting him, all in the same day. But when he reached the table and saw Ruby's face and where he was and heard her saying, "Oh, Tom, good of you to come," he withered, and then as if twenty years had fallen away in an instant, he said, "So this is far-out, Ruby, who's your friend?"

"This is Mr. Thornton, environmentalist, town gossip and philosopher. We've only this minute decided that God is dead, or I should say he has come to that conclusion. He's quite positive on the subject, or I should say he's negative on the subject but positive of his negativity."

"And how many ciders have you had, young lady?" Tom said.

Tom's anger was gone now. He saw that Ruby was trying to enjoy herself, which was a rare event these days. On her face was an expression he hadn't seen there in years, an expression of youth and vitality, and he wondered how, in defiance of her illness, she was doing that. How was she able to look twenty years younger with a glance, a smile, and a turn of the head?

Ruby said, "Don't be patronizing, pastor, I know your history, and alcohol abuse is not the best subject for you to choose as sermon material."

"So, I see you're at the nasty stage," Tom said.

Tom sat down, grinning. He then nodded at Jesse, who was regretting that he had landed on this planet, and that he had encountered these two alien creatures, who, he perceived, were engaged in a rehearsed ritual that was the opening act preceding the expected marital blood-letting scene.

Tom said to Jesse, "Sorry about this afternoon. I was too pushy."

Jesse's lower jaw dropped, leaving his mouth open. To cover the exposed hole he lifted his glass and drank, swallowing three times and thinking he was able to play this game too; he had the potential to be more gracious than this pastor any day.

Jesse said, "Had I known your wife was such a delightful person I would have gladly heard your message and donated to the cause also."

"Mr. Thornton's a Yale man you know, Tom," Ruby said.

Ruby was oblivious now to her illness, and to the Cowichan Valley, and to its Christian inhabitants.

To Jesse, she said, "Forgive Tom's appearance. He's really called to be a furnace man. Notice the streak of soot on his coat sleeve. I just know it's from a furnace. Can't keep him away from the things."

Tom acknowledged Ruby's taunt by brushing his sleeve, his initial delight in finding her enjoying herself now shifting into straight-faced passivity.

He said, "So you went to Yale, did you Jesse?"

Ruby said, "Oh, so you two are on a first name basis, are you? In that case, Jesse, just call me Ruby. Isn't this cozy, Tom?"

Tom looked down at his Adidas and then at his coat sleeve.

He was not cozy. Ruby's wit might have continued to be entertaining if he were not being scalded now by the years of unspoken discontent boiling beneath her amusing remarks. What was he guilty of? Maybe he would just have to get used to the idea that she held him responsible for her life and everything that had happened to them. But why wouldn't she open up and talk to him about it, so he would know what to do? He didn't want to leave their relationship like this.

Seeing Tom's displeasure, Ruby said, "Well then, Mr. Editor, how about you. Are you cozy?"

Benny raised his chin and eyebrows in Tom's direction, questioning him whether or not he wanted another round. Tom shook his head. Jesse was disgusted that the pastor was too cheap to buy a round. But he wouldn't let Tom's lack of manners distract him from being gracious himself.

"Ruby's a lovely name," Jesse said.

"My mother picked it," Ruby said. "She was Jewish."

What a combination, Jesse thought, part of the Zionist conspiracy, and a Christian besides.

"My father was Greek Orthodox," she said.

She lifted her cider in a secret salute to the image of her airborne father in his pink Cadillac, and then she gulped a mouthful of cider, swallowed it, and congratulated herself for not choking.

"Greek Orthodox, really?" Jesse said. "I'm Catholic."

"I thought you said you were an atheist," Ruby said.

She shook her finger at him, the cider enlivening her communication skills.

"Yes, I am, but I was born a Catholic," he said.

Jesse looked at Tom in the hope that being born into the church would count for something.

Tom struggled to refrain from preaching to Jesse twice in the same day, and won. Preaching to someone who was under the influence of alcohol was like singing to the moon, you exercised your vocal chords but its orbit remained unchanged. And besides, why risk being stomped on by beer-driven belligerence and then being embarrassed in front of Ruby, who was having enough problems with her own faith these days?

"There's hope for you yet," Tom said.

Tom now felt an urge to impress Ruby with his skillful witnessing to the faith, but he knew that self-glorification was a bad motive for spreading the gospel, even if all he wanted was some affirmation from Ruby.

"The only hope for me is right here," Jesse said.

Ruby and Tom stared at him and then at his surroundings.

Jesse said, "I mean this world, of course."

"I don't know how they could have let you into Yale," Ruby said.

They all knew the joke was stale now, and so was the beer inside Jesse. He excused himself, omitting all of the usual polite comments concerning his destination, and walked to the john, his imitation of a normal gait betraying his inebriation.

Tom said, "So what brings you to these parts, ma'am?"

Ruby applied a fingernail to the label on her cider bottle and tried to smooth out the wrinkles.

"Nostalgia," she said.

She hated the confusion she experienced when he tried to charm her. He could be captivating when he made the effort, which was seldom. So what was she supposed to do now? Try again to believe he was the man she thought she married? It was nonsense even to try. Still, he amazed her. After all these years he was able for special occasions to rouse a witticism from among those sleeping beneath the blanket of humility he cultivated as essential to his pastoral calling.

"But you never liked the place," he said.

"Nellie phoned today from Toronto. There's a 20-year

Maple Bay reunion planned, for the summer, in August. I thought I would come and get a feel for it now. I went through some old pictures yesterday. You were something special to behold, Tom."

Tom absorbed with grace the implication that in her opinion he was no longer something, since the revelation wasn't a new one.

Jesse sauntered back to the table, sober as a judge, wiping his damp hands on the thighs of his jeans, hitching his belt, and adjusting his lapels.

"Have to be on my way," he said. "It's been a pleasure Mrs. Pollard, and don't be a stranger, Tom."

He was good at exits, he thought, put on a solid show, smile, enhance his reputation.

"Keep dry," Tom said.

Jesse's smile shrank at Tom's remark to form pursed lips.

"I mean the rain," Tom said, attempting to redeem himself from the sarcasm that had slipped out. "And come over and visit me at the Center, maybe do a story, or who knows, you might even dig up some dirt on crooked evangelists."

"It might just happen, you never know your luck."

Ruby asked, "Do you believe in luck, Jesse?"

"Only when it's good, and it's mine."

He bowed his chivalrous head to Ruby and then departed. Jesse enjoyed getting in the last word. It created a good impression. A clever man, on his way up. Was he sober enough to drive? Of course he was. What a question to ask himself.

"All that man really needs is salvation," Tom said.

"That's right, look what it's done for us," Ruby said.

"Come on, Ruby, let's not take that attitude, and let's go home. You've had enough."

"How do you know if I've had enough?" Ruby said. "You don't even know when you've had enough."

"Do we have to go into it here? Come on, let's go, I'll follow you home."

"No, I'm not going." Ruby was weakening but remained determined. "I'll follow you home when I'm ready. I want to stay here for a little while longer – alone."

Tom reached for her hand, which was resting by her glass on the table, but she withdrew it in time and slipped it beneath the table to hold the other one, her eyes turning away from his.

"Fine," Tom said, pushing his chair back and standing. "I'll see you at home. Be careful how you drive."

She nodded at Tom's departure. Yes, she would be careful. She wouldn't want to kill herself on the way home. The initial euphoric effects of the cider were fading, and her stomach was queasy. And what kind of game had she been playing with Jesse? A few bottles of cider and a fatal disease and she'd created a new persona for herself. There she had been in all her glory, impersonating the perfect English gentlewoman, and she an American too. That was it for her; no more Jane Austen novels, no more cider, but as for the cancer there was nothing more to do about that, except pray. But who was listening? No. She was tired of thinking about that. Instead, she would vow to make it to the reunion. That's what she needed, something to look forward to. In August she would see all the old faces, most of which she had despised at the time, but never mind, nothing was perfect when you went for a trip down memory lane. No, nothing was perfect.

Outside the rain pelted the window, the drops running in short twisting streams before playing themselves out and dissipating on the glass. Yes, she would make it to the reunion. And yes, she would be noble and brave, a woman for all seasons, and yes, she would be a shining witness to her faith for all of them to see. She coughed a dry, quiet little cough to herself, and imagined her life continuing on, her cancer gone.

But then what? Years to live. Years to live with Tom, in ministry somewhere. What a thrill. She knew she wasn't supposed to see life this way, but right now, to her, it was hopeless.

CHAPTER THIRTEEN

Jesse sat in front of the keys, stirring his thoughts into his next editorial. Whales and seals were his topic this week, with a dash of garbage tossed into the brew. He hoped that his considered opinion would whip up in the minds of his readers a volatile mess that would begin to fester and then ooze over into indignation, enough indignation that they might recognize themselves as part of the problem and, if only to ease the consciences of their effluent producing selves, buy a few of those environment-friendly items the corporate opportunists were peddling at the supermarket. Oh, the power of the press!

And how about a catchy and concise ending such as, *Garbage is for keeps.* No, that wouldn't do it, too final. It needed something open-ended like, *Can the community, leaders and citizens alike, muster the collective courage to act decisively and sacrificially to thwart planetary annihilation.* Too strong maybe, but let it stand; *thwart* was a good word, should be used more often.

Think ahead. Next week, how about trees. Brazilian rain forest going up in smoke. The Greenhouse effect. It could have an upside though; kids would grow faster and taller in a greenhouse. But the environmentalists wouldn't be amused; he would be ostracized for that wise remark. No, trees had to be protected. People in the Pacific Northwest identified with trees; promoting their protection was good for his newspaper's circulation, too; it showed them all that The Cowichan Leader cared about the forest and was a good corporate citizen. Don't mention the mill and newsprint, and watch out for the lumber people. Don't step on toes. Balancing act. Only did the trees topic once before. Won't peek back at it. Start from scratch, showed integrity.

Pleased with this week's effort and confident he had plenty of material for next week's editorial, he swiveled in his chair to look out the window again. He had been checking every few minutes, since he saw her go out for her coffee break. And, aha, yes, finally, there she was across the street, darling, radiant Isabel, springing out through the door of the Totem Café, restraining her nimble legs at the far curb, pausing for the traffic to stop; then descending to glide through the crosswalk past bulbous Jonathan Hobbes, walking his wife's rat on a string. And onward she came past that ogling motorist, and nearing the curb up she sailed and down she floated to alight on snow-white cushioned boots; and with a toss of her head above scarlet flying scarf ends, she burst toward him. And did he have a chance? But wait, there on the front steps to greet her with a quip was Ed, the sly Cowichan Leader' Sales Manager, hands in the pockets of his black overcoat, holding his stomach undercover, and doubling up to the god of laughter, a deceitful worshipper, only a ploy to win her. But, good, she saw through him, gave him a nod and a humoring smile and into the office she came, growing in Jesse's eyes. But were his eyes bigger than his belly? Not a chance, and that was his main problem, how to lose ten to fifteen years and their accumulated flab in two weeks or less. Before-and-after photos. Before in a Hawaiian tent shirt, and after in red bikini briefs, standing poised on the white sand, red and white beach ball spinning on upward-pointing finger, other arm akimbo, thighs bulging below rippling torso, all the measure of a man. He would swear off beer for her, bathe his cynicism in love's gushes, and also buy some sweats.

He heard her heavenly feet stroke the floor and turn into the ad office across the hall. Heaven. Hmm. That reminded him. That evangelist was coming to the Cowichan Theatre tonight. Maybe he should go and cover the gathering of the faithful. But why? Nobody really cared. His readers wouldn't miss it. But what if he did uncover some dirt? The Reverend Chester Thomas offers buckets of bombast and then bilks the faithful. Describe the giant offering baskets; interview the disgruntled and disappointed; throw in a fanatic's opinion of the proceedings to add a touch of absurdity to the piece. Great stuff. Take a camera, get a miracle on film: Evangelist's clutching hands are removed from the congregation's wallets without the aid of a surgeon's knife.

Then he remembered Ruby. She would be there too, no doubt hoping for a miracle, and her husband, Pastor Tom, aching for her. How could he cover the story with them there? Still, his duty was to get the truth, and mince the charlatan in the process. But why should he give Chester Thomas any publicity at all? It legitimized the swindle in a way. Christians. They were a tricky bunch. But Ruby and Tom were likeable in their own way? He should go over to his Center and smell the air for this thing tonight. But maybe later. First things first. What would be a casual way to get her in here, without her sensing restrained desire? They had radar, women did; they knew what you were up to. But what would she see on her scope? Lust? A middle-aged wimp Teddy Bear? Sincerity and serious respectful intentions? Intentions? That's right, what were his intentions? An affair? Marriage? A May-December match? And then, when he became senile, she would be obliged to dote over him, devoted to the end of his days, wiping the dribble from his chin and deciphering for him the headlines in the daily newspaper. *It says, dearest, Euthanasia Figures Up Again For 2029.* But, never mind, the way technology was advancing the odds were against their being any newspapers by then. But what if she was the feminist type? She didn't look militant. Besides, the feminist movement was going through personopause these days. Better not say that out loud; they hated those kinds of remarks, when they thought you were trying to be so clever. He might even get killed for thinking like that. He hoped they didn't have ways of finding out. There was a backlash now though. Even the liberated men detested doing the ironing; they thought there would be equality, but women wouldn't settle for that. Why would they? No, if Isabel was a feminist, all bets were off. Too hard to handle. Impossible to train. His years of experience would go for nothing. She'd show no respect; just fork over the money for small-arms instruction, and the diapers are found under the change table, dearest. No, she wasn't going to entangle him in thankless servitude. But no, that was nonsense. Isabel wasn't the feminist type at all. She was more feminine than that. Oh-oh, there was another bad thought. He hoped they didn't read minds. He'd be done for. They had no sense of humor some of them. Yes, Isabel was the homebody kind of person. Dinner's in the oven, slippers at the ready, junior's gurgling in the playpen. And there was no doubt in his mind now that he was the old-fashioned type, a conservative in his middle-age, no more manning the barricades. Age had taken over from idealism, comfort had become vital. He was no longer keen on championing women's rights either, except, of course, the right to receive equal pay for equal work. How was that for tokenism? They hated that, of course. Still, if Isabel was only a little bit feminist, that would be all right too. You needed understanding between the sexes; difficult times were being had by all.

He decided to delay enticing Isabel into his office, at least until he determined his real motives, and, for starters, lost five pounds. And to begin on the right foot, he would forego the calories waiting for him this afternoon at the Maple Bay Pub and go over to Pastor Tom's Center to ask a few questions about tonight's performance at Cowichan Theatre.

CHAPTER FOURTEEN

Tom stood at the sink washing the coffee mugs in the RCMP's former women's lockup. It was now the Center's second-hand-clothes room. Doing dishes was one of the jobs at the Center he had been unable to inspire others to do. The church volunteers and those who came daily for soup and coffee were equally resistant to such labor. To spare himself the frustration, he had discontinued his inspirational talks about service, and had instead resigned himself to work humility into his own life by washing off the coffee rings and scrubbing out the hardened dregs. He lifted a tan mug from the water whose rim sported a smudged magenta lip-print left by the accentuated mouth of Lila Baker, the wife of Elder John Baker, the man who craved the pastor's job. He erased Lila's mouth and tried to scour the unkind thoughts from his mind. The good-intentioned couple had dropped into his office a few minutes before noon to sing their rendition of *No Hard Feelings*, which his stomach had rejected by attempting to spew out at them, but after Brother John's inspired chorus of *we'll all laugh about this in heaven*, his imprisoned sentiments down there had been wise enough to grumble for his ears only. And then the Bakers were gone, their half-empty mugs deposited on his desk for disposal. But he didn't blame them for their ambition. After all, they were only deluded sheep, believing they were called to be shepherds.

He paused to survey this cranny of his kingdom before he dried and carried the mugs out to the coffee counter. The second-hand clothes, hanging from the makeshift racks, and the assortment of worn shoes heaped in boxes below added a musty odor to the room, which contrasted with the lemon scent of the recently-mopped cold cement floor. The defunct toilet cubicle was stacked with boxes filled with more shoes and clothing. They stood a good chance of getting a reprieve on the bodies of the needy. A few household items were jammed together between the wall and the toilet, hoping for another chance. There was a shadeless panther lamp with frayed cord, a crumb-filled toaster oven, and a toy computer. All junk. Why was he holding onto it? He looked out at the gray, rainy, Cowichan Valley day through the heavy metal mesh securing the cell's only window. There was no future here. Why couldn't he just let all of it go?

He dried the mugs with a clean tea-towel brought from home. When he returned them soiled to Ruby, she laundered them without comment, but he knew she despised involvement in the demeaning chores of the Center, and she knew of course that he was the mug washer. She was becoming even more ashamed of him. But he could do nothing about that anymore. He felt now that God was calling him to this abasement. He had begun to realize that the church he was losing was not truly his, never had been. The church was God's property. He had known that all along of course, but now he was experiencing that truth up close. He knew the humbling of Tom had been going on for forty odd years in its various stages, and he knew that God's Spirit was closing in to do away with the old Tom altogether, the selfish one who performed for his own motives and disguised his self-seeking as the works of God. Not that he had succeeded during his life in moving any mountains; most of his life had been a failure. But this street mission had been his dream; to return to Duncan, build a church and open a Center. All for the Lord. Sure. He'd fooled himself, but God was not fooled. He knew now that his vision had been his own creation, one that he had fashioned in reality, so that he could point to it and say that he had accomplished something in his life. But now God was exposing his folly. He had wanted to show the world what he was made of, a builder of churches, a missionary to the lost and the poor. He had craved a monument to himself. Now he had one, a fallen monument, a memorial to his failure, the wasting of a life. Yet he hoped the Lord would allow him to continue in His service in whatever way he might be suited. Humility was the key. Scripture said it was. *The Lord resists the proud, but gives grace to the humble.* The death of his vision was for his own benefit, to speed his growth in humility. It had to be. But if it wasn't, then for him there would no longer be truth in anything. The game would be over. He would lose. The bad guy would win.

Tom carried the tray of dried mugs into the main lounge area and set them on the counter by the coffee urn. He heard Geoff call to him from the prayer room and then follow his voice out, asking on his way through the door if the pastor had time today to tell him some more about the Indian spirit dances. Tom decided that a little confusion might be good for Geoff's confident upper-middle-class self. Geoff's father was a doctor; his mother was on the charities circuit. They were good and proper church people, they shunned controversy, which meant they had to agree with the majority. Such a pity, Pastor Tom had to go, who was next? The image had to be kept up; grandfather had been a doctor too. They were good sound church people, mustn't make waves. Their son would come into line, only sewing some wild oats at the Center among the riffraff. The father had his own wild oats on the side, a second adolescence out of town; he needed the church image for his medical practice, but Jesus had to be kept at a distance, if you don't mind.

Tom captured his nasty speeding thoughts before they escaped out of his mouth and crushed Geoff. One of the challenges of the job was knowing too much about people and at the same time trying not to judge them. But was that even possible?

He said to Geoff, "Sure. I've got some time. We can talk in the prayer room."

Once inside the prayer room he opened the blinds to let some light in and then sat in the recliner, ready for Geoff's inquisition.

"So, Pastor...," Geoff said.

"Call me Tom. That's my name."

He was a furnace-cleaning, coffee-cup-washing, Lord's servant who was being schooled in humility by his Master. Why hold onto authority designated by men and revoked by men, when the only true authority was spiritual authority and given by God's grace? When God decided to recognize him as a shepherd of His sheep then he would resume the title, since it would never again be taken away. But for now he was a pastor in the making, one who had yet to arrive.

"I'm really not used to calling the pastor just by his first name," Geoff said. "But okay, uh, Tom."

Tom saw Geoff make an attempt to appear honored for the privilege, but he was unconvincing.

Geoff wasn't surprised by the pastor's self-demotion. He had resented having to call him by the title anyway, well aware that Pastor Tom was on his way out. But Geoff still teetered on the fence, not knowing whether to respect the man or not, since he groveled in menial chores. And didn't he know his odd behavior was the talk of the church?

Geoff said, "It's about the Indian dances and demon possession. You said you would tell me more about them."

"Right, I did."

Tom sensed insincerity in Geoff's voice, as his eager face attempted to project innocence but was a trifle too angelic. Geoff's eyes, unable to resist a slight squint, betrayed his intentions, and his pleasant smile failed to obscure Tom's view of the young man's lurking duplicity. Tom's discerning stare forced Geoff to shift in his chair, and then for security to look down his nose.

"Why don't you go and get us a couple of cups of coffee to help us focus," Tom said. "I'll take mine black."

"I don't want one, but I'll get you one if you like."

"Thanks."

Geoff went on his coffee errand, and Tom relaxed in the recliner and closed his eyes. The reason for Geoff's curiosity was obvious to Tom. Geoff was on a spy mission. Not that Geoff was uninterested in learning about the spirit dances, but what Geoff really wanted from him was a profession of heretical doctrine. If Tom were to state a theological position that contradicted fundamental notions of the clear teaching of Scripture, Geoff would have evidence that Tom advocated views contrary to basic teaching. This proof of heresy could then be presented to the confused majority of sheep, and those who had remained sympathetic to Tom would be forced to accept the fact that the elders' decision to direct him over the hill in search of another pasture was a wise one. The elders knew they had to be perceived by the flock as honest and fair, in order for their future rule to be peaceful. Tom was saddened to know that Geoff was drawn to this line of work. Besides, to know without a doubt what the Bible taught on every subject was a curse at Geoff's age -- the stuff that inquisitions were made of. But why not at least give him something to think about?

Geoff returned with the coffee, and Tom sat up to take the cup and to offer Geoff a few insights.

"The native people," he said, "have a deep reverence for the land and for nature. Do you understand that?

"Sure," he said. "They're simple people."

Geoff wondered what was so special about Tom's revelation

and resented being talked to as if he were a child.

"You're right," Tom said. "They're simple people if you understand simplicity as being the most profound condition."

"What do you mean?" Geoff said, offended. "Our minds are supposed to be used for the Lord's glory too, aren't they?"

"Right, but our minds can be idols."

"I thought you were going to tell me about the idols the Indians worship and their demonic dances and all the witchcraft?"

"I'll get to that, but first we need to take a look at our own idols and our greedy dances. We make a habit of not looking at some of the darkness we're in and instead point to the shiny surfaces of our myths to direct attention away from our spiritually bankrupt lives."

Tom realized he was trying to impress Geoff with his intellect. But so what? Geoff deserved it.

"By us," Geoff said, "you mean the unsaved population, don't you, not those in the church?"

"By us, I mean the pride and self-seeking in us all."

"Yes, I understand that. The Bible tells us all about it. But what about the spirit dancing? What goes on at those dances anyway?"

Tom was unimpressed with Geoff's eagerness to learn.

"I don't think you're ready to hear about it."

"You promised," Geoff said, sounding like a spoiled child.

Instead of giving him the details on spirit dancing, Tom decided that now was a good time to give Geoff, the Inquisitor, something to report back to the elders, some evidence that would solidify their case against Tom the heretic.

"Okay, here's something you can use," Tom said. "What the native people are doing in their spirit dances only needs redeeming. In other words what they are doing is the demonic counterfeit of the real thing."

"What does that mean?"

"I'm saying that if the native people were led to the Lord of the universe and they asked His Holy Spirit to come and fill them instead of the demonic spirits, then their songs and dances in the Spirit would be holy worship to the Lord. And then the Longhouse would be filled with light instead of darkness. And then they wouldn't need to erect church buildings to worship in, you know the way we do, to show the world that we're the church. Understand?"

Geoff understood as much as he wanted to. Pastor Tom had stepped over the edge.

"You mean they would continue to worship like heathen?"

"Heathen to you, but what makes you think that you know how church meetings are supposed to go?"

"Well you know better than I do that the Bible gives us the answer to that."

"Oh, you mean where it tells us how to line up the pews and when to take the offering and when to have the announcements and when to send the children to Sunday School."

"You know it doesn't say that."

"No, but it does say that everything has to be done decently and in order. And in the Longhouse things are in order, and the meetings are run naturally. Even the kids are allowed to be kids. The early missionaries didn't do the native people any favors, trying to make white men out of them. The Holy Spirit is able to run a church meeting quite well without people introducing their man-made traditions. You know the ones I mean; those traditions that make sure certain people remain in power and control. The Holy Spirit isn't bound by our traditions, we are."

Geoff suppressed his excitement. He'd gotten much more ammunition to supply the big guns in the eldership than he had ever expected. This *spying out of Pastor Tom and the Indians* business was too easy. Pastor Tom would next be stomping around the Longhouse whooping and hollering to God. The pastor had stepped over into the abyss, and Geoff was confident now that the church had done the right thing.

Geoff said, "So how would you make sure that they wouldn't just continue to worship their demons. I mean, how would you know it was the Holy Spirit? Would you teach them any of the Bible to keep them on track?"

Tom knew that Geoff was being sarcastic now. He captured both of Geoff's eyes and, smiling, answered him full in the face.

"I think they're quite able to understand the Bible for themselves without being confused by conflicting interpretations the White Man might throw at them."

Geoff "humphed" the same instant knuckles rapped on the door and Tom's recliner snapped upright.

"Come in," Tom said.

The door opened, and Jesse stepped into the room. He looked at Geoff, Tom, and the shabby furniture. And then he sniffed at the air.

"I've come to spy out your base of operations," he said.

Tom stood, grateful to conclude his present interview with Geoff, and he was pleased with himself for preventing his tongue from advising the young inquisitor as he left that *what you are about to do, do quickly*, since to use the Lord's words as a vengeful witticism was profane. Besides, the quote was now irrelevant. Tom had already been crucified.

Geoff and Jesse sidestepped each other, and then each carried on in his intended direction, Geoff toward the glory of righteousness, and Jesse forward to question one of the duped about the coming night's pie-in-the-sky meeting at the Cowichan Theater.

"A neophyte?" Jesse said, raising his eyebrows, his head gesturing backward over his shoulder at the departing Geoff.

"A young man on a mission," Tom said.

"So this is *your* mission then, is it?" Jesse said.

Jesse knew that his aversion to the dingy prayer room was obvious in his voice. And now that he had seen Tom in his working environment, he regretted that in the past he had been unkind to the reverend. In fact, Jesse was beginning to feel sorry for him. His wife was dying, and here he was, reigning in his gloomy kingdom, and it was freezing in the place too. But taking it easy on him was unwise; his objectivity would be lost. But what did that matter? It was only a church story.

Jesse said, "You mean to tell me they haven't got enough money in that church of yours to heat this building?"

"Have a seat. I'm holding court in here today. Would you like my head too?"

"No, I would definitely not want that. It's about the last thing I need."

"So, what's on your mind? Have you finally come to do that story on the Center? Great timing if you have. You can describe to your readers how a vision dies."

"Your church is going to pull the plug on it then?" Jesse said.

"Right. The power is going to be shut off in February."

"So what are your plans for March?"

"The question is, what are God's plans for me? When I get that answer, I'll let you know, if you're really interested."

Jesse wondered if he was interested.

He said, "How's your wife feeling?"

"She seems to be improving."

"Is she going to be at the meeting tonight?"

"We're both going. Oh, I see, that's why you came, you're still trying to get the inside story on the money-sucking evangelist."

"That's good," Jesse said. "May I use it?"

"Sure. But who knows, if you do come tonight you might get something out of it."

"I doubt that, but if I do make it there, my only purpose will be to record the spectacle for my readers."

"So what do you want from me now," Tom said, "a tour of the Center, or maybe some gossip about Reverend Thomas's character?"

"No tour, thanks, but some background information on the good reverend would be helpful. Do you have any of the advance publicity material here? The press release that came to the office last month was deposited in the basket upon its arrival. I held my nose when I realized what it was, and I got rid of it quickly. A lack of foresight, I'm afraid."

"I see. Sure, I've got some in my office. I'll get it for you before you leave."

The thought of leaving appealed to Jesse. He'd only been in Tom's Center a few minutes, and he'd had enough of the place already. It was a jail.

He said, "Well, since you mention it, I really should be going, but first would you tell me how you honestly feel about this itinerant hucksterism?"

"Is that how they taught you to ask unbiased questions in journalism school? I'm assuming you did go to school?"

"I refuse to be insulted, I'm a reporter. So what about it, where do you stand?"

"On the Fifth Amendment," Tom said.

"You can't do that in Canada."

"Then I'll stand on the Notwithstanding Clause."

"I might just see you there tonight," Jesse said.

"I'll get that material for you."

"I would appreciate that."

CHAPTER FIFTEEN

Will climbed Government Street hill on his way home from school. He wasn't eager to get there. His dad would be at home. There wasn't much work in the bush this time of year and that made him more difficult to get along with. And to make things worse, most nights he spent his time in the Longhouse. He was becoming more intense every day. Will went in through the basement door and hoped to go straight to his study room downstairs without his dad stopping him. Once he got inside and closed the door he wouldn't be bothered until dinner. His dad was doing most of the cooking these days. Most of the stuff he made wasn't half bad. Other times he ordered pizza or picked up fast food at the drive-thru. He even shopped once in a while, so the cupboards were stocked with cans you could open, and the refrigerator had frozen dinners you could heat up. So even with his mother and his sister gone they weren't starving. But Will liked to eat alone now as much as possible, or at least have dinner in front of the TV, so they didn't have to talk much. He heard his dad moving around up there, so he went into his study room and closed the door. He had enough school work to keep him busy until dinner. If he had any time left, he would read his Bible and prepare for the trouble above.

The thumps came around 5:30, the same time as usual. His dad stomped the floor three times. That was the signal to go up and face the music at dinner. He took his time climbing the stairs. When he got up there his dad was waiting for him. The pizza was on the table. Usually he called him early to set either the kitchen table or the fold-up ones in front of the TV. But tonight the table was set. That meant the choice of watching television wasn't being offered. They would be eating at the kitchen table and doing some talking on the side. Will sat down and waited for his dad to make the first move. That was the wisest thing to do. His dad was wide enough to take up the whole end of the table. And not much of it was fat.

"Help yourself," his dad said, and reached for the pizza.

Will took a couple of slices without comment. If there was any talking to be done, he wasn't going to start it. He was just as happy to focus on the pepperoni with extra cheese for a while. Will had a glass of milk to wash his down with. His dad was drinking coke out of the can.

"How'd school go today?" his dad said.

"You know," Will said.

"If I knew, I wouldn't have asked."

Will had learned that Christians were supposed to be a good example, and part of that good example was to honor your father and mother. He didn't want to talk, but it looked like he didn't have much choice.

"The school work went fine," he said. "But relationships lately could be going better."

"What do you mean?"

"You know Tim Richardson. He's been over to the house a few times."

"Sure, what about him?"

"We used to be friends, my only real white friend, but he doesn't like Christians, so now he's been avoiding me."

"I don't blame him. He probably wonders what a nice Indian boy like you is doing hanging around with a bunch of born-again idiots."

Will figured it would be best to continue with his end of the conversation and pretend not to hear his dad's insults.

He said, "None of my other friends are talking to me, either. You know, the ones that are the same color as me. The word is out. I'm what they call a pariah."

"Don't think you're teaching me some fancy new word. I know what a pariah is."

Will knew now that he'd gone far enough on the subject and concentrated on eating his pizza. But he suspected there was more trouble to come, so he decided he would try to delay the inevitable by heading off on another track.

"How are things going at the Longhouse?" Will said.

"Why don't you come down and find out, instead of spending your time at that Center for losers that you like so much."

"There are lots of losers in this world," Will said. "And a lot of them are losers only because they don't know where they belong."

"That's great. Now you're turning into some kind of philosopher. If I'd gone further in school, instead of going out and making a living in the bush, I'd be thinking up wise sayings too. But at least I know where I belong, and so should you. And I do know for sure you're not meant to be a token Indian in that white church you've been going to."

"Mom went to church."

Will saw his dad flinch, but instead of yelling he just said, "Don't bring her into this. She wouldn't be proud of what you're doing either."

Will considered talking back on the subject but decided on second thought that he didn't want to get martyred in the middle of dinner.

"I still miss her," Will said.

"I know. Life's the shits without her. There's nobody ever going to replace her, either."

"Mom didn't like you swearing, I know that for sure."

"Don't get smart. That self-righteous bunch of *skwati hwunitum* you hang out with probably talk worse than that when no one's around."

Will stopped himself from making a clever remark about being impressed with his dad's use of the Cowichan language.

Instead, he said, "I'm old enough to make my own choices."

"I know you are. If you weren't, we wouldn't be having this discussion. And if I didn't care about you, Will, I would have packed your bags before this and left them on the front porch. But what I know for sure is that something has to be done about the direction you're heading in. You can make the right choice, or the choice might have to be made for you."

Will turned his attention back to his pizza. He didn't want to understand what his dad just said to him. He didn't want to know that his dad had just told him he had to make the right choice, or else. But there was no avoiding it; he did understand and he did know. His dad had threatened him. And he knew his dad wasn't afraid to back up what he said with action. The image of the three men in the white sedan appeared in Will's mind. Maybe the decision about his future had already been made.

Will looked at his dad and then down at the four crusts on his plate. He finished off the last of his milk and looked for the first opening to leave the table.

"I need to go," Will said. "I need to do a lot of praying about this."

"That's nice. Put in a good word for me, too. And while you're at it, ask Him why he had to take your mother away from us."

Will took his dad's bitter comment as permission to leave the table.

"Yeah, go on," his dad said. "I'll clean up. But don't forget, even though you think you know what you're doing, there's more at stake here than you know about."

Will nodded and left the table. He would let his dad have the last word. He went back downstairs and felt the sickness coming on again. Things were pretty bad right now, but he tried not to cry. His dad was alone in this life, and it looked like so was he. The only difference between them was that he had God to talk to, but his dad only had himself.

CHAPTER SIXTEEN

The pre-spectacle tumult in the Cowichan Theater resonated through Jesse's brain, which, receiving bad news all around from his sobering nerve endings, clenched his teeth and ordered his eyes to bulge. He should have downed more than two draft before mixing with the faithful, and from the looks of the multitude around him, mixing with some of the not so faithful too. There was the wife of the Congregational Church minister, Mrs. Standeven, who bowled on Saturday afternoons for the sake of the working folk in her church, but on Saturday nights could be found sipping cocktails with some of the other ladies who lived on Kingsview, while her husband toiled at home, crossing the Ts on his next day's sermon. And there in the front row was Safeway manager Rolly Polterman appearing for all the world like the angelic gratefully redeemed, in stark contrast to his less important and less public role as pornography buff and touring massage parlor enthusiast. Hypocrisy was ugly stuff and much too easy for Jesse to find. He pressed his arm against his side to confirm the location of his flask of rum, which he had stored in his inside jacket pocket lest the Revival scene sicken him overmuch, which it already had. A washroom cubicle was the required venue. Up from his back row seat he arose, and away to the men's he went.

In her seat three rows from the stage Ruby was in turmoil. What was she doing here? The anxiety in her heart forced her to breathe faster, and that was uncomfortable, not that much of anything was comfortable anymore. To avoid turning her stiff neck, she shifted sideways in her seat to survey the valley's Christians who had come for the show. She pitied them. And

Tom was there beside her.

Tom had been strong until now, but now his faith was wavering. There was nothing for Ruby to receive here. God hadn't told them He would heal her. What were they doing here, with the rest of the crowd breathing down their necks? Still, maybe someone would get saved, and then the whole thing would have been worthwhile. But what about Ruby? He repeated his silent uninspired prayer, asking God for a miracle, his elbow taking turns with hers on their shared arm rest.

Inside the cubicle, Jesse focused on the speedy downing of his rum. He estimated that four or five ounces would be enough to kill the stench he expected to inhale in the hour to come. But hold on, what was that he heard? A woman's voice? Bringing her boy into the men's washroom. She was supposed to take him into the women's. Christians were scary. They'd be the first to condemn such rude behavior in others. He should go out and fill her in on proper bathroom etiquette, but he still had a few more ounces to go. Down the hatch. Ignore the foul disinfectant smell. Don't gag. Good. About time they left; now force a bit more down for the cause. Cap on, into the pocket. What's that? Another woman in here? No, it couldn't be; he'd been in here many times before. Still, think back; no, he didn't remember seeing the urinals this time. Did they have urinals in the men's here? Certainly they did. That settled it, time to sit down and become very small. Roll up the pant legs? No, women wore pants, too. His hairy legs would sink the ship; though some women had hairy legs, too. He snorted a laugh. Good, the rum was doing its job. He needed an escape strategy and an excuse. How about, *God made me do it*? He controlled the local press at least, so he wouldn't make the headlines. Somehow he had to get out. Good, she left. All quiet. Nothing to worry about. To anyone out there it would appear as a momentary error in judgment. He was only in and out. Screw up his courage to the sticking place, out of the cubicle, no women around, good, and now out the door...and...and, there was Mrs. Long walkering his way. No, that just couldn't be her there with Mrs. Long. Why did it have to be her there?

"Some investigative journalism, Mr. Thornton?" Mrs. Long said.

She looked up at the young woman beside her and smiled.

No use lifting weights now, or getting in shape. When the object of your affection has caught you in the women's john, the jig was pretty well up. And surprise, surprise, dear Mrs. Long was no doubt a Christian on top of it all. That figured. He should have known.

"It's those bloody symbols," Jesse said to them both, and then flustered to Mrs. Long, "Why can't they just spell it out." And then to Isabel, "Women don't wear skirts anymore anyway." And back to Mrs. Long, "What kind of symbol is that?" And to Isabel, "Why don't the feminists do something about it?" And in conclusion to Mrs. Long, "Disgraceful."

Then feeling the need to relieve himself of his embarrassment, he wheeled away from Mrs. Long and Isabel without saying goodbye, and with a sharp left-face, straight-armed his way through the men's room door.

So Isabel's the enemy in disguise, he muttered at the white tile floor. Didn't that just top off his whole life quite nicely? There was nothing left to live for. If he did away with himself right here he at least would die in the john of the appropriate gender. He stepped into the cubicle, closed the door and swallowed about an ounce. Upon reflection he decided that committing suicide over a young woman he didn't know would be a trifle hasty. He decided to let his stomach and his emotions settle first and then take one last pull on his flask of rum, before sallying forth to spear the flanks of that evangelist pervert, Chester Thomas.

Tom had escaped into the lobby to relieve his anxiety. He waited for no one. After a few minutes of dazed gazing at the entrance, he was rewarded for his absence of mind by the royal arrival of John and Mrs. Baker. The important people always arrived late, he thought. But did the Bakers really think they were something special? Of course they did. But it was his own spite that was now accusing them of pride. Maybe if he had done a better job of shepherding them, they wouldn't be in the mess they were in now. He was the one at fault. There was no way Baker was prepared for the job, even as an interim pastor.

"Good evening, Tom," John said.

Lila Baker acknowledged him by lowering her chin to the level of the common folk.

"Bless you both," Tom said.

The Bakers accepted his blessing as their due, breezed by him and pressed onward into the theatre. Then blasting from the men's room, head down, hot on the heels of the Bakers, blazed a ruddy streak. It was Jesse. He had come. Perhaps there was hope for the man after all. Sure, there was always hope.

As the doors swung closed behind Jesse, Tom heard the Baptist minister, John Derry, call for quiet in preparation for his words of welcome and his opening prayer. Tom had to go in now; he had to return to his seat next to Ruby. The worship would soon begin, and he had to go in and face the music. Either she would be healed, or she would not. Only God knew which. But as for him, his faith was gone.

Inside the theatre, Jesse lounged in a back row seat. He hadn't seen her yet, but just in case her eyes were upon him, he assumed an unruffled air, casual, taking in the whole scene, as a good journalist should. But where was she? Never mind, he would see her down there soon enough, but he would only search with his eyes, keep his head still, he shouldn't appear too anxious to find her. Yes, of course he still had a chance. He felt the rum warming his disposition enough for him to mock his paranoia and to put a rosy glow on Isabel's reaction to his recent foray into No Man's Land. She would conclude that he had been lost in thought, *such an intellectual, busy in his mind, forming the next day's news, only an absent-minded slip, what a dynamic sort he was, a man to be admired, and he recovered so well too, and he was right about those silly symbols, must talk to him, get to know him, hope he's approachable, he's the editor after all, and I'm just an ad clerk.* Yes, that's right, she would understand, he still had a chance, but how deep was she into this Christianity thing? What a way to spoil a relationship even before it began. Ah ha, at last, out of the corner of the right eye, over there, far side, one aisle forward, sweet Isabel sitting beside what's her name, the old darling. She had to be here as a volunteer, helping the less fortunate get out and around, community service, that sort of thing. What a good-hearted young woman. He had a chance yet. A person of her warmth and insight would have thought his brief indiscretion amusing. She had a great sense of humor, anyone could see that; hadn't she stifled a smile when he burst out upon them, yes, try and remember, close the eyes and visualize, yes, there's her face beside what's her name, and yes she's holding back a smile, yes there was no doubt she thought his predicament amusing. Of course she liked him, her loving vibrations had electrified the air, and there was every possibility she would take him as he was, and let the devil keep the exercise.

Open his eyes. What was going on now? Derry gone, curtain up, singers and a band. They were all beginning to stand; not this reporter, not allowed to join in, unprofessional.

He didn't care what they thought; had to sit tight, endure. He had a few good shots of rum left, save it for a taste later. But there, down at the front, was dear Ruby. She wasn't getting up either.

Ruby doubted whether she was able to praise God tonight, whether He healed her or not, and then she imagined the scene if she were healed, and then she saw herself healed and realized she would still be empty, unless God also filled her with His love, leaving no room for lonely spaces. And there he was beside her, Tom, standing and praising God. How could he?

Tom's lips were forming the words to the song he had sung hundreds of times before, but his mind was elsewhere. He could do the two things at once now, worship God and continue to think about other things. He had years of practice. He was a professional. He sang the words, but his mind was at home before the meeting, reviewing his dispute with Ruby. *I don't want to go and be prayed for, what's the use?* COME AND WORSHIP, ROYAL PRIESTHOOD. *There's hope, that's all we need.* COME AND PRAISE HIM. *What hope?* HOLY NATION. *God does perform miracles today, you know that.* WORSHIP JESUS. *I haven't got any faith.* YOUR REDEEMER. *You don't need to have any.* HE IS PRECIOUS. *Oh, come on, Tom, have you got any? No, I didn't think so.* KING OF GLORY. *But Ruby, you know that it's Jesus who heals.* COME AND WORSHIP. He couldn't go around again, so he stopped singing and tried to focus his thoughts on asking God to do what he had been asking Him to do for months, but he lacked any new angle from which to present an argument that would reinforce his petition. *Help* was about all he could manage. He repeated the word over and over again in his mind.

Jesse had continued his defiance and remained seated during the singing, even though he had enjoyed some of the music. It had a soft rock sound, and, in his opinion, was a welcome addition to the hymn singing scene. The rum had helped his appreciation. But that part of the agenda had now ended, and coming up next was the show he had been waiting for. The evangelist Chester Thomas was being introduced.

Reverend Derry said, "This man is God's man, whose mission is to liberate the lost and dying from an eternity separated from God."

Eternity, what a concept, Jesse thought. If there was an eternity, it would include the present and the past, not just the future. Infinity went backwards and forwards didn't it, and also included the now. Or maybe it didn't in theological thinking, and maybe this was a theological concept that Derry was trying to put across, and maybe the rum was having a splendid effect now. And what about this *lost and dying* bilge? Who did Derry think he was calling him one of the lost and dying, simply because he disagreed with the whole born again stuff that he knew they were peddling? And would he still be lost and dying if he were a Muslim or Jewish? Surely if there was a God, He was bigger than the small, neat and tidy box this Christian bunch insisted on stuffing Him into.

"So here he is, Chester Thomas."

Identical to his picture, Tom thought, focusing on the green eyes behind the horn rimmed glasses. The bow-tie was a little much, but passable. Medium build, about 65, a young looking 65, and a black mole below his left eye dotting his cheek. Mark of the Beast. Not funny. Bring every thought into the obedience of Christ. Impossible! Give Evangelist Thomas the benefit of the doubt, just listen, no more judging. God hadn't finished perfecting the man yet. He looked seasoned. But did he have an anointing for healing? That was the question. He had a large following, so he had to have the gift. But was it Ruby's turn?

Ruby was panicking. She wanted to run away, but she had to stay. Or did she? Confusion. She wasn't worthy to be healed. But why worry about that? She wouldn't be healed anyway. How could she be healed? Those things didn't happen. How could they? Why was she here? She wanted to go. The whimper in her mind found its voice in a weak cough, suppressed by her lace handkerchief. And then she held herself, frozen in her pain.

Jesse from his back row seat threw down the rum-stained gauntlet in his mind, daring Thomas the evangelist to take it up. The bow-tie was a laugh, wanted to look ancient, as if he knew everything about the state of this world and forevermore. An old bigot in a bow-tie had come to save Jesse from the demon rum. The con artist had no chance; the rum was a winner hands down.

Chester placed his Bible on the oak podium and then he raised his eyes to look at the congregation. A showman, thought Jesse, the roar of the greasepaint was written all over him; he would have them thrashing and foaming in the aisles in jig time. But look at them all now, silent, eager faces, pockets ready to be fleeced, no wonder they called them sheep. Poor sheep. Still, they deserved to be shorn; gullible and stupid they were. The smarter sheep became the shepherds, lived off the others, law of nature, no worse than the rest of humanity, except for their self-righteous bleating. Annoying, pitiable wretches they were in their glistening shrouds of goodness. But wait, he speaks.

"You people here are in a lot of trouble and you don't even know it," Chester said. "Sure some of you are saved, but you aren't really sure what that means. Others of you were invited by your Christian friends to come and hear the evangelist preacher. And some of the churches who have come together to sponsor this meeting are embarrassed to be associated with me and my kind. In fact I was scheduled to be here for three nights, but I was told today that there was a mix-up, so now I'll only be here tonight. But I thank God that He's allowed me to be here for tonight at least. And, of course, after these comments, I really don't expect to be asked here again, even for one night, but I'm too old to mince words anymore. Amen?"

Chester grinned at the sheep, whose swallowing throats were tucking their chins in and pushing their heads back and away from the man on the stage as he unbuttoned his black suit jacket and opened his black book.

What the hell is this, thought Jesse? No introduction, no *thank you all, I'm pleased to be here*, just straight into haranguing the multitude. And, surprise-surprise, by the tone of his comments, strife had developed between the local church leadership and Chester, who didn't seem to care who knew it. Or was he trying to be funny? It was hard to tell with these people, and what kind of people were they anyway? Christians? And who did they think they were?

From the third row, Tom was admiring Chester's attitude. He was beginning to think that possibilities might be opening up. Maybe the Holy Spirit was here to heal, and here to heal Ruby. Faith was again beginning to rise in his fickle self.

Trouble, thought Ruby, Evangelist Thomas was just more trouble, one more person stirring the pot. She could do without any more trouble, any more tension; she had lived through enough trouble and tension. Maybe she could persuade Tom to take her home now, or better yet, maybe God would do her the honor and take her home now, permanently. She squirmed in her seat and nudged Tom's elbow off their shared armrest. He shifted his weight to the other elbow, and she, sensing his change in mood and his focus on the podium, knew he was tuned into what the evangelist had to say.

Jesse watched the grin of Chester Thomas descend into a grim, stern face of warning: "The world is in trouble, and you people here in the peaceful and safe Cowichan Valley aren't going to escape just because you're isolated on an island. The world's too interconnected now for that. It's the age of the computer, and instant communications. The electronic revolution is obliterating the boundaries that separate nations. We are in for a lot of upheaval, my friends. The world is coming together, and there's going to be a lot of strife and turmoil while it's happening. No friends, you're not safe, even on this peaceful island. What happens in Bangladesh is going to have an effect on you here, let alone what happens in the Middle East. Some of you think you can have security in this world by piling up money, or hoarding the various other kinds of riches that the world values. But the truth is that there is only one place to go for security, and it's not really a place at all, it's a Person. Sure, there are some of you here who are thinking you've heard all this before somewhere, what's the old so-and-so going on about?"

Jesse was thinking he'd heard all this somewhere before and had been wondering what the old reprobate was going on about. Chester had to be psychic, or maybe he knew that his audiences often wondered what he was on about. The man was over the hill. At his age he belonged in a retirement home, not on the road preaching. But then again what would he do in an old folks' home except be a menace? No, they wouldn't let him in. He would be raising the roof every day, telling the rest of the inmates they were all doomed. Incontinence and daily scolding. No, they'd never let him in.

"Well, I'll tell you what the message is for you here in the Cowichan Valley. This valley is filled with darkness. And that darkness has been here for thousands of years. The Indian people here have been victimized by evil spiritual forces for centuries. And now the white people are here to add to the darkness, bringing their own kinds of spiritual slavery, their cold religion and the worship of their idols of money and success. Yes, my friends, you are in deep darkness here in the Cowichan Valley. But you need not feel unique, or alone, the whole world is in the same darkness."

Tom wondered how Chester Thomas knew about the spiritual forces in the Cowichan Valley. Maybe he was just guessing, or maybe he could see them. Tom knew that some in the church were able to see spirits. But Chester had to be just guessing. The Bible said such things existed. Chester must have got it from there. Still, maybe he would get the chance to talk to him afterward and compare notes.

An Indian bashing bigot, thought Jesse, and for good measure he was hammering out that old tune, *We're All Going to Hell in a Hand Basket*. For security he again nudged his flask with his arm. His pleasant alcohol buzz was now spiraling down for what he hoped would be a soft landing. At least he had a blast or two left for another brief zoom before bedtime. He glanced down at Ruby and Tom seated near the front. They had split apart now, each leaning away from the other, elbows on the armrests of their neighbors. How was it possible that such intelligent people could swallow all this nonsense?

"So, some of you think I'm just an ignorant old bigot ready for the Old Folks' Home. Well, I'm not ready yet."

He'd better stop doing that, thought Jesse, his restless nerves firing flaming arrows into his serene rum heaven, or else!

"Right now I can feel the Spirit's anointing coming, so I'll stop soft-peddling the message and tell you the truth. And there's a lot of truth missing in the church today. But there is a new day coming both to the church and to the world. In fact, that day is upon us now, my friends. The walls are coming down all over the world, the walls separating nations, the walls separating peoples and tongues. And the crumbling of the walls is going to cause upheaval. We're in for riotous times, my friends."

What's this got to do with so-called evangelism, Jesse wanted to know? Probably prided himself on being an expert on world affairs. And dear tender Isabel was over there, all ears, listening to the old crackpot. Rape of the ears, rape of the mind, it shouldn't be allowed, beauty defiled; one of those walls should fall on Chester, a merciful act it would be too, put him out of his misery, and into eternity.

"The question that we in the church have to ask is, when are the walls coming down that separate us from one another? The answer is that they're going to come down very soon. God in His sovereignty is going to tear them down, and those who oppose His Spirit are going to step aside, be pushed aside, or be ground to dust. His church, His body, is coming together, and those church leaders with vested interests, who persist in resisting this move of God, will be seen for what they are."

Some squirming going on, Jesse noticed, in some of the seats of the most established church people. No doubt cursing themselves under their breath for having invited the old goat, and for being forced to burrow into their own souls for an unwanted peek at the slippery motivations that had aroused them to blunder out on a night like this, only to be snared by a fractious interloper. And there was Chester, grinning at them. He had no shame.

"Yes, the walls are coming down, my friends. God is not going to allow his people to be separated any longer. His Holy Spirit is moving on the earth, and He is falling on the just and the unjust alike. The just will welcome His Spirit, the unjust will avoid Him like the plague. And those who receive His Spirit will be persecuted by those who reject Him."

Paranoid too, Jesse thought. An old paranoid bigot; it was a wonder he was invited anywhere. By rights they should have locked him up instead of giving him a microphone; and they were going to give him money for this, too? There was no justice.

"So my friends, you who are here tonight wondering if you can delay the decision again, you should consider that now is the time. God is raising up an army now. He's searching for recruits, not to warm a seat in a church building, but to be active warriors in His Kingdom, to fight the battle of the ages against the kingdom of darkness, which is fast taking control of the whole earth. You can see the enemy's work every day. On television, in the movies and in books and magazines and in the attitudes of your fellow citizens, and in the environment...."

Jesse's mind sat up when it heard environment. Any input was welcome, no matter its source, provided it contributed to his editorial crusade and helped fill the space every week.

"Ask yourself," Chester continued, "how Satan would change the earth's environment so it would be a suitable place for him to rule. Well, he's doing it now. Nature's walls have been breached. Picture what the world is going to look like if he continues to have his way. Picture the kind of world Satan would feel at home ruling over."

Hmmm, interesting concept, thought Jesse. Change the Satan bit, though, to impersonal evil, working through men to destroy the ecosystem, and add to the mix the evil of unrestrained capital, raping the good earth. No, no good. Still too heavy. Germ of an idea though, Jesse thought, as Chester hammered on and on, unstoppable.

The image of a dead earth was too much for Ruby. Satan enthroned, ruling the world, pitchfork in hand, his subjects groveling in the putrefying remains of civilization, the atmosphere utterly polluted, the rivers running filth, the earth poisoned, the scene lit only by the red glow of brimstone. What was it that she had come here for again? She didn't need this. The words of Chester Thomas were intended to convict the unsaved of their need for a Savior. But she didn't need this at all.

Tom, feeling the weight of a lonely future, looked at his darling Ruby, and held her there alive in his mind. He clenched his jaw to keep her from dissolving into his tears. She wasn't enjoying Chester Thomas, he could see that. He ignored her demand to leave that she shot at him from the corner of her eye. No, they had to stay until the end. There was always a chance.

"It's time we actively engaged the enemy," Thomas continued. "But the problem is that most of the church doesn't even know there's a war going on, including many church leaders. They think there is a middle ground where they can be safe, with one foot in the world and the other in the Kingdom of God. Well, my friends, the time has arrived here in the Western World when we're going to have to stand up and be counted. Are we in, or are we out? And if you're in then it's going to cost you something. Maybe even your life. Salvation has been soft-peddled, especially here in North America. Repeat a prayer and you're saved. But listen up people, that kind of grace isn't going to wash anymore."

Well, hallelujah, Tom thought, maybe there was a future for the church in North America after all. And maybe there was a place for him to function in it, that is if the old war-horse knew what he was talking about. But the problem remained. How were affluent North Americans going to be attracted to the church if membership meant total commitment and sacrifice? The answer had to be that God was going to do it somehow.

"This new army the Lord is raising up will be completely devoted to the Lord Jesus Christ. No part-time soldiers need apply. God wants spiritual warriors, not churchgoers. And this new army won't be bound by the traditions of men. People don't want or need another organization to belong to. You want the real thing, don't you? You want the truth, don't you? So for you out there who have come here tonight to hear the Christian message, and are wondering whether or not you would be better off if you committed your life to Christ, I've got news for you. A commitment now will cost you your life, it really will; it will cost you a life of service, and perhaps even the ultimate sacrifice. Now I know for a fact that some of you are hearing what I'm saying, because the Lord has been speaking to your hearts. The Lord has been speaking to you for some time now, and you are ready to make a serious commitment. I thank God for you, and also for those of you who desire a deeper life in the Spirit. And for some of you who have been ignoring the Lord's call, I pray that He will begin to awaken you to the reality of His presence, so that your lives will become increasingly incomplete until you answer His call. That sounds like a curse, doesn't it? Well forgive me."

May you lose the faith, Chester, and drown in a rum vat, mumbled Jesse, offering a curse of his own. It was insidious, all this spiritual stuff. Ahh, but wait a minute, Chester looked just about out of wind. The end was near.

"Yes, my friends, the Lord is calling you to service. The walls are coming down. Especially those walls that have been built with the untempered mortar of the traditions of men. People have sought relative safety behind the walls of sectarianism, but now these walls only serve to insulate members of the Body of Christ from one another. And as God's people come together they will begin to do battle against the true enemy, instead of fighting among themselves. The days are here, my friends, when the battle of the ages will be fought. Whose side are you going to be on? If you choose the side of the corrupt world system, ruled by the Evil One, you will dwell for eternity separated from God. Don't delay your decision, my friends, now is the accepted time, now is the day of salvation."

Jesse forced his mind to imagine the kind of mentality that could envision the world ruled by a serpent in a red suit, his demons slavering through the countryside, tormenting the common folk, quartering a malcontent here, sacrificing a virgin there. No, the man had to be deranged. And over there was sweet Isabel, still listening. Wait a minute, was that a glance she shot his way? A warm glance? Of course it was. Why so surprised? Perhaps they would meet on the way out, bump into each other in the lobby, a few words, and then into the elevator, a precious chuckle shared, loosed by his amusing critique of the evening's fare. Kindred spirits. But hold on, the old dear would still be there, tongue flickering, ready to strike, ruining his plan. Ahh, but there was always a chance this farce would be too much for the old dear, her heart seizing up right in the middle of Chester's harangue. Whisked off to heaven, hallelujah. Then he would be obliged to console Isabel, the least he could do. Show his mettle in time of crisis, the mature male taking charge, his manhood and his age no longer in question. Kill two stones with one old bird. Miracles could happen.

Jesse's muse was interrupted by Chester, who was saying, "I believe the Lord wants to heal a few of you people here tonight. As I call out your illness or physical condition, make your way to the front, and when all of you are up here I'll pray for you. Meanwhile, those of you who need to leave please leave quietly. All right, now there's someone here with a bad case of laryngitis, you've had it about a month now. Yes is that you ma'am, okay, come on up, that's it. There's someone else here, a man by the name of Frank who recently fell off a roof and has a serious lower back problem. Right, is that you? Fine, come on up."

Jesse watched gray-haired Mable Thorpe, owner of Berkey's Corner Cafe, walk slowly up to the front, hands clenched under her chin, choking her emotions. Then he saw Frank Connelly, father of four, and unable to lift a two-by-four since his injury, rise gingerly and make his way forward, while Chester continued to call out miscellaneous maladies. Must be an informant in town, Jesse thought. How else could Chester do it? Now that kind of chicanery had the potential to make a good story. Find out who. Impossible though, unless the person wanted to be found.

"There's a man here who has a drinking problem and would like to be delivered from alcoholism."

What was that? Chester had better not be looking his way. Besides, who asked to be delivered? But hold on, delivered? What did that mean anyway? Chester wasn't going to make Jesse, an editor, start thinking in that strange Christian language. Why couldn't they just speak English? Oh, oh, there was Sid, he was answering the call, no shame; one drunk signed, sealed and delivered, joining the rest of them. The front of the stage was now filled with the poor duped wretches. But Ruby was still in her seat. Good for her. Well, that was enough for him. He would wait in the lobby for a glimpse of Isabel on her way out.

Tom had prayed and listened for Chester to call Ruby out of the audience, but the call had not come. But they had one last chance; they would stay and see if he would pray for her afterward. People had been healed at his meetings before. Why not Ruby tonight? He glanced at her dark eyes. They were staring into meaningless space.

Ruby knew the night was almost over. The meeting would slide into oblivion along with her life. Enough was enough.

"Let's go, Tom," she said.

"Why don't we wait and ask him to pray for you later?" Tom said into her ear.

He was coaxing and desperate.

"No. I'm not going to subject either of us to this anymore. Maybe God's healing them, but I don't believe He's about to heal me."

Tom slumped in his seat and watched Chester praying for Mable Thorpe. There was no hooting or hollering. He wasn't putting on a big show, and Mable looked like she was talking now, and she was raising her hands. She looked like she was healed.

Tom said, "Look, Ruby, Mable seems to be talking, she's healed. Let's stay for a while, come on, Ruby, let's wait and then go up later."

"No! If God wanted to heal me, I would have been called

up. Besides, if He did want to heal me, you could pray for me and I'd be healed. Chester Thomas can't heal anyone."

"Yes, but he's got a better track record than most."

"Let's stop now, Tom, and face the facts. I'm dying. I've had to faced up to it, and now so do you." And then to soften reality for him, she added, "I'll be having a wonderful time in heaven with Jesus, and you'll be down here dodging Satan's fiery darts in a foul environment. Who will be better off, Tom? I should be praying for you."

Jesse waited in the lobby, hoping that Isabel would emerge minus the old woman and her walker, but he was disappointed when after a few minutes the six-legged beast appeared, walking beside Isabel. There was no chance. He wouldn't even attempt to get past the old dear. She would humiliate him somehow. Older people couldn't be trusted.

And then he noticed at the far end of the lobby, among a few of the exiting redeemed, Ruby and Tom, walking huddled together. He suspected there was something wrong with Ruby. He started to go over to ask if he could help, but stopped when he saw that Ruby seemed to be all right. In fact, he could see now there was something wrong with Tom, and that she was consoling him. Tom raised his head, and Jesse could see that Tom's nose and eyes were red. And then Tom bowed his head again, as Ruby guided him through the main doors and out of the building. Oh, but there, he had missed her, he had missed Isabel going by. He should have been paying attention. She was disappearing into the crowded elevator with what's-her-name. The old dear could move faster than he thought. There she went, the doors were closing. Did she look back? No, couldn't see.

There was no sense waiting around here any longer, Jesse thought. The Chester Show was over. Isabel was gone. It had been a night to remember. But how in the world could people like Ruby and Tom believe the way they did, he asked himself, his arm once again squeezing his rum flask? Maybe if they didn't believe the things they did Ruby wouldn't be sick. That was nonsense of course, but it was all he could think of to dismiss the feelings for the two of them that were beginning to insinuate themselves into his emotions. She was a lovely woman. But why get involved? She was going to die. And that was a fact. He interrupted his thoughts about Ruby to entertain an image in his mind of him in the parking lot behind the wheel of his '75 Valiant, drinking the last few ounces of rum, and then driving home, the lone warrior, battling corruption wherever he found it. And then he chased the image outside, where he soon merged with his vision.

CHAPTER SEVENTEEN

Jesse's office door opened and Isabel's head poked in.

"Are you busy?" she said. "Oh, I'm sorry. I see I'm disturbing you."

Superb timing, Jesse thought, snapping forward in his swivel chair to project an innocent face to Isabel. She hadn't bothered to knock and had caught him with his eyes closed, his chin raised toward the window's light, amusing himself by jerking around the floaters on his retinas. Her suppressed smirk led him to suspect that she was now thinking he often entertained himself by performing Stevie Wonder impressions behind closed doors.

In his best businesslike tone, he said, "Yes, what can I do for you?"

He showed her the whites of his eyes, and offered her a smile, forced there by the face's muscles pulling the mouth's corners back.

"I've come about tickets," she said. "They're for our church's Christmas play, performed by the children."

"A children's play?"

"Yes, they're only five dollars each. A good cause."

"So, you just want me to buy a ticket. You don't expect me to come."

Isabel smiled, and Jesse knew he was skewered. She had caught him in the women's john during the Chester Thomas fiasco, and now she had discovered him playing the fool in his office. He had to pay; there was no question about that. A rough brush-off would make him look even more foolish. Besides, maybe he really did have a chance, but then again did he even care now, since the worst had happened? She was one of them.

"How much did you say, five dollars? That's a little steep, isn't it, for a kids' play? I usually go for free, you know, the Press and all that. But I suppose I could buy a ticket, for a good cause, but that doesn't mean I would have to go, would it?"

"We would like to see you there, Jesse."

Impertinent cheek calling him Jesse, as if she knew him. Who was she, coming in here, interrupting his muse, embarrassing him and then extorting money? He loved it.

"When you say *we*, what *we* is that, might I ask, and may I call you Isabel?"

"That's an all-inclusive *we*, meaning that's everyone at our church. And feel free to call me Isabel anytime."

Jesse liked the sound of that. He hoped his face was too old to blush.

"I see," he said. "Well, here's my donation to a good cause."

He stood and extracted a blue bill from his money clip and handed it to her in exchange for a green ticket.

"Thank you," she said.

"My pleasure. I like to help where I can, unless, of course, it compromises the objectivity one requires for one's service to the community."

She turned to leave, and smiling said, "I'll see you there then?"

"Perhaps," he said.

Jesse observed her exiting curves.

"Good," she said, from the other side of the door, her voice soft and captivating, suggesting she and Jesse now shared a secret.

Dazed by the sudden pulsating prospects brightening his dismal view of the future, he fell back into his chair. Could a woman love a man when she knew he was an ass? And an older ass at that. But for that matter, would a man want a woman who was that desperate? And a younger woman, too, immature, and naive about the terrors of cohabitation? And while he was on the subject, *who were people at their core?* The handle on his desk drawer didn't answer, as he slid down in his chair, his chin on his chest, his back humped, his head level with the keyboard, his perfect meditation position achieved. And who was Isabel? And was she what you would call a good person? Would he call himself a good person? Or were there any good people in the world at all? There was Mother Theresa of course, but who else was there? There were some dead ones. But they weren't any good now. He concluded that the world was fresh out of good people. There were a few politicians in the world who said they were trying to do good, but they were excluded by definition. Maybe you never heard about the good people, because they never made the news. There were the environmentalists, of course, chaining themselves to things, but were they committed enough to take that final journey for the cause and add their chunk of fertilizer to the soil, while their dynamic young flesh remained energy packed? Martyrs to the environment. Fertilize a seedling, Manure of Martyr, a new gardening brand. And then their souls would be free to reincarnate into whale bodies, re-populate the oceans. Learn to hold their breath, learn the whale song, freed from their chains at last. No, goodness was a myth. But wait, what about Edwin, a cousin on his mother's side? Now there was a good gentle soul. A house-husband at 42. Married above himself. Died of a heart attack one bright spring morning last year, while in the act of fluffing up the pillows in her bedroom. They found him on the floor, face up, clutching her non-allergenic pillow, his eyes fixed on a drifting cobweb hanging from the ceiling, his visage a peaceful gray.

Jesse's insightful meditation was interrupted by his flashing cursor. He read the last words he had written before signing off in his mind to study the world of the floaters: "We know that many in the local churches were horrified to realize that this town could be subjected to such a disgraceful exhibition of chicanery." The image of Isabel's departure formed in his mind. Perhaps he had been a little too harsh. Chicanery was too heavy a word to describe the meeting, besides he didn't have proof. And were the local church denizens as horrified as all that? He didn't know that for sure either. And maybe there were a few people who had benefited from the whole performance. What about Sid, for instance? Maybe as a result of the meeting he had decided to swear off the demon rum. And what about Mable? She seemed to have been talking at the end. Her throat might have been healed. And as for old Chester Thomas, he was just senile; why not give him the benefit of the doubt? Ignore the whole matter. Nobody cared anyway. Christians were only four per cent of the Valley's population. And there were a few profitable advertisers among the Christian bunch too. No sense making waves. No, not with Christmas coming. Why offend?

Still, he needed an editorial. What was Chester's pitch last night about Satan and the environment? Could tone that down a trifle. No, too heavy. Jesse pushed himself up from his meditation posture. How about garbage? Yes, garbage was always a good one. Plenty to work with. New angle. North America was in the business of making garbage. Yes, excellent start. Taking elements from the good Earth and fashioning them into garbage. Milking the environment to create masterpieces of consumer garbage, and then leaving it that way by stacking it in dumps. Take the good stuff, make garbage, leave it in dumps for the poor to pick through. The faster it was made the better; speedy garbage. Bring in the Third World. The Western World is teaching the Third World how to make garbage because they can make it cheaper. But now they're selling it back to North America. North America is collecting cheap garbage from the Third World and later leaving it in dumps. A triumph of capitalism. That's it, make the money-boys the villains. They could take the blame for the rest of the folks.

His thoughts organized, Jesse began to write his weekly editorial, which he titled, "Garbage Galore," a title which he realized would have served as well for his planned piece on Chester Thomas. To expedite his task, he primed his pump with a quick pull on the flask he kept in his desk drawer. And then he hit the keys in full flight, soon releasing his soul from the gathering rubbish by humming along with the whirring in his mind, until, with the end of his work in sight, his awakening heart broke into song, chiming over and over again, *A bell is a bell is a bell.*

CHAPTER EIGHTEEN

The light above the sundeck beamed the soft snow down. Perfect timing. A snowfall on Christmas Eve. Gently falling snow was covering Ruby's world. All of them were different, no two the same. Hard to believe. Wrapped in a red blanket in her white armchair on Christmas Eve, she felt she should purr, but instead the thought provoked two short and painful coughs. But she was ready, everything was ready for tomorrow. That was the main thing. The preparations had been made. Christmas dinner for the needy. Every year the same; Christmas dinner for the needy in the church basement.

There was no tree in their house this year, or last. When was the last tree? No children. Why have a tree? They were sensible. *What was the point?* they would say, and agree not to have one. Decorate the tree at the church instead, for the needy. Since the beginning, no two alike. Unbelievable. Couldn't be proved. Sometimes science came up with the damndest things.

Christmas at home as a girl. She was spoiled then. An only child, and presents, lots of presents, remember the pony. And always a tree for their California Christmas. The season was celebrated even though mother was Jewish, but she wasn't strict. Father taking them, *his girls*, to Midnight Mass, once a year they went, a tradition in his family, to Midnight Mass at the Greek Orthodox Church. Full house. And then back at home in bed anticipating the presents that would be under the tree Christmas morning, and her parents, the two of them, stirring their mixed marriage, and him drinking, and her screaming, and then tired silence, waiting for Santa Claus in California and the presents under the tree. An upper-middle-class only-child at Christmas time in California. She had been spoiled then.

Ruby heard Tom unloading dishes from the washer, and then she heard the rattling pans and pictured him squeezing the stew pot back into its rightful place, and all the while he was humming *The First Noel*, a happy soldier shouldering the weight of kitchen duty for his beloved corpse in the next room. She wondered what he could be thinking. Was he dreading a future deadened by continuous housework? Or plotting a union with younger hands? Sarah Durning, pianist's hands, early thirties, and a Sunday School teacher, fine prospect to begin again. *Merry Christmas, Sarah, you witch.* Oh, weren't we bitter tonight, of all nights. Give it up, give it up. Still, it kept one's mind from noticing the discomfort.

Tom placed the eating utensils in their respective slots in the drawer and contemplated the celibate life, one devoted to fasting and intercessory prayer, a life of sacrifice for the next forty years, unless he died before he was eighty or the Lord returned first. Forty years. He could do a lot of praying in forty years. And a lot of fasting, if he had the will. But would Ruby leave their will with him when she left?

"Come in and sit with me," Ruby called, finding some strength in her voice, "and we'll watch the snow fall and speak of wondrous things and futures yet to unfold."

Tom wished she wouldn't do that. Bravery in the face of the enemy. Or was it sarcasm? He jammed the clumped dishtowel through the oven-door handle and then pulled at his wedding ring, straightening his knuckle and sliding the band off and on.

"Like some hot chocolate?" he yelled.

"Nothing stronger?"

"There's some shooting sherry, left from last year."

"Great. Pour me a few fingers."

Tom retrieved the bottle and a wine glass. The thought of joining her for a drink teetered through his mind, but instead he found the carton of eggnog in the fridge and poured himself a mug full; then he filled Ruby's glass with sherry. On his way into the living room the thought of getting drunk returned, but was dismissed by the sight of Ruby snuggled in her red blanket.

"Thanks, Tom," she said, taking the sherry.

Her fingers felt numb and colder than the glass.

"Beautiful, isn't it?" she said.

"What, the snow? Sure, it's beautiful, beautiful and cold. I'm glad I'm in here."

"I'm not glad I'm in here," she said.

"Where would you like to be?"

"I would like to be in another body. It's fine for you, living in your healthy body, but as for me, I'm not as comfortable in here."

"Let's not get complicated."

"It passes the time."

Tom sat down on the sofa and anticipated a fight. But the hostilities would not begin with him. He had to remember not to mention anything about tomorrow.

Ruby sipped her sherry and looked past him.

"Good vintage," she said.

"Sherry doesn't have a vintage."

"Yes, we must be correct, mustn't we?"

"No," Tom said. "It's not important."

"I see. Well, vintage or no vintage at least it's warming me up."

"I'm happy to hear that," Tom said.

"I was thinking earlier," Ruby said, "this will probably be the last year that I work with the ladies at the church, putting on the Christmas feast, I mean."

Tom refused to be drawn in, even though she had combined in one remark his greatest fear, her death, and his greatest failure, his church. He turned his head to look at the snow falling.

"There are no two alike," he said.

Tom wanted to retract his inane observation, but it was too late.

"Do you really believe that?" Ruby said, now irritated and raising her voice.

Tom didn't have an answer. Either way he was doomed.

"Well do you?" she said, insisting on a response.

"I don't know either way," he said.

"Science says there are no two alike," Ruby said. "Science is an ass."

"Sure, science is to blame," he said.

Hearing the tone of his own response, Tom realized he was becoming annoyed.

"Even scientists can make mistakes," he said, covering his mood with a chuckle. "They're not infallible."

Ruby wasn't to be put off.

"Yes, but what do you believe?" she said.

"It doesn't matter to me. I really don't care."

"You never cared about anything but yourself, and that ridiculous bunch of people you call a church. And now look what they're doing to you."

"I care more about you, and you know it, and now look what you're doing to me."

Tom regretted taking that shot.

"That's perfect, it's always what's happening to you that's important, isn't it?"

"That's not true. Let's just stop. We're not seeing things clearly right now."

"I'm seeing things clearly enough, and I can see that it's you who can't face up to this mess we're in, not me."

Unwinding himself from their argument, Tom said, "Sure, there had to be two alike sometime."

"Yes, I think so, too," Ruby said, cooperating with his peacemaking effort. "Science is a pervert."

Tom fabricated a laugh, but he was angry at her. He lived every day in pain at the thought of losing her. But at the same time he was angry at her because she was going to leave him here. How could she do such a monstrous thing to him?

"We've never been too much alike," he said.

"Let's blame it all on that then, shall we?" she said.

She swallowed another sip of sherry and then another.

"Why don't you forgive me for whatever it is I've done?" Tom said. "Unforgiveness is poison...."

"Let me guess, it could kill me, right?" she said.

"I know you haven't had a great life married to me, but since we're being so frank this evening, what is it that you have been so angry about all these years? Was it something I did?"

"You haven't done anything that you should be strung up for. Maybe you are right, maybe we should blame it all on the fact that we were a poor match to begin with, and maybe we've done pretty well considering."

"How are you feeling?" he said.

"The swelling has gone down in my ankles, but my fingers are numb, especially my right index, see? It's a funny color too. I hope it's not gangrene."

"Let's see," Tom said. "Is it the end of your finger?"

"The tip of my finger, if you don't mind."

"Right, the tip of your finger," he said. "I don't see anything. It looks normal to me."

Tom collapsed back onto the sofa. They both knew he couldn't take anymore health discussion right now, so the subject was closed. They contented themselves with silence. Tom stared across the room at the brass and glass fireplace insert. Behind the glitter there was no fire. The previous owners had blocked off the chimney when they had redone the roof with cedar shakes. Tom understood from the realtor's pitch that they didn't want messy wood chips in their living room. Ruby had decided if it would have been too messy for them, it would be too messy for her, too. That was fine with him. The cost of opening the chimney and extending the brick through the roof was more than he could justify. The fireplace looked great though; you just couldn't light a fire in it. But who needed a fire? The wood furnace at the Center had disgraced him enough. So why bring his work home with him?

"Funny," Tom said, "Leonard's face just popped into my mind. I haven't thought about him for years. And suddenly there he was, dying in a ditch, stoned on Acid. Did that really happen? We were all pretty strange back then."

"He was a jerk," Ruby said.

She was now annoyed at Tom for bringing up the subject. Why did he need to bring that up? Just to take a depressing trip down memory lane?

"You didn't know him," Tom said.

"Forgive me for speaking ill of the dead, but I knew him well enough. And just for the record, you were strange back then, I was a regular person."

Ruby finished her sherry, and then someone from her past popped into her mind too. There he was standing on the beach in California that summer twenty years before. Todd. Muscles and also sensitive. She had known him in high school, and gone out with him a few times. That's why it had been so easy. Todd had been her silent revenge on Tom. Who did Tom think he was treating her the way he did? Just because she had never been with anyone but him before. He was so sure of himself. And why had he let her go so easily, that summer twenty years before, when they were living together in Maple Bay, when they were young and when she threatened to leave him? And he called her bluff and she went to California to visit her parents and met Todd again, more mature, and way more attentive. And she, licking her wounds, gave herself to Todd, who thought she was liberated, and then she hated Tom for doing such a thing to her. Of course she was already pregnant by Tom. At least she thought it was Tom's. Only two weeks apart though. And her guilt, and getting preached to by the Jesus Freaks on the beach, and getting herself saved. And then freedom and joy, and then later her certainty that the baby had to be Tom's, and returning to Duncan and Tom getting saved and then the news of the baby coming and Tom wanting to get married. And then the baby born dead. And anguish, and fear that it had not been Tom's after all. And then barrenness.

"Whatever are you going to do when I'm gone?" Ruby said.

She and her sherry expected an answer.

"I've always wanted to try my hand at pimping," Tom said.

He turned his head back to resume the business of observing the empty fireplace.

"Fair enough," Ruby said.

Of course the baby's death had to be her fault. It was punishment for what she had done. Free love. She hated those words now, and she hated herself, and now she needed to be let off the hook. Why had Tom let her go to California so easily? But at least she had been saved in the whole process, and now twenty years later she was going to her reward, except she didn't believe she deserved one. Not after what she did. Why not just tell him? But she had never been sure, and after the baby was born dead what was the point? Certainly it was Tom's fault for letting her go to California so easily. At any time in the last twenty years she could have told him about her affair with Todd, and for twenty years she had planned to tell him, but also assure him at the same time that the baby was Tom's. But of course she had never been positive. How could she ever be positive? But no, why lie to herself? The baby couldn't have been Tom's, since they never had any others, and the doctors said there was nothing wrong with her physically. It was only psychological, they said. No reason to test Tom, either. No, what a ridiculous idea. It was her. It was in her mind. No, the game would be over if she told him about Todd. She would have to reveal all of it then; that she had never been sure. She could tell him now, but then what would be the point now? Besides, God knew whose baby it was, and she would be able to ask Him about it soon, and Tom would be none the wiser.

"I had an affair twenty years ago in California," she blurted.

"Interesting," Tom said. "Is that the sherry talking?"

"I'm serious, Tom. Remember when I went to visit my parents that summer, when I moved out of our place in the Bay?"

A curious woman, Tom thought, the seriousness of her words becoming clear. His mind travelled far away from Tom and Ruby. He was in the place where the bludgeoned go before the decision is made whether they will live or die. He remained there out of time, until he began once more to feel he was inside his skin. Returning to the land of the living, he wondered whether down deep all women were alike. Solomon certainly thought so. Or did gender have anything to do with it? Was everyone alike? His experience told him everyone was, and of course *everyone* included him.

"I don't believe you," he said. "You're just trying to ruin Christmas. I know you hate Christmas dinners at the church, but this is ridiculous."

"I'm not trying to ruin Christmas," she said.

Tom said, "Okay, so what are you telling me, the truth? If it's the truth, why didn't you just keep it to yourself?"

"What kind of advice is that, coming from a pastor?"

"I'm not a pastor, I'm your husband. And if you're telling me the truth, then it makes the last twenty years too ridiculous to imagine."

"Fine, now at least you won't miss me so much when I'm gone. Worshipping my memory and all that sort of thing would have been bad for you."

"What? Now you think you need to give me advice on grieving?"

"Never mind, I just want you to forgive me, that's all. I've been carrying it for twenty years and I need relief from the burden. And anyway, what about you? You could take some responsibility. If you hadn't let me go that summer none of this would have happened."

"I see," Tom said. "It all makes sense now. That's what you've been holding over my head all these years."

"There's no real point in getting upset now. Anyway, Tom, I'm sure the baby was yours."

"The baby? What do you mean, the baby? What! The baby! You've got to be kidding."

Tom's anger and confusion began to dissipate and were replaced by numbing disbelief. From a great distance away, he heard: "Why have we stayed together, Tom?"

"I couldn't get along without you," he explained to the far-off voice. "At least that's what I thought." The female voice then said, "And I couldn't get along without you needing me. And I suppose I thought I had to make it up to you."

He located the source of the voice. And there she was, his wife Ruby.

"A strange way of putting it," he said.

"What do you mean?"

"The *it* was guilt, wasn't it, which you managed to dump on me for twenty years?"

"It works both ways Tom. I know you blamed me because we couldn't have any more children."

"Oh, yes, sure. I see, it's clear now who the person is who can't have children, isn't it?"

"We don't know that for sure."

Tom felt the room imploding.

She said, "Impending death simplifies relationships, doesn't it, Tom?"

He fell into himself now. It was all true then. But why did she have to do it? Why did she have to tell him now?

"There was no point to it all, then?" Tom said. "Our lives were lived for what?"

"God knows, I don't," she said. "It seems we wouldn't have had it any other way."

Tom's ability to reason was leaving him again. His mind was beginning to overload as the rushing of memories, of incidents, began flying through his mind, faces and situations, scenes and words spoken, all appeared in their predestined order. His anger was unable to arouse itself. He was weak. His alcoholic father appeared in his mind and began to drink gin, but tonight Tom was even too weak to follow in those shaky footsteps. Why had she confessed to him of all people?

He might have wished she were dead if she weren't going to be. But why not forgive her? Their life together was over anyway.

"I forgive you," he said. "It would be absurd not to."

"And I forgive you, Tom, for letting me go," she said.

"That's kind of you, Ruby."

"Look, the snow has stopped," she said. "Why did it have to stop?"

She was behaving as if nothing had happened, he thought.

That was perfect. Sure, he would follow her lead, and then go to bed and sleep. Losing consciousness was what he needed now.

"It was too good to be true I guess," he said. "Things are never perfect."

"But you would think the weather might have tried to show the Christmas spirit at least until midnight. Christmas is always spoiled one way or another, isn't it?"

"That's the Christmas spirit for you. It's a mean one. I'm going to bed. Do you need help?"

"No, I can manage, but it's a little early, isn't it?"

"Santa Claus comes sooner when you're asleep," he said.

"Don't forget to hang your stocking."

Tom got up and made his escape to the bedroom.

"I suppose I should hang something," he mumbled to himself.

CHAPTER NINETEEN

Tom was enjoying the drive. The Christmas Eve snowfall had powdered the Valley with holiday white. The weather report on the Volvo's radio explained that the icy road conditions this Christmas Day were being caused by the high pressure area that had been building up over the coast after the storm, accompanied by a cold Arctic outflow. It was nice to know. He piloted his station wagon across the Silver Bridge, where the Cowichan river below, maddened by run-off from rain that had fallen before the recent freeze, slopped and frothed, shooting a burly cedar log under the bridge for a free winter water slide to the bay. He had decided to live in eternity today. Ruby's Christmas Eve surprise had removed the sting from everyday living, and now, Christmas Day, he was off the hook, and there was nothing here in this world to hold him. He was a sojourner on earth compelled to finish his mission, after which he would live in eternity with his Lord. Several times on their journey to the church he had the urge to break into hysterical laughter, but had stifled it, fearing that Ruby might think him deranged. As for presents this morning, he and Ruby had only exchanged glances. He had never believed in the commercial aspect of the holiday, only the sacred, and Ruby in recent years had followed suit, humoring his humbuggery with her own brand of Yuletide cynicism, a legacy, he suspected that was left by her mother, who had been partial to Chanukah.

Ruby was content this morning. She had convinced herself that she was thankful this would be her last Christmas. And a stunning one it was. The cold sun reflected off the snow, piercing her sunglasses, her eyes squinting to shield against the barrage of light. The tailpipe of the car in front of them puffed its light gray carbon-monoxide exhaust fumes at her. He sat beside her, driving.

"I suppose you'll be wanting a divorce," she said.

He could hold his craziness back no longer and out it came in bursts of rolling laughter. In his self-conscious hysteria, he imagined that the approaching motorists were noting the Christmas gaiety exploding from the visible bust of the passing pastor. *What a joyful time for the man of the cloth, one of the highlights of the year for him, oh, the thrill of Christmas!*

Tom choked his laughter with a question.

"A divorce?" he said. "What for?"

"Adultery, of course."

"Adultery? That was twenty years ago, and we weren't even married."

"Well we were in a way, and then there was the fact that...."

"The fact that what, you were pregnant with my child? Oh, come on, Ruby!"

"Methinks I hear a touch of bitterness in your voice."

"You wouldn't be bitter?"

"As a matter of fact, I am," she said.

"Well this is cozy," Tom said, "and here we are the loving couple ready to preach the Good News."

"You're the preacher, not me."

"You're guilty by association," Tom said.

"That's no way to talk to a terminally ill person, even if she is an adulterer."

"I'm sorry," Tom said. "I forgot for a moment that you're terminal. But to set the official record straight, you're a fornicator, not an adulterer."

"It depends on how you look at it," Ruby said.

"Oh, come on, we both know the facts."

Tom pulled into the church lot and parked in his spot.

Ruby watched Tom get out of the car and come around to do his duty and open the door for his dear dying wife. Why hadn't she just stayed home? That's what she'd wanted to do, but she hadn't wanted to disappoint Tom. Or would he have been disappointed? She doubted he would have, since their relationship had changed overnight. So why bother now? He wouldn't appreciate her sacrifice. She shouldn't have told him of course. Nevertheless, she felt a new freedom in their relationship. She felt he had loosened his grip on her, and she could breathe a little deeper. But now she was afraid he had become hysterical. She shouldn't have waited so long to tell him. Years ago there might have been hope. There was a good chance he wouldn't have divorced her. And she, the guilty party, wouldn't have divorced him. That just wasn't done. She looked at him as he opened her door; he was grinning. She suspected his current condition might inspire a Christmas message to cherish. That would be her fault too. No, she shouldn't have told him. There were things you were supposed to take to your grave. Still, she did feel better, emotionally at least. Confession was good for the soul.

Ruby sat in her usual place in the front and center oak pew and steeled herself for the coming show. Cold flowers, frozen in the clean church air, stared back at her from the platform. The church's four elders seated in their chairs behind the pulpit projected concrete resolve. Deacon Jensen approached the lectern and opened the proceedings with an ardent prayer. Then the praise group led them all in song.

The congregation, the Holy Day faithful, was all aglow. The men stuffed into their holiday suits bellowed hymns and the women fresh in their festive dresses high-pitched the carols, all proud to be Christians on Christmas Day. The children, wearing their *don't you dare get them dirty* clothes, were sworn to best behavior and bided their time. Adding bulk to the assembly the twice-a-year worshippers mumbled the choruses and hoped for a pardon. Tom stood beside her. Since his time of trouble began, he had disdained his place of honor on the platform. God only knew why he sang.

Ruby knew the kind of lives most of these people lived. The secrets. And she knew also that the world was an intolerable place to be. Everyone got tortured here. The people lived their lives, suffering every day, most of them believing the others were happy, that there was some standard to go by, and if only the required conditions were met, happiness would follow. Skeletons hidden in closets but today brave faces singing, every one. Doomed to torment, their only hope a Savior they could not see. Faith and tears; a child born with a club foot, heartache and tears; torment in homes, one a Christian, the other on drugs and out of a job. Single parents, what's under the tree? Will there be a tree? More tears and despair. The seniors who had seen it all, some hurting with spouses deceased, but trying to help the younger ones make it through the pain. The successful ones no different, the problems of the affluent; one teenager pregnant, abortion on the way, another teen caught shoplifting, another on drugs, alcohol use epidemic. Were the people in the church just the same as the people in the world?

Ruby could feel the pain of the unseen war. Always there was evil at work, always wars. Mothers marching their children off to battle, fathers reveling in the nobility of the supreme sacrifice, and her friend, horny Todd, one of the last to go, dead on a battlefield in Vietnam. Absurd. And a special wall there in Washington, a black memorial wall erected, so the Baby Boomers could go and look up their dead. She saw it all on PBS. There they were, her generation, seeing themselves reflected in the spit and polish black wall. She cried for hours after she saw it. There was too much pain there for anyone to bear.

No, who was that? You had to be kidding. Who was that in the back row? Jesse Thornton and what's her name? Isabel. And they were looking cozy, and Jesse was wearing an adorable face for the occasion. How the mighty cynical had fallen. Perhaps he had come to uncover more corruption in the church, or maybe there was an environmental scandal afoot. She had an environmental story for him, a real scoop. Here she was, dying on the unredeemed earth; every particle of her body groaned. The earth was enemy territory, and her body was made of the same stuff. Her cells, like nature, were on a rampage. Equilibrium was destroyed, creation was groaning; earthquakes and famines, flooding, polluted water and air, the consequences of the disease of the human spirit, earth out of whack along with her trivial lump of clay. The earth had cancer. Why should her own little bit of dirt be spared? She knew the earth would try to throw off as many of the diseased as it could. That was what the earth did, when people smothered it with their corruption. She had an excellent headline for Jesse. Ruby's Earth Dies of Cancer, no one on planet left to mourn.

Jesse teetered between hoping no one saw his lips moving during the singing and wanting to convince Isabel of his nonchalant acceptance of church status quo. He was safe in the back row, only a few gawkers, and they were smiling. Were they wearing smug smiles or smiles of welcome? Or better still, who cared what they thought. And that dear old lady Long three rows up on the right side had sneaked a few peeks too, nose into everything. But Isabel was warm there beside him, no real touching yet, but close, a kindred type of agreement heating their connections. A miracle at the kids' play two nights before; she came and sat with him. The church had been dark enough to hide his swallowing apprehension and blushing face. Or at least he felt as if his cheeks had been ablaze, but perhaps not; after all, he was too old for that sort of thing. And what did she see in him? She was alive, vital, and young, but not all that young he discovered when later she let it slip that she was twenty-eight and a whole lot closer to his age than he thought. What was sixteen years between lovers? But wasn't he jumping in over his head? He was having some doubts. After all, when she would be coming into her sexual prime, he would be nearing fifty and on the grave-side slide. But why think long-term? Live for today. Except what about this church stuff? It seemed to be a serious affair to her. He wouldn't get away with a fling and an adios, or would he want to do that anyway? Life was becoming complicated. Confusion. And what about kids? He didn't deserve any. But why not? Marriage? Good God. And him in church on Christmas Day, a Protestant one at that, without a whisky flask. He was going to hell fast.

So what was coming next, Jesse wondered? But what did it matter? Radiant Isabel was beside him, lighting up the pew, her perfume alluring, and meant for him? Hard to believe. Oh, here we go, announcements, read by a stern black suit topped by black hairpiece and jowls. Announcements finally over, up pops Tom, sermon time no doubt. And Ruby there, waiting. A darling woman, she'd turned to look his way earlier and tossed him a surprised smirk. And oh, look at that, look at those broad smiles greeting Pastor Tom pasted on the faces of those same elders who were tossing him to the wolves. What a performance. Oops, no, now what? Why was Tom looking his way and smiling? You've got to be kidding. Oh no, he wouldn't.

"Good morning, Mr. Jesse Thornton," Tom said. "We are

pleased to have you here with us today."

What a cruel thing to do. Were you supposed to respond? Better not, nod of the head was all that was required. Stare them down, that's it, all of them turning around. Be calm, don't look at Isabel, take it all in stride. Affect a confident air, now glance at her casually, in control, share the moment in mutual amusement. Good, well done. Oh, it's love. She glows.

Tom said, "This morning I would like to talk about forgiveness."

Ruby kept her groan to herself as she felt the Christmas spirit drain from the assembly. He could at least have chosen a seasonal topic, and let everyone off the hook on Christmas Day. But then she remembered they all deserved to feel guilty.

"This time of year reminds us," Tom began, "that Jesus came among us that we might be forgiven...."

As Ruby often did during recent sermons, she turned her mind to other things, to thoughts of her childhood and her university years, times that were uncomplicated. This morning she travelled to the spring of her last year in high school. There she was now, being advised by her guidance counselor, who was giving his sage assessment of her intelligence and aptitudes. He said the whole world was her oyster. That was what the counselor said. But she didn't want the whole world. She wanted her fear to go away. But he wasn't equipped to help her with that. His job was to encourage and direct the bright ones and offer hope to the mediocre, not exorcise fear. Such memories for her now were not so much an escape into a simpler time as they were a re-discovery of a beginning to go with her ending. As for the time in between, she liked to keep it vague and preferred it be forgotten. Those in-between years she had only just lived. But her confession last night had given her a new defining moment from which to spring into eternity.

She and Tom would begin again in the time they had left. She would leave him in a creative way, one that would enhance his life ahead. Now that she had come clean, they would be able to communicate. And there was hope now that Tom would be able to cope with his coming freedom.

She tuned back into Tom, who was citing Mark 11, which said that if you failed to forgive others for their trespasses, yours would not be forgiven by your Father in heaven, either. True. She hoped he remembered that. And then she travelled to her university graduation and reveled in the sight of herself in cap and gown, receiving her Bachelor of Education degree, and afterwards at the reception having tea with her parents, her father beaming, on his best scotch-whisky behavior, no inappropriate boisterousness or infelicitous remarks, simply enjoying his daughter, proud to be her father, her mother when necessary reigning in his strings with a slight firming of the eyes, a lovely picture for the scrapbook, a day to remember. There, she had done it, she had remembered her mother, and they were having a good time, too. So maybe life was now beginning to flow back into the memory of her mother. Yes, there she was, her mother, and she was laughing. Only a slight hint of unpleasantness directed toward father, restraining herself, not being hard on him for her daughter's sake. Ruby wanted to stay there, with her mother, for the rest of Tom's sermon, but her mind drew the curtain and returned again to the Christmas morning church. And there he was, her Tom, letting them have it for all he was worth. As for herself, she would not take his message to heart right now; though of course she would think about it later, at a more appropriate time, but not now, not here, among all of them, who didn't deserve to be forgiven, and certainly not on this her last Christmas morning before her final graduation day.

CHAPTER TWENTY

The church basement air was redolent with Christmas dinner odors. The severed parts of the golden brown birds had flown in formation from the kitchen and blended their fragrance with the jellied cranberries, pasty mashed potatoes, and shriveled green beans, all carried by the Good Samaritans, who were sacrificing their afternoon on the altar of conscience. There were some sincere people serving the poor this day, but Jesse preferred to see all of them as hypocrites, except for himself, and Isabel of course. Tom and Ruby didn't count; this was their job. His judgment on the faithful served, he knew, to distract him from the unavoidable truth that here he was on Christmas Day, shuffling plates and carving gobblers as if he were Mother Theresa herself. Wasn't love grand?

After Tom had said grace, he and Isabel, their duties completed in the kitchen, had found two empty settings at the end of one long table, covered in white roll paper for the affair, and had commenced eating their dinner. All things considered he was thankful to be here. He had nowhere else to go. He was short on family now, parents dead, a postcard and a pudding sent from his older sister in England, a few cousins in Alberta, no warm family haunt to return to, no traditions, no past to conform to. And as for friends, who bothered with those anymore. His only regret this evening was his lack of liquor. He had left his flask in the car out of respect for the alcoholics in their midst.

Between bites of turkey and eyes for Isabel, he surveyed the merry scene. About fifty diners had been dug up from below the poverty line to consume the church's offering. Jesse recognized a few of them as outpatients from the psych ward.

Today, a special occasion, they were smiling their way through their Christmas dinners, living in peace on their medications.

"I recognize some of these people," he said to Isabel. "They're outpatients from the psych ward."

"How do you know?" Isabel said.

"How do I know? Why it's because I sit at the information center of this Valley. Nothing escapes my notice."

Isabel laughed. Jesse was pleased she was amused by his self-mockery, and then he, entranced, the room a distant buzz, got lost in Isabel, in her hazel eyes, in the way her chestnut hair was parted in the middle and flowed back, her meticulous braid caressing the nape of her neck. A few wayward, tantalizing, shining wisps left loose on the sides of her forehead were beckoning him to take the lead in pursuing their mutual happiness. Meanwhile, a piece of turkey breast, ascending on his fork, caught his attention in time for his mouth to open in order that the resulting hole might be stuffed with the hot fowl, his eyes yet absorbing his sweet Isabel. Chewing his catch, a self-satisfied tight-lipped grin appeared on his face to acknowledge his tasteful rhythm.

"The turkey's delicious," she said.

Isabel's insight prompted Jesse to wonder if she was an airhead. And did she really look this good? He knew that love might do rude things to you later on. And he was old enough to know that this love stuff was all an illusion. But so what? Why not just go with the feelings for now. Go with the whole magical thing. Enjoy the romantic program. Even stretch the moments out. Get as much out of first blush as possible. Learn to enjoy abandonment and to milk opening caresses for all they were worth and revel in the adventures of escalating intimacy. And so on. And to hell with wisdom. But maybe there was no *so on*. Marriage. That was her plan. And then he realized how conceited and over-confident he had become. Why would she want to marry him? Good question. But the fact remained, here they were together. But did she intend to change him, to whip him into shape? Yes, she had to have a plan. She would have him out jogging yet, getting him in condition for the long haul. He sighed an ambiguous sigh as he imagined his future with the beautiful Isabel and also running laps around the ugly track. He forked in some mashed potatoes for ballast.

Ruby had no use for the turkey and no fondness for the guests. Her husband sat across from her at their festive table. He was seated beside the regular inhabitants of his Center. Will sat on Tom's right, and on Tom's left lolled boiled Phil, a candidate for spontaneous combustion if ever there was one. Yes, this was her last Christmas. What a joy. To pass the time she had dug a well in the middle of her ice-cream scooper portion of mashed potatoes. The gravy she had spooned into it had breached the walls and had now begun to meander toward her traditional favorite, the dark meat from the thigh. Yes, what a joy Christmas dinner was. But it was more fun to watch her dinner this year, to watch the way it just cooled there and merged. And oh, the company this year was beyond compare. But still, Tom hadn't done away with her during her afternoon nap. That was something to be thankful for, or was it? Instead, he had been considerate and recommended she stay home and rest, but she wasn't the kind of person to risk disappointing her husband, or miss out on such a merry time. She would never do that no matter how sick she felt. Such cowardice was not to be found within her. Smiling, happy faces, that's what Christmas was all about.

Talk about smiling. Old goat Jesse was over there, smitten. Perched there beside him was the young, oh so young Isabel. It was hard to find a fault with her though. She was tall, but not really a beanpole, her nose a trifle too thin, but not hawk-like or sticking out; sharp, that's what it was. Her torso was a tiny bit too long for her legs, not that her legs were short, just a fraction out of proportion. But she had beautiful auburn hair and a kind heart. Too kind, that was her trouble. But she would learn, after a few months with Jesse. A few months with a man was all you needed in order to learn. Still, men couldn't help themselves. Their behavior was programmed from birth. Yes, everyone got tortured here.

Tom looked up at her. Was he reading her uncharitable thoughts? She could see that his peaceful smile was guarding his hurt and confusion.

He said to her above the clatter, "We should talk to Jesse. Haven't had a chance yet today. By the look of him, he'll never be more open to hearing the truth."

"Ever the optimist," Ruby said.

She saw Tom's peace shatter, and then he regained control of his face. She studied her full plate, her head bowed, ashamed of the surfacing unconscious urge to wound him. She had to face her crime. She had been manipulating him for years. And she had to recognize her control methods as just that, criminal. At the least, dishonest. She couldn't use his weakness as an excuse for her behavior any longer. She had used his guilt as a weapon against him. His guilt was his failure to succeed in the world on his own two feet. She'd been the strong one in their relationship. But now he would have to stand on his own. And perhaps now that she had confessed, he would be free. She hoped their relationship would be healed before she died. As for her, she would face her sins too, and confess all of them. But not today, for it was Christmas.

Most of her gravy had now succeeded in escaping from its potato well and was flooding her shriveled green beans. She picked up her fork and, under the gaze of boiled Phil, goaded her turkey into the gravy and then flattened the potatoes into neat corrugated rows. For old times' sake she cut off a sliver of meat and delivered it to her mouth. In appreciation of her effort Phil dragged his red plaid shirt-sleeve across his nose.

Her joyous time of picking at her plate finally came to an end. The servers arrived to remove the remains. Ruby bowed her eyes to Elder Baker, who shook his disappointed head at her poor effort, and then he looked at her, and then he offered her a sympathetic smile, dredged, Ruby knew, from the depths of his compassionate self. Then he took her plate away, his gray-flannel rump departing for the kitchen. She glanced at Phil and Tom and Will and the rest of the merry company and fabricated for them a pleasant smile. She knew the next item to appear on the menu would be the plum pudding, a seasonal delicacy whose arrival was imminent. She scarcely could contain her delight and her expectancy that presently its sauce would congeal right there in front of her very eyes.

She decided to appease Tom and at the same time eat as little of the humble pudding as possible.

Ruby said, "I'm ready, let's go, if you can drag yourself away from your soul-mates. Let's have our dessert with Jesse and Isabel and, you know, we can pry a lot, and protect Isabel, and mock Jesse and embarrass him. Let's have some good-natured fun."

In response to Ruby's sarcasm, Phil's mouth fell open and his glazed brown eyes cleared to flash his understanding of Ruby and her words, and then he gave a puzzled shake of his head, and then a shrug, and then his mind returned to glorying in his Christmas dinner bliss.

Jesse's throat was in the act of swallowing coffee, when his eyes observed through his wire-rimmed glasses, along the sides of his cup, past Isabel's golden aura, Ruby and Tom, heading his way. Down came his cup to meet its saucer, and Isabel turned to share his view.

"Oh good," she said. "They're coming to join us."

Jesse stood to welcome them and to pull out a chair for Ruby.

"May we?" Ruby said to Jesse.

"Do you mind if we join you?" Tom said to Isabel.

"Yes, excellent," Jesse said.

Isabel glowed.

The four were seated together when the pudding came, all but Ruby beginning to nibble. Jesse knew that Tom was waiting for his chance to ask him how he enjoyed the morning's sermon. Jesse also knew that Ruby was dying to bait him about his age, and there was his beautiful young Isabel, a blank slate, and here he was, remaining calm, inwardly squirming, sober, and all things considered in a moderate amount of trouble. But perhaps they would be Christian about the whole thing, but on the other hand perhaps that was the attitude he should fear most. Which aspect of the faith was coming, love or condemnation?

Tom took the bull by the horns.

"So," Tom said to Jesse, "what does forgiveness mean to you, if anything?"

"Forgiveness? I haven't done anything," Jesse said.

He looked to Isabel for support and then offered an innocent grin to Ruby.

"No, I mean my sermon," Tom said.

"Oh right, your sermon," Jesse said. "I knew you were going to ask me about that. Do you use a word processor when you do your outlines?" And to show Isabel he was up to date on current software, he added, "I've heard there are some excellent Bible programs out now."

Tom suppressed his curiosity, which wanted to know why Jesse's memory would have retained that piece of information, and asked instead, "You told us you were Catholic, if I remember right. So you must know the Bible."

For Isabel's sake Jesse feigned humility and said, "Oh certainly, I've read it a few times."

Tom admired Jesse's ambiguity. Had he read the entire Book a few times or only a few verses here and there? Tom guessed the latter was the case, and that Jesse was trying to impress Isabel. Before Tom could pursue the subject, he saw Ruby shifting forward in her seat to come to everyone's rescue.

"The Bible is a wonderful book," she said. "Tom has spent the last twenty years studying it. And I'm sure, Jesse, you've had plenty of time over the years to read it, too. I suspect your work requires you to use it as a reference from time to time. For instance, there was the Flood, and we all know how all that water was terminally bad for the environment."

Dying didn't give a person that much license, Jesse thought. And Isabel, Jesse noticed, was also shocked at the remark spoken by the pastor's wife.

Tom decided that Ruby's witticism was at the expense of the Bible, and that she had stepped over the line. He frowned at her, and then, again in reference to his sermon, said to Jesse, "You can only be forgiven if you want to be." He glanced at Ruby. "Some might blame others for their condition instead, but that's their affair."

There was a real battle brewing between them, Jesse thought. The stress of dying and all that, what a shame, but he must protect Isabel from any unpleasantness. Protect Isabel? Such a noble thought. Yes, wasn't love grand!

"Forgiveness brings peace, all right," Jesse said.

Jesse was aware that his dinner companions, in response to his pronouncement, were staring at him. To deflect their attention he shifted his eyes to view the psychiatric patients at the next table, hoping to blame them by association for his impulsive revelation.

"That's exactly right," Tom said.

But Tom was unsure whether Jesse had been sincere or had thrown out a flippant remark to humor them. Ruby wondered too. Was he agreeing for Isabel's sake? What a question. Of course he was. Lechery motivated his every move. They were all lecherous at his age. On the other hand there was a slight chance he had been listening to Tom's forgiveness sermon this morning. As for her, maybe she would forgive the church tomorrow. That would be a better day. She was enjoying her bitterness too much to ask for forgiveness today. Her stored anger continued to release in bursts of malice in her mind, but she regretted now that some of her uncharitable thoughts had found expression on her tongue.

"It's a peaceful time of year," Isabel said.

"Amen," said Jesse.

Maybe she was an airhead, Jesse thought. No, that wasn't right. She was just young and sweet. He sighed.

Amen? Tom suspected that Jesse was simply mouthing Christianese for Isabel's sake. Tom cleared his throat, Ruby followed suit, and so did Isabel, covering her mouth, but Jesse reneged, the increased stress on his belt and shirt buttons, caused by his ingestion of ample turkey and pudding, diverting his attention.

"Yes, well," he said.

Deciding to lighten up on Jesse for the moment and thus redeem her nasty self, Ruby said, "I notice you pronounce it *Eh-men*, the same as Tom does. I prefer *Ah-men*, American you know." And in a burst of inanity she felt compelled to sing, "Tom says *Ehmish* and I say *Ahmish.*" And for added effect, she asked, "Are you one of those great Canadian eh-sayers too, Jesse?"

"Eh?" Jesse said and smiled at Isabel. He hoped his good-natured response was received by Ruby as a thank you for her unexpected kindness and at the same time might silence her. As a bonus, he was delighted to see that Isabel was impressed with his gentle handling of the troubled woman.

Tom was beginning to feel embarrassed for everyone. For Ruby because she was presenting a poor role model to Isabel; for Jesse because he was lost and didn't know it; for Isabel because she was being victimized by an older generation; and for himself because he had been deceived for twenty years. And though he had forgiven Ruby to her face, anger and disgust lingered in his heart. So in his current condition what business did he have trying to save Jesse, and what was his real motive? He knew the answer to that. He was occupying himself with a sense of noble purpose to delay the inevitable end of this Christmas day. He and Ruby had to go home and face the rest of their lives together. He decided not to pursue the subject of forgiveness and conversion any longer and save them all from further embarrassment.

"So, do you enjoy working at The Cowichan Leader?" Tom asked Isabel.

"Very much, thank you," she said.

Isabel smiled a warm inviting smile at Jesse, who didn't know whether to return her warmth or, conscious of Tom and Ruby's protective presence, head for the hills. He decided on a compromise. He turned his bemused head to face Ruby and Tom, and then turned it back again to smile at Isabel. He then noticed on his plate a small spoonful of pudding, which he dispatched with vigor, ignoring his already straining belt and buttons. He chased the black nugget down with the dregs of his coffee, hoping to project a sense of closure to his meal and to their dessert conversation. He had no such luck.

"Must be exciting," Tom said to Isabel.

Tom realized how patronizing his statement was. How

exciting could the newspaper business be in the Cowichan Valley?

"I only work in the ad office," Isabel said to Tom. And then to Jesse, she said, "The excitement is in the news."

She is an airhead, Jesse thought. No, hold on, wait a minute; she was just young and out-numbered.

Ruby said to Jesse, "How do you stand the pace?"

"Speaking of pace," Tom said, interrupting Ruby's enjoyment of Jesse's anxiety, "we'll have to do some heavy exercise to work off this meal."

Tom saw Ruby's impish smile crack, and then he realized that neither had she eaten nor was she able to exercise. He had been careless with his words. No matter what she had done, he didn't want to hurt her.

"Jogging," Isabel said.

The shock of hearing Isabel's confident utterance knocked the wind out of Jesse's hope for the future and cramped his enthusiasm for mating. Even though his system was overheated by his stirring passion and his food intake, he now felt his blood cooling. He shivered. That was one of the first signs. A winter cold was coming on. He needed a drink.

"I'm sure jogging has its place," Jesse said. "But not in the winter, of course. You can't be slogging away in the snow."

Until now he had ignored the obvious fact that Isabel's lithe athletic form must have been the result of devoted exercise. Genes couldn't have been the whole story. It was obvious that she had been skipping over the countryside for years. Anyone, with eyes to see, could see that. He had a choice. A lifetime of pounding the pavement with Isabel, or drinking by himself in the pub. It was a tough one. He craved a smoke.

Tom could see that Ruby was really winding down now. He said to Isabel, "Well, it's getting late. What do you say, Ruby? Elder Baker will take care of the rest."

"Bless his heart," Ruby said.

Tom received her remark as a typical stale sentiment filtered through her increasing fatigue, but then on second thought he wondered if she had weakened to the point of meaning it.

"It's been a pleasure," Jesse said.

Jesse was relieved that he was going to be let off the hook. No preaching, no major embarrassments. Isabel intact. Still, there was this demon run business hanging over his head now, an ominous cloud of evil, threatening, for the sake of love, to invade his body.

"And I hope you have a pleasant Boxing Day," Jesse said.

He saw Tom and Ruby share a quick glance, and then he regretted his thoughtless comment. Ruby rose from her chair, equal to the occasion.

"Yes, this year Boxing Day should be extra special," she said.

"See you in church then," Jesse said.

In response to their frowns, he offered a good-natured laugh to let them know it was a possibility. He added, smiling at Isabel, "We'll be staying here for a while, we've got clean-up duty."

Unable to resist, Ruby said, "That is excellent, Jesse, we should do our best to keep everything clean, shouldn't we?"

Jesse nodded, and Ruby and Tom said goodbye to Isabel. Then away they went, Tom supporting Ruby's elbow. On the wall beside the door hovered a painting of the glorified, resurrected Jesus, floating in the heavens. Jesse watched them pass by it.

"They have been a real blessing to all of us," Isabel said.

"They are definitely different," Jesse said. "But I do know they mean well."

He turned to admire his shining Isabel. His disbelief that Isabel could be here with him enjoying his company had vanished. He was content, jogging or no jogging. And his mind was calm. Here he was, at his age, on Christmas Day in the company of a delightful young woman, who seemed to care for him. Not seemed. She did care for him. But he realized there was something even more incredible than that. He had sat through his whole hot turkey dinner and, to its everlasting credit, his nose hadn't even run once.

CHAPTER TWENTY-ONE

Tom leaned on the window ledge in the Freedom Center's lounge, staring out at the people tucked into their winter coats, bustling in and out of the post office. He suspected most were depressed now that their Christmas expectations had been converted into credit card debt and their New Year's hopes had sobered, the January weather hanging over them, drizzling news of a few more months of despair left before spring. They would be better off to be like him; he always did his best to ignore most of the whole Yuletide business. There was no let-down that way. He liked to keep an even keel throughout the year. Yeah, sure, who was he kidding? This Christmas had been a Christmas to top all Christmases. He had discovered that for twenty years he had mourned the loss of a son who was of no relation, except to his wife. *Get tested? No, don't be silly, Tom. There's nothing the matter with you.* She had played to his ego. She said she was the one who had the problem; it was psychological. And who could say for sure how a problem like that might be solved? But the fact was he had weak sperm. The tomb of the unknown son. What was there to mourn for? The truth? It had died twenty years ago along with the baby, but its grave only uncovered Christmas Eve, after Ruby had blown the lies away. Promiscuity had been his way of life back then; he didn't deny that, but it had been essential for Ruby to stay pure. He could only worship her if she were pure. Otherwise, the joke was too grotesque. But grotesque or not, Ruby was real now; she had fallen from her pedestal. His days of idolatry had ended Christmas Eve.

Tom turned and looked at Will, who was sitting on the couch reading his Bible. The regulars had vacated the Center after slurping down their soup. About five of them had come in today, the usual needy band of misery. There was no new life coming in. The place was dying. But it didn't matter. He'd already let it go anyway.

"You feeling okay, Will?" Tom said.

Will lifted his head from the Book.

"It hurts inside," he said. "They're going to get me, I can feel them."

He stared at Tom, waiting for agreement or denial. He needed the pastor to tell him everything was okay, that his fears were just his imagination.

"There's no way they're going to grab you," Tom said.

Will had wanted the pastor to reassure him, but when he heard the words spoken they were not convincing.

Tom's paranoia surfaced to tell him he was responsible for Will's condition, but that was a lie. God had saved Will. He had only been the one who brought the message. And now his role in Will's life was becoming unimportant. But what about the pain Will said he was suffering from, was it real or not? Or was pain his birthright? And were there thousands of years of Indian culture pulsating in his genes and telling his body and mind that every fiber would suffer until he succumbed to the dance and took on his spirit guide and sang his song? Or was Will just being melodramatic? When it came to spiritual matters such as this, how were you supposed to tell? Maybe they really were out there ready to grab him.

"They're out there," Will said.

"Even if they are, they can't have you," Tom said.

"Who's going to stop them? They're working on me now."

Will grunted, as if he had been punched in the abdomen, and then, in pain, he held his breath.

Tom decided not to go along with it. From a spiritual perspective he knew that witchcraft might affect people physically, but to have Will suffering from the effects of it, right there in front of him, was too much for his rational mind to accept. Theory was fine, but the real thing was unbelievable, so for now he decided to file Will's present behavior under melodrama. Overacting had to be a trait of Will's race. He examined his last thought and wondered if he was a racist. And then another thought came to him, the one that often tried to force its way in, the one about Ruby's sickness. But that was impossible. There was no way she was the victim of a witchcraft curse sent in retribution for his ministry to Will. No, he just wouldn't allow that to be the truth, that he and his ministry were the cause of Ruby's cancer. Besides, if they were to go after anyone it would have been him, not Ruby. Witchcraft was unable to cause cancer anyway. There was no way they had that kind of power.

"Why can't God stop them from grabbing me?" Will said.

"I told you, nobody's going to grab you. You're protected."

Tom turned to the coffee urn on the counter and poured himself a cup. He was trying to believe what he had just said.

"Are you sure?" Will said.

"You're one of His kids," Tom said. "He'll take care of you."

"Even me, an Indian?" Will said.

Tom saw that look again on Will's face. The one that said the race barrier had again materialized between them. Most of the time it was invisible, but it was always there.

"Jesus was a Jew," Tom said. "He's not just the White Man's God."

"Tell that to those wild Indians out there. They're going to grab me, and nobody is going to do anything about it."

Tom slumped into the shabby brown armchair that inhabited the space below the window. He had that familiar feeling in the pit of his stomach. Helplessness, mixed with fear.

He knew the pattern. First came fear, then discouragement, and after that came rebellion. And then he would be very far from God, and struggling with everything.

"Is that a prophecy?" Tom said.

He knew if they grabbed Will, there would be nothing he could do about it. He could call the RCMP, but they wouldn't interfere with what they considered native culture; to them it wasn't the same as kidnapping. So what else could he do? Only pray.

"It's the truth about the future," Will said, "so I guess you could call it prophecy."

Jesse poked his face into Tom's mind. The power of the press; that might be an idea. But if they did grab Will, would Jesse help? He could ask Isabel to pull some strings. No, he wouldn't do that. Unethical.

Will said, "That Bible College on the mainland has students coming from all over, doesn't it?"

"Sure, from all over."

"Other Indians are going to be there too, probably."

"Sure, you already know that," Tom said.

"It's a long way from here though."

Will groaned and held his stomach, the pain returning.

"Only a twenty-mile ferry ride," Tom said.

"Well then, I'm lucky," Will said.

"Lucky? What do you mean, lucky?"

"At least these days, thanks to the White Man's ferry, I won't have to paddle all the way over there in my canoe."

Tom laughed and said, "At least we're good for something."

Will stood up with his open Bible in his hand and said, "I'm a Spirit-filled, Christian Indian, and when I finish college I will be a Bible-educated Indian, and then I'm going to lead my people out of their bondage and oppression, right past the open mouths of the White Man."

"You're going to be dangerous, Will. That's why the enemy wants to stop you. He doesn't want you to get out of here."

"So you agree," Will said. "They are out there, and they are going to grab me,"

Before Tom could answer, the door opened and in from the rain came Elder John Baker, his hands in his pockets, flapping his raincoat.

"Hi, Tom," he said and nodded at Will. "Boy, it's miserable out there."

Tom stood. He was uneasy. He should be doing something, not sitting in a chair talking to Will. What was he getting paid for? They were right to get rid of him. Then he sat down again, dismissing his sudden panic. Why should he think John Baker's thoughts? The eldership didn't know what the job was anyway. They didn't know that the pastor's primary responsibility was to carry the spiritual weight of the church, they only knew they wanted tangible results. And besides, why should he care what they thought. He was fired.

"Want a coffee?" Tom said.

"Thanks," Baker said. "I'll help myself."

He poured himself a cup and then hovered beside Will, who was hunched over his Bible. Tom was about to ask Baker if he would like to go into the office, when Baker said, "I just came by to ask whether you would mind if I gave the sermon next Sunday."

"You've got a message for us, then?" Tom said.

Tom wondered whether he'd sounded sarcastic. Baker's request had caught him off guard. Here Baker was, in the flesh, making his bold, inappropriate request in front of Will. But since Baker had done his best to undermine his ministry and take over the pulpit, why was he surprised?

"Yes, I believe I do," Baker said.

If Tom's voice had been tinged with sarcasm, he sensed that

Baker hadn't noticed. Baker stood beaming in the light of his imagined revelation, expecting a positive response and contemplating the clever spiritual insights he would present to the congregation next Sunday.

"So what's the message?" Tom asked.

Baker glanced down at Will, who, hiding his physical discomfort, was impersonating a studious young man engrossed in his reading and ignoring the conversation.

Baker said, "It has to do with tithing."

"Tithing? And what led you to that topic? Did God inspire it?"

"Well, it's our building. It's old and cramped. And, if you must know, the Lord gave me a vision."

"A vision! Well, tell me about it."

"I saw some property, a few acres just outside of town, and I saw the blueprints for a new building. It was a glorious vision."

Will shuddered in pain. Tom guessed Will's pain had been compounded by Baker's vision.

"Is he okay?" Baker asked Tom, avoiding the bother of talking to Will directly.

"He's got the sickness, we think it's because of the winter ceremonials."

"The what?"

"The Indian spirit dances. You've heard of those?"

"Is he in them?" Baker said. "I always liked Indian culture. It's so colorful. As a matter of fact Geoff tells me you know quite a lot about this spirit dancing business."

"Only a little," Tom said.

Baker had leaked his spy report, and Tom could sense that he was enjoying this bit of intimidation.

Baker said, "That's not what Geoff tells me. He says you have a plan that sort of mixes pagan with Christian."

Tom noticed Will's eyes open wide on Baker's remark.

"Say, excuse me, Pastor," Will said, "I couldn't help overhearing and...."

Baker interrupted, "Don't get me wrong. I'm not referring to you, Will. I know that *you* are fairly orthodox in your beliefs. And I think it's tremendous you're going away to Bible College. Led correctly, you people have a wonderful future in the Kingdom."

Agitated, Will stood and moved over to lean on the wall beside Tom's chair.

"Do you mind if I say something, pastor?" Will said.

"Go ahead," Tom said. "You don't mind, do you John?"

Tom could see he minded.

Baker smirked, and shrugged, and said, "No, go ahead."

Will said, "I know that I've pretty well been the token Indian around here, but I sort of thought that I was accepted by most of *you* people."

"Oh, you are," Baker said.

"Then you must think I'm deaf or ignorant, or...."

Tom interrupted, "Careful, Will, it's not helpful to attack...."

"He's not attacking me," Baker said, deflecting the unpleasantness. "Let's just drop it. There's no sense in pointing fingers."

"Well then, sir," Will said to Baker, "I'll change the subject." He waved his arm toward the window, "There's a bunch of wild, ignorant Indians out there who are going to grab me and put me in the Longhouse."

"We don't know that for sure, Will," Tom said.

"Yes, I do know that for sure. And that's going to be the answer to the Indian problem in this church. I'll be going back to where I belong."

Baker said, "I don't know why you have such a negative attitude toward your people. It's disrespectful. I mean you're one of them, aren't you?"

"I'm not being disrespectful," Will said. "I just don't want to be thrown into the Longhouse to be beaten with deer hoof rattles, and starved, and almost suffocated, and then thrown into the river to freeze, so that I can be taken over by an evil spirit and do my spirit dance. But maybe I'm being unreasonable. Oh, I forgot, Indians aren't supposed to reason, are they?"

Baker frowned.

He said, "I think all this spirit nonsense is overdone. It's only one of your Indian traditions, isn't it? You don't have to do it if you don't want to. Who's going to make you?"

"When they grab you, they grab you," Will said. "You don't have a choice."

"Do you go along with all this, Tom?" Baker said.

"It happens."

"It's not for me to say, Tom, but aren't you going a little overboard on this demon nonsense."

Tom said, "We're in a war. Most of us don't know it, that's why we're always losing."

Tom reflected on his last statement, and on his current failure at work, and at home, and understood why Baker's face began to grin. But Tom knew that Baker's grin was inspired by ignorance. Baker didn't understand that he and his wife Lila had been aiding and abetting the enemy by causing dissension in the church. Rather, they saw themselves as emancipators, freeing the congregation from an eccentric shepherd.

"While I'm on the subject of losing," Tom said, "I guess with the Center gone, there'll be more funds available for your vision."

"We don't want you to be bitter about that, Tom. After all, your Center isn't exactly packing them in. By the way, you don't plan to continue here, do you?"

"No one's been knocking the door down to donate money for the lease, if that's what you mean," Tom said.

"Well, you know better than I that the Lord has His ways of giving guidance, but I for one haven't seen Him encouraging us to continue operating this place."

Tom was irritated now, because Baker was right, even though for the wrong reasons. He knew that Baker preferred that Baker's church have a clean, upstanding image, but the Center gave Baker's church a bad reputation in the community. There were undesirable elements hanging around the Center, people who had no business being associated with Baker's church. Feeding them on Christmas Day was fine, a charitable activity that looked good to the community, but having them congregate at the Center all year round was a black mark on the reputation of Baker's church, and now with this Indian business and Tom's continual preaching on sacrifice, so was Tom. Tom was dragging Baker's church through the gutter, and the bums and the tramps were getting a free ride at the expense of the respectable church citizens.

Tom said, "No tithing message this week, John."

Tom enjoyed the way Baker's mouth fell open, and the way Baker forced his eyes to squint as he processed the words, and the way Baker then frowned and said, "I see."

"Good," Tom said.

"Well," Baker said, "we only have another month or so to enjoy your preaching, so I suppose we should take every advantage of hearing it while you're here. See you Sunday, Tom. And goodbye, Will."

"Goodbye, sir," Will said.

Tom had to give Baker credit. He'd made a good recovery, a professional job. But how about his own performance? Ruby would have been proud of him, the way he had defied Baker. Not that he cared to impress her these days. So why had he bothered to stand up now? What difference would it make now? Should he have humbled himself instead and allowed Baker to preach? No, that was cowardice not humility. For too long he'd been calling his cowardice humility. On the other hand, he hated confrontation. Why make waves? But the Bible was clear about confronting sin. There was that word again. Nobody wanted to hear about sin. How could you keep members of the congregation happy by confronting them with a word like that? If you did, they would run away to another church. Or worse. All he had done was confront them with the simple principle of sacrifice, and they had given him the boot.

"He's a plenty upset White Man," Will said.

"Plenty."

"Loving is hard," Will said.

"Love your enemies, bless those who curse you, do good to those who hate you, and pray for those who spitefully use you and persecute you."

"Easy for you to say, pastor."

"How are you feeling now?" Tom said.

"Better. Elder Baker's visit cheered me up. I can see the enemy more clearly now. But he was right about one thing. The Indian people are going to have a great future in the Kingdom of God, if they are properly led, that is."

"You can be the one to lead them, Will."

"Maybe, but right now I have a strong feeling they are the ones who are going to do the leading."

"Don't start that again," Tom said.

"I'm sorry, pastor, but they're out there and they're going to grab me."

"Are you feeling well enough to go back to school?"

"I hope so. I better get going. I've only got a few minutes before my next class, and I haven't been able to train the school to run on Indian time yet. It wouldn't be good for me to be late, because I sure wouldn't want to give us Christian Indians a bad name."

CHAPTER TWENTY–TWO

Jesse was in his office, seated in front of his own words, doing what he did best. He was a reporter, an editor, a writer, a commentator on the events of the world. He was where he was meant to be. And across the hall, not five seconds away, his angel hovered. They had been weaving their souls together for a few weeks now. Or at least that was his ardent interpretation of the mating proceedings to date. Physical contact had been elusive, but on the plus side she had let the jogging issue drop since it first sprang from her tongue Christmas Day. The last three Saturday nights they had gone to movies in Victoria, sixty kilometers away. Their pleasant relationship continued to be formal. He picked Isabel up at the family farm, where she lived with her mother, although she hadn't yet introduced him to her. And that was odd. Isabel's father had been killed five years before in a logging accident. When she told him the touching story, he ignored the passing impudent thought that she was attracted to him because he was a father figure. Why be too psychological about it? Last Sunday he had gone to church, the first time since Christmas Day. But his intentions had been frustrated by Isabel's absence. Fate had decreed that she stay home to care for her mother, who was down with the flu. Isabel's mother had sworn off church. She held a grudge against God for the death of her husband. And rightly so. The two Sundays prior to that, Jesse had skirted the pitfall of becoming a habitual pew sitter, not wanting his church attendance to be taken for granted, or for him to appear too accepting of Christian marriage, or any other kind of marriage for that matter. He had continued to be cautious. They were seen in Duncan together at Christmas, and that was enough.

He had not want to encourage town gossip.

His editorial this week concerned the abuse of the forest by logging companies and the splendid work environmental groups were doing. He had done the forest topic once before, or maybe twice. It wasn't fair to look back and take a peek though. Make it up as you go, that was his motto. He finished his last sentence: *Therefore progress will be minimal until government fulfills its obligation to the future and initiates legislation to protect the forests from abusive practices and to insure an aggressive reforestation program.* Excellent, Jesse thought, scanning his work. He was in his element. He was a commentator on vital matters; he was the insightful editor of The Cowichan Leader.

He had his editorial in the can before lunch, and today he had decided to make a bold move, to throw caution to the wind. At the risk of igniting office gossip, he would invite Isabel to lunch. He had felt it necessary until now to keep their relationship under the Leader's radar. He was afraid that if they were seen dating and if their relationship were to fail, then everyone in the office would know it, and he would look foolish. Besides, office romances were disruptive. Still, he was going to take a chance. There was no fool like a middle-aged fool. But would he be risking more than a red face, that was the question? And a dumb question it was. Of course he would. He wasn't so love struck that he was blind to the implications. Such a public declaration would lead either to public humiliation or a trip down the aisle to the altar of sacrifice. Taking her to lunch amounted to one of the two. And if it was marriage, then there would be no way to back out. People wouldn't believe that he had rejected her. He would prefer marriage than to look foolish in the future if it appeared to the staff that she had rejected him. *What would a lovely young woman like Isabel want with a disagreeable old degenerate like him anyway?* That would be the sort of thing they would say. A simpler route was to have a sordid affair and then afterward she would quit her job on her own steam, heartbroken by his later rejection of her loose self. But she wasn't that kind of person. And if they did get married then it would be inappropriate for her to work in the office. Therefore she would have to quit her job and devote her life to him. That would solve the office problem, except he would be married. There was no doubt women complicated life.

Decisions, decisions, he thought, looking at his watch, stalling. Which was correct? Should he *take* the decision or *make* the decision to invite her to lunch? He wasn't certain anymore. He couldn't decide. He suspected his indecision was Margaret Thatcher's fault. He couldn't remember anyone *taking* a decision until she came onto the scene. Now everyone who held public office was *taking* them. Prime Minister Mulroney was *taking* decisions all over the place. Probably got the bug from chin-wagging with Thatcher at Economic Summits. Was Bush *taking* them now too? He couldn't recall. But he knew that the person in the street wasn't *taking* decisions. The average person was still *making* them. Ever since the politicians had begun *taking* decisions, economic conditions had worsened for the middle-class and the poor. *Taking* decisions was just a little too high and mighty for the average person, who was better off when decisions were simply *made*. And to where were they *taking* these decisions? When you *made* a decision it was right there in front of you, but when decisions were *taken* who knows where they might end up. Still, he had better move on with the times. Why be a rebel in the Nineties? He decided he had to *take* the decision. He pushed his phone's front-office button and asked if Isabel would come in to see him. A minute later his door opened and in she came.

"Yes, Mr. Thornton," she said.

He was unable to appreciate her humor, sitting, as he was, at the center of his power. Her playful affront for a moment assaulted the dignity he thought due his position. But he recovered. After all, she was young. She would be good for him; she would liberate him from his rut.

"I wonder," he said, "if you are free for lunch today, would you care to dine with me at the Totem."

She feigned shock at his bold proposal.

"I bring my lunch," she said. "But today, I'm sure my mother will forgive me for not eating it."

He was delighted to hear her mock her age. She was far from being an airhead.

"Fine. Why don't you get your coat and I'll meet you outside." he said.

She spun and sprang out.

Jesse was excited now. He might as well go for it, or rather it seemed as if he had already gone for it. He stood and tucked in his shirt. But prior to donning his overcoat he remembered he needed to clean a spot off the left elbow of his tweed jacket. The sticky spot was on the suede patch. Earlier, when he was composing his brilliant editorial piece, each time he leaned on the arm of his chair, his jacket sleeve had stuck there, just enough to annoy him and disturb his concentration. At first he thought the sticky stuff was on the arm of the chair. His attempt to remove the invisible spot by rubbing the chair's arm vigorously with his handkerchief failed, since the annoying stickiness, as it turned out, was on his jacket patch. Somewhere, he had leaned on a wad of someone's forsaken gum. He glanced at his watch and then dribbled a blob of bubbling spit on his white handkerchief. He then began to rub the suede-leather patch, remembering in the process that she often chewed the stuff. But it was no use. The jacket would have to go to the dry cleaners. As he put on his overcoat, the image of a gum chewing Isabel flashed in his mind. Marriage, he thought, had the potential to be a sticky affair.

Jesse felt every eye of the noontime crowd in the Totem Cafe follow him and Isabel to their booth, where, defying them, he helped her remove her coat, the fragrance of fries shooting up his flaring nostrils, and the establishment's dishes and cutlery clattering in concert with the chattering diners. The giant laminated menus arrived with the jaded waitress, who, pushing coffee, produced two saucers and their cups, which she proceeded to fill, the creamers in dribble mini-cups along for the ride. What a place to bond, Jesse thought, studying the menu and regretting his choice of eating spots. The advantage of the place was its convenient location across the street from the office, but hearing the titters behind him coming from the booth of the newspaper's production staff, he decided that its location was also its disadvantage. One of the fast-food joints on the other side of town would have been better. Still, Isabel seemed content.

"I think I'll have the special, veal cutlets," Jesse said. "How about you?"

"Sounds good," she said.

Jesse wondered if she did prefer the cutlets or if she felt compelled to act out the pre-nuptial custom of being agreeable. Maybe he should have asked her to the Maple Bay Pub for a beer and a sandwich. They could have taken the rest of the day off, and made an afternoon of it. But how would she have reacted to the suggestion? No, that would have been pushing it. Besides, there was no sense turning over an old leaf already.

The waitress returned and they ordered their cutlets. She noted their choices and left. So far so good, Jesse thought, but then he noticed that Isabel's expression had changed from contentment to deep concentration. She had something on her mind.

"Is there something wrong, Isabel?" Jesse said.

He amazed himself by how sensitive and caring his voice had sounded. He sipped his coffee and waited.

"Well, yes there is," she said. "I need to tell you something."

She lowered her head, hesitating. And then she looked up, her luxuriant eyebrows accentuating her hazel eyes, and he was captivated. Her face filled his universe.

"What I mean is, well, I haven't told you about one important detail of my life. I mean, I haven't been completely honest with you."

Isabel's confession of dishonesty brought Jesse down to earth. He imagined the worst. Had she been leading him on? Making a fool out of him? But what for? He had an urge to escape from the booth and hightail it down to Maple Bay for a beer and a smoke. Jogging. Man, he had almost fallen for the whole ugly mess. His earlier suspicion that she had a young jock boyfriend, sweating in some gym somewhere, was probably right. So why had she bothered with him?

"What do you mean, you haven't been completely honest?"

"I don't know how to tell you, except to just tell you."

"That would be the best way of going about it, I think."

"Yes, I agree. So this is the situation. I have a six-year-old daughter."

Jesse was astonished, but relieved. She hadn't been making a fool out of him; she had only been misrepresenting the merchandise. And that was fair enough. Still, he was confused, so to steady himself and present a solid image to her, he assumed his familiar seasoned reporter role.

"So you've got a six-year-old daughter, then?"

"Yes, six years old."

"A six-year-old daughter, you've got one."

"Six years old, that's right."

"You didn't mention it before."

"No, no, I didn't, I'm sorry. I just mentioned it now."

"So you had a daughter about six years ago, then."

"In Saskatchewan, yes. I went back there to live with my older sister and her husband while I had the baby. But I couldn't bear to give her up for adoption, so the two of us came home."

"You kept your figure well."

"Thank you."

"Where is she now, then?"

"With my mother at the farm. That's why I've never asked you in. I was embarrassed to tell you, since I'm supposed to be the virtuous type, a Christian. Do you see what I mean?"

"So you've got a daughter, then."

"That's right, her name is Rowena."

"Does she jog?"

"No, not yet."

"That's in her favor. You were never married, then?"

"No. Her father now lives in Alberta. He isn't interested in us at all."

Well, wouldn't you know it, Jesse thought, waxing philosophical, there was always a catch, and it looked like he was it.

Jesse said, "So, let's see, you were embarrassed, and you didn't think I could handle the fact that you have a daughter, was that it?"

"Well, no, that wasn't exactly it. I didn't want to complicate things. It didn't matter before, because I didn't really know your intentions. I still don't really."

Why had she waited until now to tell him? Why indeed! He had taken her to lunch in front of the office staff and the whole town. He might as well have gotten down on one knee in front of them all. Well, he wouldn't put up with it.

"I'm sorry," she said.

And then she captured him with a genuine hurt look. In his dazed state he was at least positive of one fact. She wasn't the feminist type. And down deep he was a chauvinist for sure. He was too old to be liberated. Slippers brought to his chair and a daughter who might even call him daddy. And Isabel was so young and lovely. He leaned forward, shifting his left elbow on the gray table-top, the gum residue on his jacket-patch hardly sticking at all.

"I don't know why you were so concerned about it," he said. "It makes no difference to me. What I mean to say is, that it makes a difference of course, but I can live with it. That is if we have an understanding. What I mean is, if you're agreeable, that we should carry on, if you see what I mean. Is that all right with you?"

"Yes, if I understand you, that is all right with me."

"Good."

Jesse was unsure himself whether he had just taken the plunge or had been ambiguous enough so that if it became necessary he could talk himself out of the whole thing later. And how she thought she could understand his proposal was beyond his grasp. But he knew now that she was not an airhead, and he had a premonition that if he did get to know this young woman, rather than reveling in his romantic idea of her, then he would be in danger of falling in love. And she had a daughter already. They would be a family. Worse things could happen.

"Have you ever wanted more children?" he said.

"Not without a husband, no. I'm old fashioned. Other than that one lapse in judgment, I'm without blemish, if that's what you mean."

"Uh, no, that's not what I meant."

"Well then, yes, I do like the idea of having more children."

The waitress, returning with the special of the day, broke Jesse's fusion with Isabel. He was again aware that he was in the Totem Cafe and that surrounding the two of them, a world still existed, filled with noises and smells and objects and people.

"Looks good," he said.

"Yes, but nothing beats my mother's home cooking," she said.

He watched Isabel thank God for her meal, and then he, as he ate, contemplated her last statement for a very long time.

"How old is your mother?" he said.

He took a deft swipe at his nose with his coat-sleeve while her eyes were on her cutlets.

"Fifty-eight," she said. "Why? Is it important?"

"No, no, of course not," he said. "I only wondered how long she had been cooking for, that's all."

CHAPTER TWENTY-THREE

Jesse sat in the prayer room at the Center and waited for Tom's response. He'd brought his confusion to the pastor. The move was logical, since Isabel was a member of Tom's flock. In his prime, his pride would have prevented him from confessing his inability to make an important decision concerning his future. Now he was middle-aged, insecure and desperate. And he was wise enough to know that his emotions were untrustworthy. And he knew that Tom was safe, a person with whom he could share his fears and desires. Since diplomacy was now a necessity, he retreated from his previous position of mocking Tom and his ministry. He had even gone through the motions of humbling himself. And as he had hoped, Tom had not taken the opportunity to make him squirm before offering his services.

"The simple answer is no," Tom said. "The Bible is pretty clear about Christians not marrying unbelievers. Marriage is already difficult enough without having fundamental differences of belief. So the main problem is not your age, which seems to be what you're worrying about, it's about faith."

"So you recommend that we not get married?" Jesse said.

"That's what I'm saying, and I'll say the same to Isabel. But it's still her decision, as it is yours. I do understand that you are concerned about the age difference. It is a factor, but as I said, the main challenge to a successful union is the fact that you're not a Christian, and the two of you would be unequally yoked."

Jesse was now annoyed that Tom did think his age was something to consider.

"Now wait a minute," Jesse said, "What do you mean I'm not a Christian, I'm Catholic, and I'm as good as the next person?"

"Goodness has nothing to do with it, but that's another subject. If I remember right, I once heard you say you were an atheist. If you were a Christian, you would know it."

"I also said I was baptized a Catholic as a baby," Jesse said.

"When you show up at the Judgment Seat, don't count on your infant baptism as proof positive," Tom said.

"Now hold on. That's a little much, isn't it?"

"Okay, it was a low blow. I was just trying to make a point."

"And I think I know what your point is. You're leading up to all that born-again stuff, like Chester Thomas and all the rest of your crowd spout every chance you get."

"The point is that being born again isn't optional for a Christian. You can't be a Christian otherwise. Jesus said that you can't see the Kingdom of God unless you are born again."

"So you're saying that unless I fall for the whole born-again pitch hook, line, and sinker, there's no point in joining the church, if my reason for joining is so that I can marry Isabel."

"That's it exactly, now you've got it. We have enough nominal Christians to go around already. But you might think about coming to church anyway, something might eventually rub off."

Jesse began to wonder now why he had come to Tom for advice. If he had taken the time to think about it first, Tom's response would have been simple to predict. But was it possible that he had unconsciously hoped Tom would advise him against marrying Isabel? Whether he had or not, now that Tom the pastor had brought down his decree, Jesse was angry at being told he was inferior, and furious at the unwanted confirmation that he might also be too old for her. And what about love? That subject hadn't even been brought up. He was about to disagree with Tom's assessment, when a bloodshot head appeared in the doorway to slur the news that a man was here who wanted to see Tom.

"He says it's important," Phil said. "But just to let you know, there's something I really don't like about him."

"Thanks, Phil, for telling me that," Tom said. "Please send him in." And to Jesse he said, "If you'll forgive the interruption, I'd like to see what the problem is."

"I've had enough anyway," Jesse said. "I've got to go."

The intrusion of Phil's head had given Jesse a moment to reflect, and he was thankful for that. An angry outburst might have jeopardized future maneuvers. His emotions told him that despite Pastor Tom's advice he was still in the running for Isabel's hand. And then he reprimanded himself for thinking a bad word.

"If you could stay," Tom said, "I'd appreciate it. I've been meaning to ask you about something."

"That's fine, I can wait, but I would appreciate you sparing me any more preaching today."

"Fair enough," Tom said.

Jesse turned to see a man come in and stand for a few seconds, staring at the ceiling, and then he sat down. Jesse looked over at Tom, curious to know how he was reacting to the man's rude, abrupt entry. Jesse tried to catch Tom's eye, but he was focused on the man.

"I'm Tom and this is Jesse," Tom said.

"My daughter told me last night about you," the man said to Tom.

"Your daughter? What's her name?" Tom said.

"She lives in Victoria. She had a dream about the Controllers shutting things down."

Jesse was baffled by the man's continued impolite manner,

and then he felt an irrational fear creep into his abdomen. But Tom seemed calm, so he decided he would try to relax too. Yet why was this man in shirt-sleeves in the middle of winter? And why was he rolling them up to his elbows, as though he was preparing for something? Jesse looked at the man's exposed forearms; they were red and raw. Either they were badly burned, or they were covered with severe eczema.

The man shook his head and said to the floor, "What me? Oh, they have been contacting me for years now."

Jesse was confused. Who was the man talking to? Tom was nodding his head at the man. As for him, the editor of The Cowichan Leader, he had no idea what was going on. Then Jesse noticed that the man, who was in his fifties or perhaps early sixties, looked like the twin of the grandfather on the Munsters, except his face appeared to alter and shift, but not just its expression. His face's structure seemed to change.

The man said, "She saw it in a dream."

"Do you live there?" Tom asked.

What kind of question was that, thought Jesse? Did Tom understand this guy?

"Sometimes," the man answered. "They know what's going on."

"What happened to your arms?" Tom said.

Jesse wanted to know that too, but he felt cautious about asking anything, which was an unusual feeling for a reporter.

"It's resistance. I don't flow through exactly right."

What the hell does that mean, Jesse asked himself? And then the man's face did it again. It blurred and changed, not into another distinct face but, Jesse speculated, perhaps into some other distinct facet of the man's being.

"How do you know that?" Tom asked.

"I'm an engineer."

Interesting, Jesse thought; he looked like he might be an

engineer. But what was he doing here? His dark gray pants were wool and tailored; he wore new black loafers, and his blue pin-striped shirt had a Pierre Cardin symbol on the pocket. So what was he doing in a drop-in center, talking gibberish? He wasn't drunk. Drugs maybe, or insane?

He said, "You don't understand. Nobody does. The Controllers. They do it with beams and force fields and electrical impulses. See."

The man held out his arms for Tom to see.

The man said, "Too much resistance. I'm being punished for my blockages. They beam down the punishment." The man lifted his eyebrows toward the ceiling. "They're up there."

His face began to shift again. From where Jesse sat, the man now looked like the Pope, peaceful now, not threatening, like everyone's ideal grandfather. A man you could relate to.

Jesse decided to be brave.

"Where do you work?" he said.

Jesse watched the man turn his head toward him, exuding the warmth and understanding of the Pope about to bless a peon.

"I'm resigned," said the Bishop of Rome.

Then the man shifted back into his Munster role. Jesse was stunned. But at least he had received a straight answer. That was as good as Tom had gotten. It was obvious that his reporter's skills, his years of conducting interviews, had been recognized and respected by the man.

"You haven't got a clue how it all works," Munster man said to Jesse.

Now even more confused, Jesse looked at Tom for guidance, but Tom was occupied, concentrating on the man, or men, or whatever was going on there. And who did this man think he was? He couldn't talk to the editor of The Cowichan Leader that way.

"How does it work?" Tom asked.

"You know a bit. You're the straight-shooter. There are others that shoot straight, but you're a gunslinger, okay?"

Whatever was happening, Jesse thought, the man seemed to like Tom, flattering him the way he did, or at least he thought it was flattery.

"The Controllers do it," the man said. He rubbed his forearm. "This is nothing."

"Where are they?" Tom asked.

The man tried to laugh but sputtered instead.

"You don't know," he said.

Jesse was unable to discern whether it was a question or a statement of fact.

On an impulse he said, "I don't know either, Mr....ahh, what did you say your name was?"

The Munster man rolled his eyes, and for the first time since the man had come into the room, Jesse had gotten Tom's attention.

"Cool it," Tom said.

And then, changing his persona again, Pope man added his cryptic input, "Cool hot arms."

"What was your dream?" Tom asked.

"A trick," he said, shaking his head. "You tried a trick. You know it was the daughter who had the dream. You will never find out in time. You know it's too late. It's coming down."

"I knew it was the daughter," Jesse said, beginning to get a feel for the conversation.

Tom frowned at him.

"Arms are burning," Munster man said. "Yes, I'm going, got to go. I know. Message is clear here."

Munster man nodded and said to Tom, "You got the message."

"How are they going to do it?" Tom said.

Rising from his chair, the man said, "A secret naturally, but you know the way they always do it. Fire. They always do it that way. The fire comes down. Shooting rays, you know, straight-shooter. Power coming down. You know. The straight-shooter has quit around here. The straight-shooter has lost."

Tom said, "May I pray for healing for your arms."

"No hope," he said and laughed. "Goodbye straight-shooter."

The man turned and walked out the door, ignoring Jesse as he left. Jesse jumped up to look out the window and Tom followed. They saw the man get into a late-model Oldsmobile and drive away into the January gray. Jesse read the large bumper-sticker letters: IS THIS BIG ENOUGH TO READ?

"What was that all about?" Jesse said.

That fear was rising again in Jesse's stomach. And he wanted Tom to tell him right now what was going on.

"I think I've just been had," Tom said, and collapsed into the recliner.

The purpose of the man's visit was becoming clear to Tom. Everyone knew he had given up. It was obvious. And for sure the enemy knew it. Even though he was about to lose financial support from the church, there still had been a chance for a miracle to save the Center, but he had lost heart months ago. He had quit in his mind. He had been too discouraged to go on. There was no way he wanted to spend another freezing winter in this building, feeding the fiendish furnace. The enemy knew that too. And that demonized man had walked right into the prayer room and done something right in front of Tom's uncomprehending self. But what had he done? That was the question. And why had he allowed the man to take control? He should have confronted the man and stood up to him right away. Instead, he had been fascinated, and entertained. He was continuing to chastise himself, when Phil came into the room.

"Who was that guy?" Phil asked.

"I don't know," Tom said.

Phil said, "He looked at me kind of strange on the way out." Phil swallowed hard. "His eyes were flames."

"It's okay, Phil, we know."

Jesse made an attempt to be sympathetic to Phil's distress, but he knew that the weak condescending smile he forced onto his face betrayed his overriding aversion to old drunken-bum Phil.

"Pastor," Phil said, "do you think I could stay here tonight? I haven't paid my hotel room rent yet this month, or last, and they're starting to hassle me. They won't give me my things until I pay up, either."

"You know we're not zoned as a hostel."

"I know, but just for one night, it wouldn't make much of a difference for one night, would it? I'll try to find another place tomorrow, or find the money maybe."

"Sure, Phil, why not? At this point it won't make much difference."

"Thanks, Pastor," Phil said.

Phil lurched out of the prayer room and then out through the Center's main door. Tom guessed he was going to the hotel to try and liberate some of his things. He also guessed that there had to be another reason besides money that would cause Phil to ask to stay at the Center tonight. And he had seen that reason on Phil's face. It was for security. Phil was half-sober and terrified.

Jesse was annoyed at Tom, but he wasn't going to ask him again what the man's visit was all about. His fear lingered, but he wasn't going to let Tom know it. He had already been humiliated enough.

Still standing by the window, Jesse said, "There was something else you wanted to talk to me about?"

"Yes, there is," Tom said. "And as for our visitor, you wouldn't believe it if I told you."

"As mysterious as that, eh?" Jesse said.

Jesse's sarcasm and Tom's irritation at being deceived by their visitor prompted a frank response.

"Not that mysterious. He was demonized. They were the ones in charge, not him, whoever he is, or whoever he once was."

Jesse digested the information for a few seconds, while Tom shifted back a few notches in his recliner.

"You mean The Exorcist bit?" Jesse said. "Spewing green vomit and spinning heads and that sort of thing?"

"That's close," Tom said.

"So, this is what you do here all day? It might make a good story after all."

"Not every day," Tom said. "This was unusual, a full frontal assault, as bold as you can get."

"Hold it a minute," Jesse said. "What do you mean by assault? I didn't see him do anything. We had a chat with multiple personalities, that's all."

"Didn't you hear him?" Tom said. "He threatened me and the Center, or really the Controllers did. He was gloating too. I guess it's all over."

"Whatever you say. All I saw him do were a few impressions, and then he left, what's the harm?"

Jesse was fed up with the whole thing now. He could see that he wasn't going to get any straight answers from Tom, the demon hunter.

"So, anyway," Jesse said, "what was that other matter you mentioned? I've got to get back to the office."

"Right," Tom said. "It's a bit of a coincidence, but I wanted to talk to you about a potentially dangerous situation that also has demonic elements."

"You mean you're going to tell me that the town is about to be taken over by the Controllers, and that I should warn the citizenry in tomorrow's Cowichan Leader."

"Maybe this is the wrong time to talk to you about it," Tom said.

"No, come on, let's hear it. I'm all ears."

"It's about Will Joseph. They might grab him."

"Who's Will Joseph, and who's going to grab him, are the Controllers at it again?"

"Will is a young Indian in our congregation," Tom said. "His people might be planning to grab him and throw him into the Longhouse. And I was wondering if you might be able to do something about it if they did. You know, the power of the press."

"And I suppose you have something against Indian tradition and Will taking part in it."

"Yes, I do," Tom said. "Spirit dancing and Christianity are not compatible."

"Now how did I know that a simple thing like native tradition was going to get more complicated once you got hold of it?"

Jesse was even more irritated now. First Tom had told him he was not good enough for Isabel, not to mention too old, then he was humiliated by multiple personalities, and now Tom expected him to agree with his bigotry.

Jesse said, "So if I were a Christian and an Indian, why wouldn't somebody such as yourself advise me to participate in my cultural traditions?"

"I'll make it plain and simple for you. The spirit dancing rituals are demonic."

"Please excuse a question from an unenlightened pagan, but

if there really were demonic spirits, and if spirit dancing actually was a means to contact them, and the interaction was bad for the Cowichans, why would they want to take part in the rituals in the first place?"

"They think they're good spirits, and that they're going to help them."

"So, if they do exist, maybe they are good," Jesse said.

"The native people wouldn't be in the state they're in if that was true. The conditions on the reserve aren't all the White Man's fault."

"I don't know about that," Jesse said. His anger was rising now. "I would say the White Man is the problem. We stole their land, infected them with disease, introduced them to alcohol, shut them up on reserves, polluted their salmon rivers, made it impossible economically for them to live in their traditional way, tried in the early days to make good western-dressed Christians out of them, while we outlawed the potlatch, and now we are chopping down their forests and continuing to desecrate their burial grounds. Not to mention the atrocities committed at the residential schools. And now it sounds to me that if you had your way you would complete the job the missionaries started and once again shut down their rituals and traditions. And you have the nerve to say to me that I'm the one who needs to be converted?"

Jesse's liberal education was probably the most offended, Tom thought, grounded as it was in the bleeding-heart goodness of man, and in his burden to restore the aboriginal to his former condition of natural greatness, living off the good earth, in harmony with nature. But those who were filled with such great human compassion omitted mentioning the gentle native's occasional forays into enemy territory in times past to butcher and plunder, and then there was that other often forgotten tradition of capturing slaves. Tom knew that being native didn't make you any better than the rest of the human race.

"So you do know something about native culture," Tom said.

"It's my job to know a few things about the valley where I work. And for your information, while we are on the subject, I might mention that I haven't yet had the pleasure of meeting any evil spirits in my travels around here."

"Until today."

"That's your interpretation. A sane person might come up with any number of reasons for that man's behavior. For instance, he could have been rehearsing his nightclub act, who knows?"

Jesse knew there was at least one thing wrong with that explanation. Why did the man's face change the way it did? Right there in front of his eyes the man's face transformed itself like a liquid plastic mask, shifting in a blurry Twilight Zone aura. Nobody could do that without help.

Tom said, "Can we talk about Will. It's him I'm concerned about. If they grab him, he most likely will resist. And that might be deadly."

"It sounds to me like you're more afraid that if he returns to his Indian roots there's a good chance his current zeal for Christianity will be lost in the process. But I'm sure you would just blame the demons for that."

Jesse knew he was being unkind, but after all Pastor Tom had judged him unsuitable for Isabel, so he was no longer compelled to be nice? Plain Tom was okay, but righteous Tom, the hunter of demons and the destroyer of cultures, was a pain in the butt.

"You did see what happened here today, didn't you?" Tom said.

"Yes, I did. But if I'd known I would be given a front row

seat to view the floor show here in your so-called prayer room, I would have forgone the pleasure."

Tom said, "Okay, I'll make it simple. As a newspaper editor, what would your response be to a person being taken against his will and tortured, and then the police and everyone else did nothing about it?"

"The answer's obvious. I'd look into it."

"If it was a white person?" Tom said.

"If it was any person," Jesse said.

"It happened right here, two years ago, and you didn't do anything about it."

"You're referring, of course, to that Indian who died. Yes, I remember, he was 19-years-old, and the RCMP were involved. And there was an investigation. And if memory serves, the cause of death was ruled accidental."

"Swept under the rug."

"Are you saying there's some kind of conspiracy?"

"No, it's not a conspiracy. That's just the way it's done. It's tidier. Nobody's going to challenge Indian tradition."

"If the rituals are so terrible, why don't the Indian people do something about it themselves?"

"The only way you can stay out of the Longhouse is to sign a statement with the RCMP beforehand, saying you want them to come and get you if you're grabbed."

"Okay, there's your answer. If they want out, that's all they need to do."

"If they did go to the RCMP, they'd be shunned by their people. The last person to do that had to move to Vancouver."

"So you're telling me you want me to help you keep your Indian convert out of the Longhouse."

"You can't keep him out, but if they grab him, will you do a story?"

"If he's grabbed, I'll look into it. But I know one thing,

Christian or not, he won't testify against his Band elders, especially in a White Man's court. And who is your convert going to turn to if he does get out, the White community?"

"Christians will back up other Christians, regardless of race."

"So that's been the history, has it?" Jesse said.

"Maybe not, but we're going to back up Will."

"Who's we? And how many Indians are in your church?"

"Will's the only one," Tom said.

"And you'll be going down the road soon, isn't that right? And I suspect you are the only one in your church who really knows or cares about this."

"That's why I'm asking," Tom said. "If Will were grabbed would you investigate?"

"So, do you think Will would issue a complaint, and testify against the elders, if it came to that?"

"I don't know. Right now he would, but afterward, I don't know."

"Well, we won't know till then, will we? That is if this so-called kidnapping happens at all."

Jesse was pleased. He had won that one. Stay away from the spiritual mumbo jumbo and play on a level field, and he was a winner.

"Here's just a thought about you and Isabel," Tom said. "You might try the church's new pastor when I'm gone. He might go for it."

Jesse caught Tom's sardonic tone, and asked, "Who is the new pastor?"

"John Baker, one of the elders, he's going to be taking over as a lay minister until the search committee can find someone else more qualified. My hunch is they'll need a shoehorn to get him out of the pulpit once he gets in."

Tom regretted his last comment. His bitterness had once

again managed to wag his tongue.

"You mean John Baker, the real estate developer?"

"That's him."

"He owns a lot of property south of town, doesn't he?"

"I wouldn't know, but I do know he has some plans for a few acres there. Did I tell you I was in real estate years ago?"

"Who? You? I don't believe it."

"My father-in-law was a big developer in Southern California. I wasn't suited to it."

"What was your problem?"

"I was never cut-throat enough," Tom said.

"It's obvious you're still not, or you wouldn't have lost your church."

"So now you're an expert on church politics?"

"No, but I do know a little bit about politics, and about people, and unless your God saves you, you're going to lose again the next time around."

"And now you're a prophet too? But just as a reminder, God has already saved me, and He's also your God."

"I'm a pagan, remember? And we wouldn't want me to graduate to barely nominal, just so I could marry Isabel, now would we?" He smiled at Tom. "I've got to get back to the office and get a few things done. There are deadlines in my line of work."

"Mine too, but the deadlines I deal with are more permanent than yours."

Tom grinned at Jesse's fading smile.

"If they grab Will, then you'll do the story?" Tom said.

"If there's a story there, I'll write it."

Jesse got up to leave.

"Thanks," Tom said, "I believe you would."

"You take things too seriously, Tom," Jesse said. "Give my regards to Ruby, would you?"

"Sure, and watch out for all those multiple personalities running loose out there."

"No problem," Jesse replied. "I'll just send them over to see you."

"Thanks."

"No problem," Jesse said, and then he left.

Tom pushed back on the arms of the recliner. He decided he would have a nap before he went home. He might as well. The Center was dying. No one came to him for counseling anymore. There was even a lull in marriages and funerals. And today for entertainment he had sunk to the depths. He had tried to reason with the tangled nonsense of demons. A bad day for sure. Still, he had been given the opportunity to talk to Jesse about Jesus. That had been worthwhile. Telling people about Jesus was always worthwhile. Jesse was pompous, but he did have a lot of insight. And Jesse was right about one thing. He would probably repeat the same mistakes in his next church—that is if he ever served in another—unless he surrendered his self-will and allowed God to be in charge.

But more troubling to Tom right now was his lack of sensitivity when he was counseling Jesse. He had ruled like a judge and only given him the spiritual facts. But on the other hand what was so bad about that? Why couldn't people just marry into their own spiritual tribe? A lot of problems were eliminated that way. But people refused to do that. Still, he should have shown more compassion. But how, when he hadn't felt any? He wasn't going to put on an act. Phony compassion gave off an odor. But Jesse had been desperate. He wouldn't have come to him otherwise. He should have at least softened the blow, or reserved his opinion and suggested he talk to them both first. To affect other people's lives in such a powerful way was an onerous responsibility. Who would ever want the job? The answer was simple. Those who longed to serve and those who thirsted for the power of the position. And he knew that for many in his line of work the two motives were often intertwined.

In the moments before he fell asleep, an image of Jesse, sitting in the prayer room, formed in his mind. Round wire-rimmed frames and a beard, a tweedy intellectual, an ex-revolutionary type with a paunch. Except for the intervention of Jesus in Tom's life, he might have become like Jesse, a kind, liberal thinker, prone to cynicism, with nowhere to go. So how were Baby Boomers like Jesse to be saved? Most of them had experienced everything the world had to offer, so why wouldn't they give God a try? Why? Because God had been eliminated from their thinking years ago. *God is Dead*, and He had stayed that way for most of them, or had transformed Himself into Self. But yet, in one significant way, he and Jesse were alike. They shared the dilemma of being confused Baby Boomers trying to muddle their way through middle-age.

CHAPTER TWENTY–FOUR

Tom parked in front of his Center and turned off the Volvo's engine. There were no white wisps of smoke coming from the chimney. He saw a figure standing inside the dark open doorway. He knew his Center was dead. The RCMP hadn't bothered to call him in the middle of the night. When they did call him in the morning to tell him the news, he was upset they hadn't phoned him at two in the morning when the fire started. Then after he hung up, he had to phone back because he had forgotten to ask about Phil, whether he was okay or not. Thinking about it later he realized they had no reason to call him when the fire started. He wasn't the owner of the building.

The figure stepped out of the blackness as Tom got out of the car. It was Jesse. He came down the cement stairs shaking his head.

"There will be no more praying in there," Jesse said. "Not for some time anyway."

"I expected as much."

"It's not gutted, but bad enough, especially in the furnace room, and the stairs down to the basement. The rest of the damage is from smoke and water."

Tom looked over at the furnace room's ground level windows. They were black and shattered.

"It looks substantially worse than that inside," Jesse said. "And by the way, the owner was here waiting for you. He left about fifteen minutes ago. He said he had some other business to attend to, but he would be back."

"I need to go in," Tom said, "and have a closer look."

"You're not going to like it."

Inside the Center, Tom surveyed the blackened walls, the puddles and the grit, and he inhaled the smell of wet charcoal that filled the cold air. It was dead all right. He grabbed a flashlight from a shelf in the broom closet, continued down the dark hall, and opened the door to the basement. The stairwell was black. He crouched so that he could see his furnace. He shined the light at the fallen eight-inch chimney pipe. The wall next to the brick chimney was baked charcoal. The insulation on the water pipes was black and hanging. So there it was, his furnace, his heavy burden, gone up in smoke. The remnants of his long-handled boiler-brush still leaned against the wall, a few bristles sticking out from the clamps, the wood gone. There it was, summed up. Total defeat. He had only been going through the motions anyway. In his mind, he had abdicated his throne months before, and the enemy had now taken the opportunity to enter and torch his kingdom. But that was fair enough. His creation was dead now. It was a start. As he walked back down the hall to the Center's main room, another thought invaded, the cruel one about his imminent loss of Ruby. He knew he had to let her go, too. Her life wasn't his responsibility, and she wasn't responsible for him. She had to be accountable for her own life, and death, and he had to face his life without his Center, without his ministry, and without her.

His shoes squished the dirty water that had soaked the burgundy carpet, as he returned down the hall to the lounge area. Jesse was there waiting.

"Get any pictures of the fire?" Tom said.

"Yes, we did. At least I hope they're printable. Our eager junior reporter shot a roll or two. She was here about 2:30, shortly after the fire broke out and when the fire trucks arrived."

"Well that's good. The Center will finally make the paper."

"I'm sorry about this, Tom."

"Any idea where Phil is?"

"As far as I know," Jesse said, "they let him back into his room at the hotel. By all accounts, he's sober and scared."

"Did they say how it started? They wouldn't tell me on the phone."

"From what I understand about the series of events, Phil wanted to ensure he stayed warm enough overnight, so he stuffed the furnace with firewood before he went to sleep, or before he passed out, or however he does it. As it turns out he's a regular Boy Scout when it comes to building fires. The fire chief thinks the blaze started because the fire was hot enough to send the flames up through the pipe and into the brick chimney, where there was a heavy buildup of creosote. The creosote exploded and sections of the chimney blew out sending the flames into the walls downstairs and up. Which brings us to the question, when was the last time that old chimney was cleaned?"

"Thanks for the summary," Tom said. "You do a nice job of reporting. But to answer your question, chimney cleaning wasn't in the budget."

"A lack of foresight, it would seem. But at least you don't need a budget now. And just as a word of caution, you would be wise to prepare your responses beforehand to predictable questions the owner of the building and his insurance company are going to ask you."

"I wonder why he built such a big fire."

"It certainly was big."

"No, I mean it was a fairly warm night for January, and even though alcohol thins the blood, it's not like Phil to do that much work."

"I knew you would get to that. I suppose our friend yesterday paid him to do it."

"No, there wouldn't be any money involved. He triggered something in Phil, spirits to spirits, you might say."

"I see," Jesse said, "I'll write up the story that way. The Controllers ordered demons to do it. That would make a great headline. Suitable for the tabloids. Demons Burn Down Christian Center. Conspiracy Suspected. I'm sure the owner and the insurance company will be satisfied with that explanation, too. And forgive me for belaboring the point, but didn't you say yesterday this place isn't zoned to be used as a hostel. How are you going to explain Phil?"

"That's easy. He comes from a long line of alcoholics, and he was beaten as a child, in preparation for being beaten as an adult. And that's all I'm saying to the press today."

"Sensitive this morning, are we? Is that because you suspected this would happen and were unable to prevent it? I don't expect an answer. And don't worry, there's nothing newsworthy about minor squabbles with insurance companies, and besides, the condition you and this Center are in would be too much for my readers to stomach. A picture will do."

Tom said, "What did he say his daughter dreamed? No, he was the one who said how the Controllers would do it. Fire. The fire comes down. You heard it yourself."

"Coincidence. Only a coincidence."

"Aren't you the least bit concerned about what happened here?"

"I know what happened here. Phil built a fire, and the chimney was lined with a thick layer of creosote. It's as simple as that. And if I remember correctly, our friend yesterday didn't say they were going to send fire on this Center. He said the Controllers did their dirty work by shooting rays down. He didn't say they were going to shoot fire down at this Center as a special treat for you. Good grief, I don't even know why I'm talking about this."

"Because it was real, and you know it."

"Real? You must be joking. And just so we understand each other. I don't go along with your claim that a demonically inspired psycho burned down your Center, even if Phil was his accomplice, which is highly doubtful. And if you were to survey a cross-section of our fellow citizens, including people in your own church, and ask them if they thought your interpretation of events was plausible, we would soon discover which one of us has an accurate view of reality."

"Public opinion wouldn't prove a thing," Tom said.

"And you're never going to prove your theory either, but the insurance adjuster might have theories of his own."

"The owner doesn't care about any of that. He's wanted to bulldoze the place for years. He only wants the lot. Who else would want this igloo?"

"Only someone like you. But I must say I'm sorry you're out of business, even though I'm not sure now what your business is."

"Thanks, but I'm happy to be out of business. It's an easy way out. Thank God."

"I thought you said the Controllers set fire to the place, not God."

"God allowed it for a reason," Tom said.

"For what reason would your God allow it? To make sure your work here was a complete failure?"

"He works in mysterious ways."

"Your God is too scary for me, so I'm sure you'll be able to forgive me for not joining up."

"You'll have to face Him sometime," Tom said. "It's only a matter of when. And I can guarantee you, now is way better than later."

Tom was about to continue his uninspired sermon when Phil squished his way into the room.

"Phil! You're okay," Tom said.

Phil rubbed the dirty blonde stubble on his chin.

"Yeah, I'm okay. It wasn't my fault, pastor, honest, uh, the furnace went nuts."

"I know, Phil. Thanks for coming to tell me. How did you get out?"

"I was lucky, I woke up…you know, I had to go to the can…and man, the smoke was heavy. I crawled out the back basement door."

"I'm glad your alarm clock was working," Tom said.

"Alarm clock? Oh, I get it. Yeah, me too, but that's not the only reason I came to see you, pastor. There's something you need to know. I was heading for the hotel this morning, and about a block away, at the end of the school grounds, I saw a car pull over, and a couple of guys got out. They grabbed another guy off the sidewalk and shoved him in the car. They drove right by me, and I looked inside. It was Will in there, three native guys and Will. They grabbed him right off the street, just like that."

Tom suppressed his urge to flop on the soggy sofa. Instead, he found his way into the prayer room, which was farthest from the fire and had been spared major damage. The vinyl recliner was dry, and he fell into it. Jesse followed him and stood in the doorway. Over Jesse's shoulder Phil, in a hurry, said, "I've got to go…I've to go to the welfare office. Say, can you spare? I mean, never mind, see you…sorry."

Tom wondered how Phil planned to convert the tragedy of the Center into enough cash from the welfare office to get a bottle. But what about Will? Now they had him. Grabbed right off the street. That outcome was a great deal worse than the fire.

"Well?" Jesse said.

"Well what?" Tom said.

"Well, what are you going to do about it?"

"Nothing right now," Tom said, "the question is what are you going to do about it?"

"Me? What am I going to do about it? Okay, you tell me. So what's the story?"

"Come on," Tom said. "How about kidnapping? Isn't that a story?"

"Yes, kidnapping is a story. But is that what happened? I'm not so sure. But if you are, why don't you go and raise a stink about it?"

"You summed it up for me yesterday, remember? I'm only one person. But the power of the press and public opinion might be able to do something about it."

"And what do you think that opinion would be?" Jesse said.

"Sure, that's the other question, isn't it?" Tom said.

"I know what public opinion would be. The young man is only taking part in his native tradition, so why interfere? Although, that's not how some people in this town would phrase it. I'm afraid you're on your own, Tom."

"I thought you said you would help."

"If someone complains."

"I'm complaining."

"I'm sorry to say, you don't count. I think from your standpoint the only thing you can do is hope that he holds on to his Christian beliefs, and then, when it's over, he can pick up where he left off."

"That's not how it works. Like I told you before, if he doesn't submit to them, the result could be deadly."

"And as I told you before, you take things too seriously."

"I hope he does submit," Tom said.

"Why don't you try to forget it for now? Come on, let's go over to the Totem, and I'll buy you a cup of coffee."

Tom shook his head.

"If you change your mind, drop by the office later, maybe we can go for lunch. I've got a soft spot for underdogs."

"Why so kind? Are you hoping I'll change my mind about you and Isabel?"

"No, I haven't decided what to do about the two of us yet."

"Get saved, Jesse. That's the best decision you could ever make."

"This might come as a shock to you, but the idea of joining someone like you, battling his demons in a burnt-out building, doesn't really appeal to me that much."

"Coward."

"I see, well, I'll be on my way. I can't take anymore of the hard sell right now. With Christians like you in the lead, it's a wonder anyone ever joins the flock."

"Thanks for the encouragement," Tom said.

CHAPTER TWENTY–FIVE

Ruby wheeled her shopping cart down the Safeway frozen foods aisle. The cart's right front wheel wobbled, and its top rack was jammed shut, but she took the thing anyway because a burly logger type had been behind her, waiting to rip out a cart, impatient with her weakness, immune to her sex. He was angry, she guessed, because he didn't like to be seen out shopping. Bad for his image. Poor man. Frozen peas. Tom liked frozen peas, and that suited her fine, throw the whole bagful in at a boil, simple. Cook them all, throw out what they didn't eat, who needed Tupperware? Milk. In your grocer's dairy case. Two cartons. She could still drink milk. Went down easy. Moo. *Meditating cows, standing in the soft brown field, chewing their warm crud.* University poetry fun. Sophomoric. Potatoes. She had to buy potatoes. A stew staple. Idaho Russets, more expensive, but who was counting the cost? Who indeed? No, take that back, at least Tom wasn't like that. Pain in her body everywhere. She was too sick to be doing this. She should have sent him and stayed home. So nice to have him around the house since his Center burned down. Poor Tom. Mangy cart, squeak, squeak, squeak. No wonder they called them buggies. They drove you insane. Pushing them for punishment, aerobics for the near-dead but walking still. A contradiction. Good exercise though. What's next? Meat, he loved the stuff. Why begrudge him animal protein? He was taking it all well in the aftermath of her confession and the Center burning. But they didn't talk much. Where's my socks? That sort of thing. The wounds had to heal. Maddening, that's what he was. Where was his passion? He should have shot her, or himself, or both of them. But that would have looked bad to the neighbors. And after twenty years of marriage passion was hard to raise, like raising the Titanic. You think he would have complained more about her lack of interest over the years. Been more persistent. But no, he just took it. A good Christian, taking it. His poor dear was turned off, because she lost her child. Once in a while was fine. He could handle it. Idiotic. He was furious now though, underneath, you could tell, once it all sank in. Twenty years of his sex life lost. But he was doing his best to be forgiving, going through the motions of trying to be pleasant.

Stewing beef next stop. Red, bloody beef, dripped when you picked it up. Always a trail of blood. The blood hounds. She dropped the cold meat and blood, cradled in its white Styrofoam bed under its plastic-wrap blanket, into her cart. At least she would be spared menopause. No hot flashes, night sweats or irritability to perplex him with. Soup bone, $1.05, you had to pay for them now. And no problems with osteoporosis later on, save money on calcium. Oh, no, there's Sarah Durning again, nose into the pork chops. Last encountered in the produce department, fondling the English cucumbers. Tom's future honey, silly witch. Oops, discovered. Clean up my mind. What to say this time? Have to say something. Last time a comment on the prices. Oh, good, she's going to talk first. Let her be the fool.

"How's the stewing beef today?" she said.

"On sale and lean."

What business was it of hers? Had Tom been complaining about his diet? Was Sarah ready to take over? Gourmet dining and plenty of variety. Greeting him at the door in seductive black negligees. Fat buttocks though, from all that sitting on the piano bench. Cellulite galore, no doubt. Have to say something.

"See you in the next aisle, Sarah."

Ooh, she tittered at my witty remark, clever girl. Titter back, don't sound facetious. Nod and move along.

Why couldn't he have been more demanding? That's all she had wanted. More attentive. More romantic. Passionate desire, like when he was younger. Make her forget about the present. But no. A little resistance and he would retreat, filled with love and understanding, frustration seething beneath the covers. It was his own fault. Couldn't blame their sex life on her.

Bakery aisle next. Doughnuts. She could still handle a few doughnuts. Fatten herself up a little. So who was Sarah Durning, anyway? Only young. Ruby couldn't imagine Tom playing the fool like Jesse. Sarah was older than Isabel though. But to be sensible, what would she want with a failed minister? Two glazed holy ones and two apple fritters, expiry date tomorrow. Bread. Brown. Cheap. Two loaves. Tom didn't want Sarah. No way. Why did she have to entertain these ridiculous thoughts? Jealousy? To punish herself? Eggs. She had forgotten the eggs. Backtrack. Sarah had better be gone. Squeaking piece of junk, hard to steer. In danger of veering into the mayonnaise *On Sale* display. Slowing for the ninety-degree turn and reducing speed to stop for the eggs. Large. Brown. You always opened the carton, teeth on edge, to see if there were any cracked ones. Solid. No Humpty Dumptys here. At least she still had her breasts. That young woman years ago. The memory haunted now. Stringy-haired hippie type, sandals, dirty jeans, and faded black T-shirt bleach-spotted, tripping into a downtown Victoria pub. A sixties child, spaced-out and braless, one ample breast flaunting the absence of the other. The image hurt. She winced and then shivered at the sterile stainless steel case, where inside, bare and browning, turned the barbecued chickens. Take one for tonight? No. Too expensive. Could roast her own cheaper. No treats. Self-control. But at least Tom would get three months' severance pay. Guilt money, decided by the elders.

That was all, she was done. Head for the checkout. How many items? Under ten, her lucky day. There was another one of those full shopping carts, abandoned by the driver. She usually saw at least one now when she shopped. Usually full. Sometimes just a few select items. Steak and mushrooms and bakery cake. Last week she asked about them. She thought the people who filled them had only stepped out for a minute and would be back. But no. The produce man told her that people just came and shopped and then left them. People without the money to pay. Pensioners and other poor people, fantasizing a middle-class life, like on television. Being somebody. Being normal. Normal. What was that these days? An outdated concept left over from the '50s. Where had she heard that? Of course, Public Television. Normality was a '50s concept, and so said PBS.

Tabloids. A Two-Headed Man. One head a night club singer, the other an Evangelist. What a pity. UFO jockeys running the Soviet Union, a fact. Cover girls, there ought to be a law. The man ahead, oh it's Mr. Logger again, ah, ah, ah, more than ten items. Give him a dirty look. Canvass the rest of the lineup for support. That's it, let him have it. Exchange knowing sighs with the cashier, roll the eyes and shake the head. Excellent. No good, he's short on awareness. Forgive him. Goodbye Neanderthal, goodbye cart, *I think I'm going to dieyie.*

"Yes, paper bags, thank you."

No plastic bags for her. Think of the environment. For Jesse's sake. Tokenism. Why not? But there were no handles. Too heavy.

"Help to the car, ma'am? I'll ring for service."

"Thank you."

The cashier gave her a caring look. Did she look like death

warmed over? Here he comes. Cute in a bow tie. Follow him out. Open says me. Take your time. It was a wonder anyone ever got out of Safeway alive.

"Over there, the blue Tercel. Here's the key."

Dear Tom was at home waiting for his dinner. He would have a long wait tonight. Yes, of course, she could make it to the hospital. She only had to get into the car and drive there.

"Thank you," she said.

You don't tip them.

Wisdom might say she needed to call Tom or a taxi or an ambulance, but she knew she could make it. It was only a mile or two at the most, and she could stand it for that long. It would be too embarrassing, too much of a fuss, to call someone.

She drove out of the parking lot and turned left onto the road that led to the hospital. Simple. No problem. Yes, they had a future. A mission school is what they needed. She had enjoyed teaching school. Why hadn't she gone back to it? Endless church meetings, supporting Tom emotionally, a full-time job being a pastor's wife. Total dedication, be an example. Pressure. Be good. Make yourself good and righteous and holy. Couldn't be done. Definition of a holy person: One who refrained from swearing at unruly coat-hangers. No, it couldn't be done. Only God's grace could transform a person. But she had a chance now. They had a chance now. The Center was gone. The church was gone. A few miracles were all they needed. The pain was the illusion. Cancer was the illusion. First she would forgive God and the church, and then she and Tom would reconcile. They would both serve Him in a mission and a ministry that bore fruit. She would stay here on earth. It wasn't that bad here. Tom said he had forgiven her. Tom was good that way. They would fall in love again. There was a chance yet, wasn't there? Oh, God, let there be another chance. Yes, another chance. Death was too far to go. And yes, she could make it to the hospital, and God would heal her there. She had to have another chance. Oh, God, there had to be another chance.

CHAPTER TWENTY–SIX

Jesse searched for her room number above the wide doors that opened into the wards, where patients, ill and detached from the Cowichan Valley's active population, lounged in the open or hid behind drawn curtains. Fear struck his diaphragm and grabbed at his breath as he suppressed images of blood and scalpel gashes, his eyes turning away from the sight of bare sexless backs exposed by loose hospital gowns. The corridor reeked of cleanliness. Shafts of dull light from the gray day spread out through the doorways and clashed with the artificial glow from the fluorescent hall lights above. The speckled gray and white marble floor elbowed its way up into the walls, avoiding the accumulation of dirt. He was cold, and he began to sweat. He hated hospitals.

What do you say to a person who is dying? Tom had come by the office to tell him Ruby was out of intensive care. Why had Tom been compelled to do that? He remembered his visit to the hospital to see his editor in Port Moody. There they were, the two of them, people whose job it was to put words together, and neither of them had anything of substance to say. Would he do any better this time? Room 212, Tom had said, and there it was, semi-private. He hesitated at the entrance. He was about to visit a woman he cared about but didn't really know, and what would he say? A careless drop of cold sweat found a clear path beneath his shirt to meander down his side. Cancer. What do you say to a person with terminal cancer?

Through the door and to the right, and there she was, and there was Tom, too, thank God. He was there, sitting and leaning over her. The scene was too much for him to look at. Could he backtrack? No. They saw him. He must put his best face forward. Into the breach. Talk softly, muster up the guts. Good Anglo-Saxon word, guts. But today it made him sick.

"Hello there," he said.

"Thanks for coming," Tom said.

Tom leaned back in his chair, and there Ruby was, worn, but smiling.

"Hello, Jesse," she said. "Are you checking up on me, or are you making sure the hospital's no-smoking regulation is being complied with?"

Jesse was sad to see her in her frail condition but was thankful her sarcasm was intact.

"Actually," he said. "I've been asking the nurses whether or not you have been smoking in bed."

"I haven't tried smoking since Tom was a hippie, and I wasn't very good at it, was I Tom?"

Jesse glanced at Tom's vacant eyes. He guessed they were gazing at a young Ruby smoking.

Tom's eyes refocused on his dying Ruby in the bed. He said, "You were good at everything, Ruby. Why don't you have a seat, Jesse?"

Jesse pulled up a chair and sat on the opposite side of the bed facing Tom.

He said, "So when are they going to let you out of here?"

Ruby and Tom exchanged glances, and Tom swallowed. Jesse realized that in the excitement of seeing Ruby healthier than he had expected, he had said the wrong thing. And then Tom surprised him by saying, "Tomorrow, we think."

"Oh, that's wonderful," he said.

But then he understood the implication. They were sending her home to die.

"How's Isabel?" Ruby asked. "Are you behaving yourself?"

"Always," he said.

"You know what I would do if I were you, Jesse?"

"No. What's that?"

"Grab her and don't let her go."

Jesse observed the good-natured frown Tom cast at Ruby, no doubt intended as a mock protest against her defection from his sound counsel.

"Or you could make an honest man of yourself," Tom said.

"I might just do that to get you off my back," Jesse said.

"You'll see the light," Tom said. "And I'd normally take the time to preach to you right now, but I need to run a few errands and do a few things at home."

Tom squeezed Ruby's hand and kissed her on the forehead.

He said, "I'll be back later, and, Jesse, I hope to see you soon, and I also expect to see you in heaven."

Jesse had him now.

He said, "Well if that's the case, then there's no reason why I shouldn't marry Isabel, is there?"

"Exactly," Ruby said.

Tom seemed encouraged that Ruby was enjoying herself. He rolled his eyes for dramatic effect, a gesture meant to express his frustration with the incorrigible pagan.

"You two have fun," Tom said, and left the room.

Jesse's mind was so engaged in self-congratulations for beating the pastor at his own game, he had forgotten that Tom's departure would leave him alone with Ruby, the predicament he had been dreading prior to his visit.

But Ruby took charge before he had time to panic.

"I do really appreciate your visit," she said. "And I was serious about what I said. You and Isabel will make a lovely couple. She's a wonderful girl and clever enough to make up for your deficiencies. But at the same time you must remember that I'm not a professional counselor, so I'm not responsible for my advice. Unlike Tom, if my advice ruins your lives, so what? It's not my fault."

Jesse laughed and said, "I appreciate your sensitivity. And I do need advice. There are a few issues to work out, not the least of which is my age. And she belongs to a different generation."

"You do talk a lot of nonsense, don't you?"

Jesse was about to continue with his *reasons why not*, when he remembered he'd come to see Ruby, not talk about himself and Isabel.

"How are you feeling?" he said.

Listening to the tone of his own voice, he realized he really wanted to know. It wasn't just another one of his reporter's questions. He had become more caring in the last few months, and he wondered how that might have happened.

"I have felt better than this," she said. "But at least they're sending me home tomorrow. The doctor knows best."

"I came to tell you, I mean, I would like you to know that you and Tom have had a positive effect on me. What I mean to say is that the two of you have made me question certain aspects of my life. And because you don't hide behind the typical self-righteous Christian façade, I have been happy to discover you're as messed up as the rest of us."

"How kind of you to share that with me. You know just what to say to a girl in the hospital."

"Forgive me, but I think you know what I mean. You're Christians and you behave almost like real people. You're not even very self-righteous, well except maybe for Tom sometimes, so it makes it hard to put you in a box."

"In a box, Jesse?"

"Uh, yes, I am sorry for my choice of words."

Jesse knew by now that you had to be a masochist to engage this woman in conversation. He could understand why Tom was so humble.

"No, I'm the one who's sorry," Ruby said. "I can't seem to

help myself sometimes. Misery loves company. But you're a thick-skinned, hard-nosed editor type, aren't you? Oh-oh, there I go again. It's hard for me to stop. I think I've developed the habit of being nasty as a distraction. Living isn't much fun these days."

"Don't you worry about it," he said. "I've taken worse beatings."

"Oh good, then let me be serious and even a little kind for a moment. Did I say serious? What a disgusting word. Anyway, I care about you, Jesse. And I'm going to tell you the truth. It might seem strange, coming from a person lying in a hospital bed, but on the other hand it might be the best place to say it. There is a God who sent his Son to die for us. I'm telling you this now because I don't want to die and leave you thinking I had lost my faith. There's only one truth, Jesse, and I hope you find Him. Now, don't look so nervous. That's the end of my sermon."

"Why do you religious people always have to preach?" Jesse said.

"I'm not religious. God isn't religious. People are the ones who like to create religions. I'm trying to tell you about Jesus, and He is a completely different subject."

"I don't understand you. Why would you bother to preach to me when you're more cynical than I am? I would find your presentation more convincing if you were oozing with sweetness and light."

"Well, maybe I will be some day. There's always hope."

Jesse thought Ruby was without further hope in this life, but to encourage her he nodded in agreement, and then the stout crisp nurse came in to tell Ruby that she had to rest now, meaning also that he had to leave.

"Thanks, Jesse, for coming," she said.

Ruby held her hand out for him to take, which removed

from him the burden of deciding on an appropriate gesture to offer her as a token of his affection, and as a goodbye.

"Thank you," he said.

Jesse pressed her hand and then released it. The nurse, for his benefit, stiffened in her authority. He took one last look at Ruby and turned and left.

Jesse walked down the corridor, his head down. She was a strange one. Still, there had to be something to it. Why would she bother if she didn't believe it herself? Tom was no fool either. Well, he was and he wasn't. The man was hard to figure out. As for advice, he preferred Ruby's view of things. Her advice was more down to earth than Tom's. Go for it! Absolutely, why not? He was man enough. And as for his spiritual condition, Christianity wasn't all bad. He would allow Isabel to attempt to convert him on the honeymoon. But then what if he were to succumb? What would be the fate of his good liberal precepts, such as *live and let live*, and *there are no absolutes*? Oh, who cared? They weren't that crucial to his existence. His view of the world had been going to hell anyway. He had also noticed that his conservative attitude had been solidifying, no doubt a curse of middle age. He had been looking through The Good Book, too. There were some reasonable ideas in there, a few he remembered from childhood. Maybe there was hope for him yet.

He stood alone in the elevator, going down. There was no way he wanted to go all the way down. He thought of Ruby back there in her bed, and he swallowed what, if let loose, would have been a sob. Unexpected tears came to his eyes, which he, sniffling, offered up to the light above the door, which haloed 2 and then 1 before coming to rest on G. He applied his handkerchief to his eyes and then slipped it back into his pocket before the door opened. He brushed past a nurse escorting a senior plugged into a bag on wheels. Ruby was a strange woman; there was no doubt about that. He was thankful that Isabel was less complicated. She had to be. Yes, she just had to be. But at the same time, he knew she wasn't an airhead. Jesse breezed through the main doors, glad to be out in the fresh air. Considering his aversion to hospitals and his and Isabel's age difference, maybe he should get serious about his health. Some exercise wouldn't hurt, but then again, it probably would.

CHAPTER TWENTY-SEVEN

He was bounding along the roadside. Well, not exactly bounding yet. Ignore those heads peering at him from the cars. What did they know? Perhaps the red was too much. Good brand name though, in bold white lettering down the leg and across the chest. It looked professional. Besides, the red suit was on sale, couldn't pass it up, and the blue was sold out. On the feet, brand new running shoes. They didn't soften the hard ground much though; the pounding was jarring his brain. The world refused to hold still; it was shaking, and so was his gut, jelly rolling, the knees stiff and jerky. Jiggling fatty triceps too, not to mention the backside. But his suit was loose enough to hide the majority of the movement. Cholesterol on the run. No such thing as cholesterol when he was a child, could eat as many egg sandwiches as you liked, hardly any mention of bad fats either; they should have left well enough alone. Why create problems nobody wanted to hear about?

The rural scenery was hazy without his glasses. What he needed was music, or a teaching tape to take the mind off, or was that only for weekend joggers, not for serious aficionados? He should ask somebody, shouldn't take a chance on looking amateurish. Beautiful day for it, considering it was February, only a sprinkle, the odd puddle, a mere smattering of mud. Yes, there were many benefits to be had from jogging. For the body, for the mind. And it was a good time to contemplate topics for his editorial. Might forget his valuable insights though, no way to write them down, the ground was too jarring to jot. Had to stop now. He shouldn't overdo it first time out. Walk time. There's the answer, he could make notes during the walking rests. Superb solution. A man of ideas, and a man of action, that's what he would be from now on. He would take it easy on the body at first though. He knew how to break the old body in. No heart attack for him. He had been an athlete in his youth, at least until he was twelve or so in Little League. He didn't grunt so much then. He had wanted to be a baseball player when he grew up, but then he grew up. Crouch for a second, swallow the panting, stifle the urge for a smoke. Up and at 'em, quick brisk pace and then break into a run. Flying now, but no, hold it, not so fast, a stitch in the side, go back to a walk. That's it, walking was good too. There was no shame in walking. He must have hit that wall the runners talked about. And there was nothing like a brisk walk along Maple Bay Road on a Saturday in February. There was no reason he shouldn't make it all the way to the Maple Bay Pub.

Let's see, what about his next week's editorial? It was hard to think with the traffic noise, and that pounding in his ears, and those birds. Slow the pace. Man, look at her coming on the other side of the road. What a stride. Stop, look nonchalant, bend over, pretend to tie the shoes. She was close enough now for him to flash the athletic smile; look up and over, give her the ruddy-faced grin. Camaraderie of the fittest. Ignored. Glad it wasn't Isabel though.

How about an editorial on feminism? He needed a new angle. How about the world would have been a better place if women had been in charge from the beginning, if women had been the inventors of technology? No missiles. Round stationary saucer shapes instead. The result, a technology that accommodated, absorbed, included. No swords, or projectile-shooting mechanisms. Use a cosmic analogy: Not comets blazing, but black holes sucking in. Dense and infinitely powerful. The vacuum principle. Hmm, he would need to be careful that the piece didn't come out in a bad way. He had to be accurate. No sexist blunders. Expand: As a result, men the weaker sex. Their initial tendency to fashion clubs rendered impotent by the superior female compacter. All violent instruments sucked in by female technology and reduced to anti-matter. Aggression squelched. Peace and harmony, the earth safe from rapists, the environment inviolate. Mother Earth would be husbanded by mothers. Weather permitting, everyone would go around naked.

The topic was no good, he couldn't use it. The valley's rednecks would be shooting holes in his office windows. He stopped and adjusted his headband, reviewed the tenor of his most recent thoughts, and wondered what the mind was, and if it was a good thing. Probably the exercise was the culprit, creating a chemical imbalance in his brain. Frenzied endorphins running amok, hunting the once comfortable alcohol and nicotine molecules. Jogging was a rough way to go all right.

At last! There was the sign above the Maple Bay Pub, coming into view, blurry from this distance, but there it was, perfect. He'd read about those famous marathon runners drinking as much beer as they could on the night before the race. It had something to do with calories and liquid intake. Beer was good for joggers. Maybe not smoking, but beer could be justified. He would have a few draft, a reward for the first time out. After all, he had expended a lot of will power. No smoking though. But forget the original plan to jog back home. Somebody at the pub would give him a ride, at their leisure of course, when they were ready to go, he wouldn't be in a hurry. Now finish in style, a respectable sprint the last thirty yards, give the folks at the windows a show. Earn his beer. Enter sweating.

The packed Saturday afternoon bar seemed unimpressed with his outfit. The patrons at the windows ignored his finishing dash and his entrance, except for those two smirks in the corner from the Cowichan Rugby Club veterans. He removed the sweaty red and white polka dot handkerchief headband, tied at the back of his head. Why wasn't it called the afthead? Only logical. There was something wrong with that though, couldn't remember what, something nautical. Space at the bar, hop up on a stool. What a thirst! He pulled his twenty dollar bill out, hidden inside his left sock. He'd put it there in case of an emergency, like twisting an ankle and needing to call a taxi. You had to come prepared.

"Two here, Benny, my man," Jesse said.

Benny looked at him and grunted.

Then he said, "What's the matter with you today?"

"I'm feeling refreshed after my run, you know, healthy exercise, jogging. You must have heard of exercise."

"Yeah, sure I have," Benny said, "but where did you get the Satan suit?"

He should never have tried to communicate with Benny in the first place, or treat him like a human being. Forget the Father Confessor barman routine. Order, pay and drink. No small talk with Benny. He had known better, but in the stimulation of the moment a few friendly words had slipped out. And by the rules of the game Benny was justified in letting him have it. Benny had probably been waiting for a few years to stick it to him, to mock the big shot editor. Benny poured the draft, set them down, lit a cigarette, inhaled and then, leaning on the glass-washer, blew the smoke in Jesse's direction. Their relationship had changed forever. Deflated and vulnerable at the bar, Jesse looked around for a table. There was one in the corner, farthest from the rugby boys.

He should have brought a jacket or something. He was beginning to cool off. The sweat was going to dry, and there he would be, vulnerable to catching a cold. But who would have guessed he would have ended up in the bar? No problem, he wouldn't be there long enough to worry about it. A couple of quick ones and back he would go, before he cooled off too much, and he would forget about asking someone for a ride. He wouldn't want to stay in a place like this for the rest of the afternoon when the roadside beckoned him to recapture his health and win the fair Isabel. He found the corner table and sat facing the ocean, his back to Benny. He downed his first draft in a few healthy swallows, and started on his second. The view was wasted on him. He should have brought his glasses, but how? He needed to buy one of those waistbags, or whatever they were called, to carry his valuables in.

The smooth second draft beckoned for a third, but he might as well order two more. That would be perfect, he thought, just about the same amount of liquid he had lost to evaporation. There was a waiter working on Saturday, so he wouldn't have to order from Benny again. He signaled the waiter for two more. Yes, jogging was good for a person. Probably kept down the sex drive too. Why hadn't he thought of it before? He had been using booze. Not that he had an irrepressible sex drive. But wait, how was he going to jog and, if they did get married, keep up with Isabel too? That kind of cancelled the drinking. He only had so much energy at his age. No, not to worry, he thought, paying the waiter for his next two, jogging probably increased a person's stamina. That had to be the answer. Jogging was a stamina builder. But he knew a healthy body wouldn't materialize overnight. He felt the blisters rising on the balls of his feet, his Achilles tendons contracting, his knees shrieking fire, his elbow bending faster. He would order only two more after these, for the pain. He couldn't challenge the road in this condition.

He would prefer to borrow one than to buy a whole pack. He only needed one, but he couldn't ask Benny, not now; and there was no one else here he could borrow from; there were a few recognizable faces but no one he knew well enough. He would have to buy a package. What a waste, a whole package for one cigarette. Couldn't be helped. Expensive these days too.

He returned to his table with his cigarettes and a matchbook. The first drag was superb, and then the guilt. Smoking in a jogging outfit was a betrayal, shaming himself and the swoosh on his chest. Still, he was only having one, he thought, his lungs expanding with the smoke. But to keep him honest, he needed someone to give the rest of the package to. He wouldn't give them to Benny, not now. Why did the smoke in his lungs have to feel so good? Beer and cigarettes relaxed a body. So what was the big sin? Cancer! But Ruby didn't smoke, so who was to say? When your time was up, up you went, as simple as that. He lifted his fourth draft and waved for two more. Half-a-dozen was perfect for an afternoon. And maybe someone would come in later that he knew, and he could get a ride. There was no sense in overdoing it first time out. He didn't need a heart attack to ruin his future. So why did people run anyway? The answer was simple. Instinct. People ran because they were afraid. The world was a frightening place to be. He took a drag and coughed hard, and then he cleared his throat with a swallow of beer.

Isabel. He barely knew her. But that was the way to go. She wanted him, and if that was what Isabel wanted, that was what she would get. Ruby had the right idea. Of course the daughter would be angry. Competition. He would be coming between her and her mother. Couldn't be helped. She would get over it. And he would get sweet Isabel. And Isabel's mother would be no problem. She would be more like an older sister. But why did it seem so much like a business deal? Never mind, he was in love. She made his heart flutter and his knees weak and all the rest of it, but he was too cynical at his age to believe such feelings would last. Oh, well, they could settle the emotional claptrap later. And Tom wouldn't interfere; he had only been trying to talk some sense into him. First, they would work out a no-jogging pre-nuptial agreement. Second, a compromise. He would cut down on his drinking, or maybe volunteer to quit. Then a year's engagement to work out the love stuff, and then tie the knot. Case closed. His mind was clear now. A few draft and a cigarette did it every time; just what the doctor ordered to lift the jogging fog. He would go home, have a shower and phone Isabel. A Saturday night movie in Victoria was an option, or maybe there was a good one showing at the local theatre. He would look at the theatre section later to see what was on. She wasn't big on sex and violence though, but neither was he.

His last two beer of the afternoon arrived, which he greeted with respect. It was a watershed. He was about to do something meaningful in his life, an unselfish act. He would make a lifetime commitment to another human being. And they would somehow marry in church. He had been reading some more of The Book, and he had been discovering that Jesus had said some pretty good stuff. And despite the behavior of most Christians, he was attracted to the man Jesus. When He was here on earth, He had partied with the riffraff, like those in the pub today. But Ruby and Tom were the only Duncan Christians he had ever seen in the place. And there was a logical reason for that. The Duncan Christians weren't anything like Jesus.

Jesse realized that one season of his life had now passed, and he was ready to enter another. To celebrate he would call a taxi. No use waiting for a ride from some drunk. And he would have just one more for the road, and the rest of the pack he would give away to the waiter as a tip. His life was shaping up. And Monday he would go into the office and work on his spirit dancing story. His feature article was coming together. It was the least he could do for Tom. He had done some research and discovered some surprising information about the natives' winter ceremonials. He had conducted a few interviews, too, including one with Tom. Jesse's award-winning feature was coming together. Isabel would be proud of him. That is if he decided to print it. There would be plenty of controversy and interest generated, complete with a flood of letters to the editor and plenty of problems to sort out. Oh, well, you had to pay a price for fame.

"Hey, Benny," he yelled across the room, "call me a cab, will you?"

That ought to get his goat, he thought. Yes, Benny was frowning, but he was picking up the direct line. The cab had to come from town, so he had plenty of time to finish his last two draft. Oh, what a day! A jog, a few beer, a successful, award-winning career and a wonderful wife-to-be. His life was becoming a bowl full of cherries. It was about time.

CHAPTER TWENTY-EIGHT

Ruby sat in her white leather recliner beside the living room window. The rippling current below splashed foam gashes where the river's olive skin surface split, the afternoon sun flashing off the water, piercing her sunglasses and dazzling her Demerol. She could hear Tom in the kitchen, pretending to make tea. Outside the calm sunny day was enjoying itself, and she was floating in the peace that forgiveness brings. She had taken her whole life to God before she left the hospital. And He had understood. She was free from guilt and condemnation, and as for her impending death, it was an obscure concept, one that she'd heard about but had no use for right now.

The Demerol was transforming her world into a tolerable place to be. During the last few months the pain, multiplied by her total dissatisfaction with life, had stimulated her nastier personality traits, which she had nurtured to occupy her mind. But in the last few days the painkillers, united with her fresh freedom from guilt, were pacifying her awful self and lifting her up to gaze at transcendence. Transcendence was a much kinder word than death. Had it been PBS that had informed her about the human desire for transcendence? Possibly. Or had it been in a magazine? No matter. According to the research, the brain was the culprit. Drugs, TM, alcohol, frenzied idol worship, they were all pursued to achieve the same goal. The brain and the central nervous system wanted out of here, if not permanently, then for periodic bouts of relief. Science was fascinating, but would they ever discover a cure for evil?

Tom came into the living room head down, maintaining a level keel, the teaspoons rattling on the tea tray, and then he set his burden on the coffee table.

"Steeping," he said.

"Are you going to cut down those maples this year before they spoil the view of the river?" Ruby said.

"I don't own a chain saw, and now they're too big for a hand saw. I could borrow a chain saw, or rent one, but I've never used one."

"All I want to do is see the river and not have the view spoiled by maple leaves when they come out in the spring. Is that too hard to accomplish?"

"I'll have somebody come do it. Shouldn't cost much."

"Is there somebody in the church who would do it? For old time's sake?"

"Relax, I'll see."

"I am relaxed, as a matter of fact I feel wonderfully well."

Tom poured the herbal tea and handed Ruby her cup. He scooped a spoonful of sugar into his.

Ruby said, "I noticed we skipped Valentine's Day this year."

She smiled at him. He returned her affectionate offering with a sheepish nod.

She said, "Would you like to yell at me or something? Perhaps you might want to scream and swear. Don't let my fragile condition inhibit you. Get it off your chest. It's been simmering long enough, don't you think?"

"I've forgiven you, forget it, there's nothing more to do."

"Have you reviewed the charges? Adultery, a childless marriage, and a frustrated sex life.

"Let's get the adultery straight once and for all. We weren't married then, remember?"

"What a gentleman, defending my honor to the end," she said.

"We need to start again," Tom said. "We've been through

too much to allow what happened twenty years ago to come between us now. We've made it through this far. There's something to be said for that. And remember, we loved each other once, before all the misery, and I believe that our love for one another is still there, even if it's buried. And with God's help we can make it through."

"Man, that's poetic," Ruby said, "I wonder if it's a symptom of a mid-life crisis?"

"That's okay. I understand," Tom said. "I know you're hurt, and it's hard for you to be sincere."

"I've lived with this attitude for so long now, it's hard to stop," Ruby said. "You're the one who's been hurt."

"We make a good pair. The strange thing is that we might be able to survive as a couple now."

Ruby was thankful for the Demerol's help in restraining her tears.

"What's the matter with us, Tom?" she said.

"I thought we both knew the answer to that. We don't need to review the situation again, do we?"

"No, I'm not wanting to go into it all that again. I've had enough of that. No, I mean, what's the matter with us Christians. You and I aren't the only ones whose lives have been disastrous."

"No, we're not the only ones. Most of us live our Christian lives putting up a front, pretending to serve God, when we haven't really taken the time to get to know Him. Instead, we try to be good, and then we fail. We play church, smile, and pretend everything's great, but when we're alone our demons are waiting for us. We need to get real and live our faith, or else not bother with the façade. When people in the world point their fingers at us it's usually for a good reason. They know when we're real or just playing the part and mouthing the right words."

"You love to preach, don't you?" Ruby said.

"Yes, but has it done any good?"

"Don't worry about that. Your sermons haven't been wasted. I'm sure there are some in the congregation who were listening."

"Let's hope," Tom said.

"What do you think is going to happen with Will?"

"It's hard to say."

"I didn't mention it to you before, but I talked to him a few weeks ago. I was shopping in the mall, and when I came out there he was in the parking lot, just standing there. He asked if we could talk, so we went into the coffee shop."

"That's a surprise. I mean, that he wanted to talk. That's not like him at all."

"I know. It was so unusual. I'll admit he hasn't been my favorite person, but not because of anything he's done. It was the Center, and the associations I had with the place. I put him in the same category, a lost cause. Not fair really."

"No, he's far from being a lost cause. You need to get to know him, that's all. He's got a good heart."

"That's what I discovered. He was just a face before, a native face that I didn't know how to deal with. It's not that I'm prejudiced, at least I don't think I am. But the gap seems so wide. I feel more helpless than anything else."

"It's been a hard lesson, but I think I've learned something about bridging that gap. The only way is through relationships, one person at a time. That is, if we have the courage to step out and take the chance."

"Will took the chance. He said he cares about me. That's why he wanted to talk to me. He said he knew I wasn't the person I was pretending to be, and that I had a kind heart. Then he said his mother had been a lot like me. She had cancer, too."

Ruby began to weep. She took out her handkerchief and dabbed at her tears.

"Yes, I know," Tom said. "He was in his early teens when she died."

Tom hung his head, but didn't cry.

"It meant a lot to me that he would want to meet me and tell me that. I was overwhelmed. I began to think I might have had what it takes to be a good mother after all."

"Will's a bright sensitive guy," Tom said. "And he knows what he's talking about. You would have been a great mother."

"We'll never know, but it's nice to think so. Then we talked a little more, as if I really was his mother, and he told me about his fears for the future. And then he said something surprising. He said that he and I had a lot in common."

"A lot in common?" Tom said. "What did he mean by that?"

"He said that neither of us seems to belong anywhere."

"You belong," Tom said.

"And what about Will? Where does he belong? He said he could feel his Indian blood calling him."

"His ancestry has no claim on him. He's a Christian now. He belongs."

"I think you know that's not true. The church hasn't been that friendly toward him, has it?"

"No, not really. That's not the way the church is right now, right here, but the day will come."

"And what about me? I'm a Christian. Do you really believe the church and I have been a good fit?"

"We're all like that. That's just the way it is."

"What are you saying? That heaven is the only place where we will all get along?"

"No, there is always hope that the fences will come down, and that we will begin to live together as real people."

"Why don't you tell that to your former eldership?"

"I understand your anger and frustration," Tom said. "But this isn't getting us anywhere. We're finished with that church now. We both know how things are, and we need to move on."

"You're right," Ruby said. "But I am truly sorry about Will. I know how much you hoped he would make it to Bible College. It didn't really matter to me before, but now that I know him better I'll be praying for a miracle, and that somehow his dream will come true."

"We need more than one miracle."

"If we can only have one, I hope it's Will's."

"Don't say that. God is not limited."

"I know that, but wouldn't it be incredible to see him going to college. It would be good for you too."

"You mean that our time here wouldn't have been be a total loss?"

"At least one victory would be nice, wouldn't it?"

"Would it be a victory?" Tom said. "I've had my doubts lately. I'm beginning to wonder if Bible College was only my big idea and God isn't leading Will to go there at all."

"I'm sure He is," Ruby said.

"We'll see what the future brings."

"While we're on that subject," Ruby said. "I know you haven't wanted to discuss it, but what are you going to do with yourself?"

"The future is not singular yet, so let's not talk about it. Besides, there's always room for one more on the mission field."

"I would still like to do that myself. And that's something else I didn't tell you. It was strange. When I left the grocery store on the way to the hospital the idea of going on the mission field was one of the first things that came to my mind. I would still like to teach again, a mission school somewhere,

South America, maybe."

"It's a deal," Tom said. "That's what we'll do. I've got a few connections, and I know the right people to call. You can teach, and I can evangelize. We'll be a team. It's not too late. And since we're both talking to Him again, we can pray that He heals you."

"Perfect. We're agreed. And you know what else? I'm really looking forward to that Maple Bay reunion now. I can hardly wait to go."

"It'll be great," Tom said.

"That is, if we're not on the mission field by then."

"It's a date," Tom said. "Maple Bay in August."

"Right, it's a date," Ruby said. "We'll really knock 'em dead. Now, would you please carry me to bed? I'm getting tired. I can't sit up any longer, and I don't have the time or the energy to hobble that far."

"Carry you to bed? Is that an invitation? Things are looking up."

"You better not take advantage of me when I'm stoned on Demerol."

"At least you don't have a headache."

"Right. That's something else I haven't confessed. I hardly ever get headaches."

"You're a naughty girl."

"Don't you wish."

CHAPTER TWENTY-NINE

He was wrapped in blankets inside his tent in the Longhouse. He was sweating. His chest and back were sore. Every bone ached. He wasn't sure how long he had been there. They had been rough. And he was hungry. And thirsty. But mostly his heart had been taken away. The White Man's God hadn't rescued him. Maybe He wasn't allowed to. So why resist them? Except that he didn't want some evil spirit dancing him around, but why had God allowed such a bad thing to happen to him in the first place. What was he suppose to do? He felt that he was more Indian than anything else now, and that these were his people. Is this where he belonged? He was beginning to lose his belief in Jesus. He had been half Indian all his life, but a Christian for only two years now. What was he defending, if God didn't care enough to rescue him? Bible College. On the Mainland. That was a big joke. How could he get there from here? He might as well be all Indian now, and let his people make him dance. What was the difference? And if he didn't do what they said, what was stopping them from killing him? A Christian among the heathen. A heathen Christian among the heathen. Was he more heathen than Christian? He was beginning to think so. Here he was in the Longhouse, a lost human being. And there was no escape.

He had nothing else to do now but think and remember things about his life. He remembered his early school days. They were good days for him. The Indian kids who made it through the Catholic Elementary school usually started to drop out when they got into public school. They really outnumbered then, and who cared if they dropped out? They were only ignorant Indians anyway. But he had stayed in school. He figured God must have had a lot to do with him making it through. That had to be the reason he succeeded. But now it looked like he was never going to make it to Bible College. That was one thing he pretty well knew for sure now. Still, he was happy he had made it all the way through to grade twelve. But the way things looked right now for him to show up on graduation day would be a real miracle.

He saw the image of his parents come into his mind. There they were, young and laughing and having a good time. He saw himself and his sister with them, and the two of them were happy, too. There was no way they all could have stayed the way they were then. Life wasn't rosy. So who did he have to blame for the way his life turned out? His parents couldn't have done anything different. It was easy to think that they could have, and blame them. But they fell in love and got married. What was the matter with that? And what about him? What could he do about anything now? No, it was too hard, and too late. They had you. And they were him. He was both white and Indian. How could he separate himself from either of them? But he had tried to do that, to separate himself from them both. He had wanted to become just a Christian, and a savior to his Indian side, but now it looked like his Indian blood was going to save him. At least that was what these wild pagans thought they were doing. But who was right? He knew the Bible was right. But how could he tell them that? Especially when they were trying to heal him of the White Man's ways, and introduce him to his spirit that would be with him and look after him for the rest of his life. It was true that there were spirits who looked after you. But anyone could tell that those kinds of spirits weren't looking after the Indian people very well. And they wanted him now to take one for his own. But once he did that, he would be Will the pagan Indian. And could he ever find his way back to the Will he was now, or to his God? And would Jesus be found again? Would the words in the Bible say the same things afterward? Would they mean anything to him? He then would be carrying the weight of his Indian blood, and his spirit would be reading in the Indian way. He had fought to throw the weight off when he was growing up, and then Jesus lifted it off. But now the weight was coming down again, and where was his God to carry the burden? Why had he bothered to finish school, if in the end he was going to become a spirit dancer?

The drums continued to knock the thoughts around in his head, but he knew what he would do. He would fight. But he was going to lose. He knew that. He was going to become another victim of the Indian way. He knew it would come natural to him. The White Man was right. The Indian was programmed for failure. Everything was stacked against them. God was the only hope. But where was He? Was He not allowed into the Longhouse? Or perhaps He was asleep or on a journey. He knew he shouldn't be thinking those things about his God. But he was thinking them anyway, even though he knew that daring Him to come wouldn't work either. He had to face the fact that He wasn't coming. There were no lightning bolts blasting the roof off the Longhouse to rescue His servant Will. Life wasn't like that for Indians on the Reserve.

Someone began to sob far away, and then he realized it was him. He was crying for his dad, his human one. He knew it was his dad who had paid for him to be brought back to the right path. His dad had gone back to practicing the old ways. Will was a Christian, but his dad had started practicing witchcraft. He knew it was in his blood too. It had to be. As far as power went, it was hard to tell the difference between the Holy Spirit and the demons pretending to be the spirits of ancestors. There was power in ancestral spirits. And they were going to kill him. His people were going to kill the apple with the red skin but white inside, and even if they didn't kill him, what chance did he have, even if he could go to college. What kind of chance did a Christian Indian have in the world? Most of the white people didn't even like Christians. And he was a Christian Indian. What chance would he have? He might as well give up.

He knew he was in bad shape now. When he breathed, his lungs made loud gurgling noises all by themselves after the air came out. He bowed his head to wipe the mixture of sweat and tears from his face onto the top edge of the blanket. The salt stung his eyes. He was wrapped up like an Egyptian mummy. The picture of himself like that was funny. The person far away stopped sobbing and began to giggle. Maybe he would get up and scare his captors away. The mummy dance. Holler loud and moan. They would run. Then he would go to town in his blankets and sell cigars in front of the Village Green Inn. Sweaty cigars for the White Man. He would earn enough to go in and drink beer for the night. He would then be able to stagger home and look foolish like he was supposed to, like a good Indian should.

But maybe they would let him off. That was it. God would somehow make them let him go. They were only pretending to be scary and really they were happy and good people. Or were they pretending to be happy and good people when really they were bad and he should be scared? It was hard to tell. So how bad were they going to hurt him? How serious were they? Maybe they were happy and good Indians who thought they were doing their duty to their Creator, but the bad spirits behind them were the scary ones. He knew one thing for sure, the spirits behind the dances weren't pretending. They were going to kill him for sure if he didn't cooperate. The bad spirits hated Christians. But wasn't he supposed to be able to defeat them? That's what he thought. Sure, that's right, Pastor Tom said so. But he knew that Pastor Tom sometimes got things wrong. Like the idea he had about turning the Longhouse winter rituals into something good. He was wrong about that. Will knew that the winter rituals and the shaman's drum and the spirit dancing couldn't be redeemed at all. There was no sense keeping those things. His people needed to come out of that part of their culture and then bury it and leave it buried. Why bring that with them and try to make something Christian out of it? His people needed rescuing from their spirit dancing in the Longhouse. He suspected that God wasn't impressed with their culture. God probably wasn't impressed with any culture. Even the White Man's culture. And a lot of the Indian culture was centered on the Longhouse, and look what the Longhouse was doing to him. Those spirits that were fixing to kill him sure couldn't be redeemed. And they went with the Longhouse and the shaman's drum and the dancing. No. He knew something about Indian culture because it was in his blood, not like Pastor Tom. You couldn't have the Longhouse and the drum and the spirit dancing without the spirits. It all went together. You had to come out of it. That was all there was to it. Sure people could dance in the Holy Spirit, but if you let the Indian drum into the church it would be really bad news, and the church had enough problems already. No, if you let the drum in you might as well just invite the bad spirits in to run the show and then start doing witchcraft too. The spirits were real bad to have around. And he knew right now those spirits were not liking him one bit. He could feel them as easy as hearing his chest gurgle.

But wait. There had to be some hope. He would just tell the evil spirits to go away and leave him alone. Didn't Christians have power over evil spirits? He knew God did, but there was only him here. He didn't feel as if God was here at all. No, he hadn't been a Christian long enough to know what to do now. If he had been able to go to Bible College, then he might know. He had read about the great heroes of the faith. Christians liked to talk about the heroes. But what about the little guys, like him? He didn't feel like a great hero of the faith, but he did know he wasn't going to cooperate with them and their spirits. And that made him a dead Indian, a baked-apple dead Indian. He had no future anyway. A Christian Indian. That was a big joke around here.

And then He came. It was a big surprise to Will. He could hardly believe it. All of sudden He came. Will wasn't alone. His God hadn't left him alone. His eyes filled with tears, and he felt joy all over. How could he have even thought such a thing before? His God wouldn't do that. His God wouldn't leave him alone. Jesus was here with him. He could feel Him now. He could feel Him really strong. That was it. That was the answer. Jesus had come to suffer with him. Maybe He wasn't going to blast the roof off the Longhouse, but Jesus was going to go through the whole thing with him. This was great. Jesus was great. His Holy Spirit was great and way bigger than anything in the Longhouse. There was no fear now. His God had come. And it didn't matter anymore what happened. Jesus had won already, and Will was going to win with Him now. There was nothing his Indian people could do to him. There was nothing anyone could do to him. He was safe, and he was going to stay safe for eternity no matter what happened. This was really a good deal. And here he was, Will the Christian Indian in the Longhouse, where everything was strange and peaceful now. He never felt so good and so secure in his whole life. God was here with him. His God was here. There was no doubt about it. This was really worth getting grabbed for.

CHAPTER THIRTY

Jesse had two things on his mind this morning. The first was his editorial, the second his feature on spirit dancing. His plan was to search his mind for possible editorial topics, and once he had settled on a timely and pertinent one, he would then complete the final edit of his Indian feature story. And if he had time before lunch he would go back and write the editorial. A sound plan.

Air was a possible topic. He had to breathe a lot of it jogging to Maple Bay. And how polluted was it? Good question. He'd decided after his outing that jogging was not up his alley. If he had to exercise, then swimming at the Community Center was more suited to his physical and mental condition, but not jogging. The only drawback to swimming was that he had to be more upfront about his physical appearance, since it would be exposed for all to see, but he would cross that bridge when he came to it.

His Saturday evening with Isabel had proved to be more fruitful than the afternoon's jogging. He had invited her to his apartment to watch a nature program about gorillas, and she had agreed to come. He extended to her another invitation that he thought he was obliged to spring on her from a preconception of his male duty, and to show her that his virility was intact, but she declined, offering a good-natured laugh in response and saying June would come soon enough. His previous suggestion that they wait a year to get married turned out to be much too old fashioned for Isabel, and so the June date was set, but at the same time he was thankful the sensitive topics of jogging and beer had not arisen. Isabel's main concern was for the daughter and making the time for

Jesse and her to get acquainted, since once they were married she would have to arbitrate, the two of them competing for her attention. The daughter was a bright active young thing by Isabel's account, and sensitive. He and Isabel had agreed they would not be too aggressive, but would develop his relationship with her slowly, and show her that he was no threat. And they would break the news about their June wedding more toward the actual event. There was no reason to cause added stress to their courtship.

That reminded him. Stress, there was too much of it in the world these days. Even the environment was stressed. And what about the air around them? He had to have an angle. What about space junk? But that wasn't about air. In fact, space was the lack of it. But he hadn't heard the topic mentioned in some time. The space shuttles were back at it again, and there were all those satellites up there, all that space pollution orbiting the planet. The Junkhouse Effect. No, that was too far out for people to be bothered with. But how about pollution from satellites? Communication satellites were beaming pornography and violence around the globe, transmitted from earth to satellite and back down to the dishes to feed homes and motels and hotels, with millions of communications a day. A grisly rape authentically portrayed, a filthy paid telephone conversation consummated, a serial killer glorified, drugs promoted, prostitution taken for granted, greed enthroned. And all of it bouncing around up there and shooting back down through the atmosphere, polluting our beautiful blue and white orb, filling open minds, the Good Earth enclosed in an invisible network of smut, a spider web of obscene signals, encasing and heating gullible and desperate minds. By the turn of the century law and order would melt and the cities sink beneath the filth. The Smuthouse Effect.

He leaned back in his chair. Too moralistic. He had been

getting much too close to religion these days. Its self-righteousness had begun to infect him. Hadn't Tom mentioned something about the dangers of religion, or had it been Ruby? Poor Ruby. Forget space pollution. The local pulp mill's emissions would do. The stink and so forth. He had wanted to do that for some time now. It was kind of close to home though; the mill was a main contributor to the local economy, but he would temper the criticism with a smattering of applause for their recent attempts to clean up. Nothing too negative. Keep them and the publisher happy. Fill the space. Keep the job secure. There, his editorial topic was settled.

He was now ready to go full speed ahead on his feature. Here he was probing into the heart of the valley's lurking racism after all. What a fateful turn of events. It wasn't the Boys Road story, but it would suffice. A few final touches here and there and it was ready to go. He'd done a good job. Great lead:

Every winter in the Cowichan Valley a dance is held that is four months long.

The winter ceremonials of the local Cowichan Band begin at the end of November and end in late March. During that time, Indian people are chosen to be initiated into their dance and receive their song. But the methods used to initiate the dancers have become an issue that in the last few years has caused controversy in the broader community.

The controversy is not a new one. In the nineteenth century, missionaries in collusion with lawmakers outlawed the potlatch and various Indian customs that were contrary to Christian principles, forcing the Coast Salish to practice their tribal rituals secretly. However, in the early 1950s the winter ceremonials again came out in the open and enjoyed a revival. Since then, the Indian people have had relative freedom on their Reserves to exercise their traditional customs without interference from cleric or constable.

That was good, cleric or constable, neat alliteration, and unobtrusive too.

But recently debate is once again being heard. During the last five years two Indians have died in the Valley while undergoing the rigors of initiation. And among the Native Bands on the Mainland that share the same Coast Salish culture, four more Indians have died in the last ten years. Some argue that they have been victims of ritual abuse, while others, namely the Indians themselves, and in particular the ruling elders, insist the ceremony is not only benign but is the indispensable foundation that supports the spiritual and mental health of Coast Salish people.

In addition, the ritual is often used as a therapeutic technique in the treatment of alcohol and drug abuse. Those who exhibit behavior harmful to themselves or others are likely candidates to be "grabbed," the term used when the prospective dancer is taken by force to be initiated. The intended result of initiation is a rebirth into native teaching and tradition, and death to the old diseased self.

A Cowichan elder, who agreed to an exclusive Leader interview, provided he remained anonymous, defended the rite. He said that there have been concerted attacks in the last few years by certain fundamentalist Christian groups, whose intention is to discredit the spirituality of the native people for the purpose of proselytizing, and in the process undermine Indian culture.

He told the Leader: "The same kind of people who tried to destroy the Indian ways years ago are trying to do it again. But this time they won't be able to do it because we are a lot wiser now. We know the White Man's lies now, not like then. Our spiritual path is sacred, and we won't have outsiders coming in and telling us we can do this, but we can't do that."

In the local Christian community there are strong views on the subject. Tom Pollard, former pastor of Duncan Christian Fellowship, condemns the violence employed by the ritualists, and denounces the spiritual validity of the initiation, saying that rather than being beneficial to the participants, it is harmful, and overall has been devastating to the Cowichan people: "They think they are contacting good spirits that will help them in their lives, but from a Biblical standpoint, the spirits are actually demons whose goal is to ruin their lives. That's the evil in their culture that keeps them in bondage."

Tom didn't mince words. Sounded foolish though. He hated even to print it. But Tom had the Bible to back him up. Probably a matter of interpretation. They could make the Book say anything they wanted to. But Tom said it, so why not print it? Besides, Jesse had witnessed that strange man in Tom's Center who had changed his faces. The newspaper was only supposed to be a medium for objective reporting. So who was he to pass judgment on Tom's beliefs?

The Cowichan elder, when asked about the deaths that have occurred locally during the initiations, said: "See, you want to know why things happen. How can you really know that? Sometimes there are things that happen, and there are no explanations. You need explanations. We don't. And it's always the ones who need the explanations who are the ones who don't have any right knowing. They only want to get nosy and put the blame on someone. Make it somebody's fault. They need to make it neat and tidy by making a law against it and catching the guilty ones. And that way, if they have laws against dying, they think it will be harder for death to happen to them." Old Amos made sense. It was good to have contacts, to have trust built up over the years. The sign of a professional.

The Cowichan elder refused to discuss the methods used in the initiation rites, but anthropologists, who have managed to penetrate the secrecy surrounding the ceremonials, commonly describe basic techniques that are used to facilitate the initiation. The methods used are at the root of the controversy.

University of Victoria anthropologist and authority on West Coast Indian culture, Robert Bell, in an exclusive Leader interview, described the ritual: "To reach a state in which he can perform his dance the initiate must achieve altered states of consciousness - usually accompanied initially by a loss of consciousness. Sense deprivation and stimulation are used by the ritualists to accomplish this goal. During the four or five-day initiation rite the prospective dancer is routinely beaten with deer-hoof rattles; thrown into ice-cold water; forced to run for long periods; deprived of sleep, food and water; guarded in seclusion except when required to engage in physical exertion; and suffocated, usually by having his or her head submerged in water." Jesse imagined what it would be like to take the cure for his booze habit the Coast Salish way. The rattles sounded painful, not to mention having no food and minimal drinking water, and being kept under guard, and chased through the bush, and thrown into the freezing river in winter, and having your head submerged until you were unconscious, oblivious to what you needed more of, air or water. There was no doubt you would sing and dance if you survived that. As for breaking his own alcohol habit, he preferred marriage.

Bell maintains, "These methods are intended solely to achieve the result of spiritual rebirth and the releasing of the dance and song, and need to be understood in that context. We must resist condemning the supernatural aspects of native spirituality, as is our habit, since our spiritual senses have been stultified by our western rational mind-set." Bell wasn't long for this world, using words like *stultified* and *mind-set*. Probably had been known to say *assuaged* too. Had he ever said *parameters* though, that was the question? Jesse was proud to have left university when he did. Academia spun elite cocoons. You might admire the intricate spinning up there, but the moth was never to burst forth. No, there would be no Masters degree for him, let alone a PhD. He could have gone back, like Becky did, but she was more suited to that sterile environment. Leave him to his lowly editor's job. And she did. Academicians were too clean anyway.

Forget Bell, forget Becky. The feature's the thing.

But the record shows there have been those rare instances when the rite has proved fatal. However, there have been no prosecutions. The so-called Potlatch Law, passed in 1884, which outlawed the potlatch and also suppressed the right to perform the winter ceremonials, was repealed in 1951, and their inherent right to practice their traditional rituals was returned to them. But even if the Potlatch Law were still on the books, unwilling participants—or in the event of a fatality, their relatives—would be reluctant to prosecute their elders. This means that charges are not laid, and although the deaths are investigated by the RCMP, the cause of death is usually listed as accidental, the fatality attributed to the hazards of tribal initiation rites." Hmm. The piece was a bit chatty, but so what? Nobody around here paid any attention to style. Forget awards. Do the job. Get paid.

Pollard, who until recently operated the now defunct Freedom Center, maintains, "People here in the Cowichan Valley don't care about the victims. And the RCMP can't do anything unless there is a complaint. The School Board doesn't protect the Indian children either, even when they are absent from class for months at a time during the dance season. The Longhouse takes precedence in the children's lives. Our education system does nothing. The children often fall behind or drop out. If it weren't for the spirit dancing, a lot more Indian kids would have a chance in school. You would think that as a community we would find a way to prevent this abuse. And the government seems to be too concerned about the politics of the natives' land claims to do anything about it." Kind of long and wordy, but he made a few good points. Leave it all in. Lots of ads this week, lots of space to fill.

An opposing clerical view is held by Duncan United Church

minister Lawrence Bennett, who was once invited to participate in the rite himself: "I don't see Christianity and native spirit dancing as opposed. Each in its own way involves a rebirth. And I certainly don't agree with those who say that through it you become possessed by demons. I certainly cherish my experience of initiation, and though it was twenty years ago, when I was younger and hardier, I would still do it again today. It gave me a deeper appreciation of nature's forces and the oneness of all God's creation, especially the affinity of all His creatures." Perfect. The Christians never could agree.

Jesse was debating whether to include the ambivalent quote he got from Social Services, when there was a knock on the door, and Tom, head bowed, came into the office. His pale face looked even thinner than usual. Then Jesse had the image flash in his mind of Ruby in the hospital, that last time, when he saw her there alive.

"Tom? What is it? Sit down, Tom? What is it?"

Tom sat in the chair and stared at the floor.

"I just came from the hospital," Tom said.

"I'm sorry, Tom...."

"He's dead."

"He's dead? Don't you mean she, I mean who's he?"

"It's Will. He's dead. He died. They killed him. I just came from the hospital. He's dead."

Tom looked to Jesse for support, but Jesse turned and stared at his flashing cursor, not knowing what to say. He waited a moment and then asked, "What was the cause of death, did they tell you?"

Tom groaned and clutched the arms of the chair.

"No, they didn't," he said. "But you have to find out."

Jesse had no real idea of who Will was, or had been, but the feature, the one he had been enjoying writing for the hell of it, would be front page news now.

"Now, take it easy, Tom, calm down."

"How could they do it?" Tom said.

He looked up at the florescent lights and clenched his teeth.

"I mean, why?" Tom said. "Can you tell me why? It's pointless, isn't it? That's the answer, it's pointless. You have to find out what happened. You promised a story, remember? Write it all, the whole thing. You've still got that interview I gave you, haven't you?"

"Yes, I've got it, just take it easy. I'll do the story. As a matter of fact, I've just been working on it. His death will be front page news, and I'll also publish the feature article. Does that satisfy you?"

Jesse's decision to write a front page story wasn't enough to satisfy Tom anymore. It just wasn't enough. Tom felt his anger draining into despair. He was desperate, and he was numb.

"What's the use?" Tom said. "A story in The Cowichan Leader won't do much, will it, especially if it's true that most of the town doesn't care if the Indians kill each other?"

Tom knew that whether it was true or not, nobody cared enough to do anything about Will's death. But what was that, what was that he was just thinking? Was his mind beginning to fail? Of course there was nothing to be done about Will's death now. Nothing. Will Joseph, died in a pagan ritual a few hundred yards from the courthouse, in 1991, in the middle of scientific, rational, western civilization. And there was nothing that anyone could have done about it.

"Still, it's got to stop," Tom said. "Someone's got to stop it."

But he knew it was hopeless. Will was dead and Ruby was dying, and why shouldn't he take the blame himself? Why blame anyone else? But at the same time he knew he couldn't take the blame for death. He couldn't stop it. He couldn't stop death. He couldn't stop the spirit dancing any more than he could stop cancer cells from spreading.

Jesse said, "From what I've learned, nobody is going to stop it unless the Cowichan people decide to put an end to it themselves."

Tom looked at Jesse, nodded his head, and said, "So you know that too. Yes, that's right. I believe that's right. When I was driving down here from the hospital, I began to realize that they had to be the ones to stop it. That's the only way it could stop. And do you know why?"

"Yes, I think so. It's obvious from the facts. But I'm sure you know something I don't, so let's hear it."

"The truth is that there can only be a spiritual solution to a spiritual problem. We can't stop them by passing a law. We are the ones who have broken a higher law. We don't have any right to tell them what to do. Look at us. We are the ones who have sinned against them. We stole their souls."

"I wouldn't know about their souls," Jesse said. "But we stole just about everything else."

Tom stared again at the dark brown linoleum floor.

He said, "I'm sorry I accused you before of not doing your job, there was nothing you could have done about it. But grabbing Will was too much. He was all that was left of the Center."

An image of the Center formed in Tom's mind. He could see it again. There was the bulldozer, breaking the walls down. And there he was, watching. He had driven by that day, the day they converted the Center to rubble.

Jesse dismissed Tom's selfish appraisal of Will's life, since he knew that Will had meant more to Tom than simply the Center's only legacy.

Jesse said, "Don't forget, you're still here. But like I said, I'll report the story, and I'll do the feature. As for spiritual answers, I don't deal in them around here. I've been doing this job long enough to know that what I write in The Cowichan Leader won't change the world. I simply fill in the spaces left among the ads."

Jesse leaned his elbows on the desk.

"How's Ruby?" he said.

Tom sighed and remembered her sitting in her white chair, tears in her eyes, telling him about her meeting with Will in the coffee shop.

"Ruby's about the same. At least that's what her doctor says, but I think she's a little better. We're praying for healing every day. And we talk now. And we've started playing chess the last few days too. Imagine, she enjoys playing chess. She beats me, despite the Demerol. It's funny what you can learn about a person, even after so many years."

"I suppose. I haven't really known anybody that long. Anyway, I'm sorry about Will. But I'm sure you did a fine job to get him as far as you did."

"I hope so. But wait a minute, yes, that's right. He's there, isn't he. Of course he is. That's right. Thanks, Jesse."

"I didn't mean...."

Tom felt the burden beginning to lift. Will had only gone home. Why had he forgotten that crucial fact? Will was there with that other son, the one he never knew. But there was no reason that Ruby had to go.

"Yes, I know he's there," Tom said.

"Well then, you have more consolation than most of us."

"What about you?"

"You never miss an opportunity, do you?" Jesse said.

"No, I guess not. Come over and visit us, if you like, any time. Bring Isabel. You know, we can talk, or we can play Trivial Pursuit, the four of us."

"Trivial Pursuit? Yes, I'll see. I mean, I'll talk to Isabel about it."

"Sure, fine," Tom said. "I've got to go. I've got to get home and see how Ruby's doing. I've left her alone too long."

"Like I said, I'm sorry about Will, and give Ruby my regards, would you?"

"Sure," Tom said, rushing toward the door. "But don't worry," he said turning, "you'll see Ruby again, and she'll be healthy too. I can't lose her. I'm sure God will let me keep her here. Why wouldn't He? I can't lose everything. He just can't let her die."

Jesse watched through the window as a wild-eyed Tom drove away in his green Volvo. And just why wouldn't God let her die, he asked his cursor? It seemed to him that God was far from this earth when it came to such common events as dying. Was it possible to have enough faith to keep God around when one's own extinction loomed? He would have to explore that concept sometime. You needed to cover all the bases, just in case. But how was he supposed to have faith? Where had God been when dear grandfather had abused little boy Jesse? Nowhere to be found. But faith or no faith, Ruby had terminal cancer, end of story. There was nothing more to be done. Life was temporary, there was no question about it. Too bad about the young Indian, but he had taken his chances rejecting his own people. A fatal mistake. He was executed by demons, according to Tom. But why continue thinking about death? There was no sense dwelling on the inevitable. Forget it. You had to get the most out of life while you could. That was the secret. Stay positive. For him, of course, there was Isabel, ready at the altar. A life changing event. She wasn't in the office today, had phoned in sick. He would have called but what if the mother had answered? He didn't want to talk to her. Right now he needed to concentrate. His cursor was beckoning, and there were questions to be asked. But how far would he get with the RCMP? Not very. And the Cowichans themselves weren't going to talk. And the star witness was dead. But he would go through the motions anyway. That was his job.

But what was that, out the window? Mrs. Long, across the street, gliding around the corner, with wheels on that walker of hers. And at her age too. God bless her. There was hope for the rest of us, Jesse thought, if she could step up to a new and improved model at her age. But wasn't she in danger of losing control? A potential runaway, a hazard to pedestrians, not to mention the motoring public? She had better avoid inclines. No, hold on, she had brakes, handbrakes. Marvelous. Yes, God bless Mrs. Long, the dear old bat. And yes, of course, there was hope for the rest of us. There was even hope for him.

CHAPTER THIRTY-ONE

Tom stood in the graveyard on the hillside beside the Native Catholic Church. The late morning sun had fought off the clouds and was shining on Will's grave. The funeral Mass held in the sanctuary had been dark and heavy, the people in deep sorrow. Tom knew that the traditional native Mask Dance had been performed earlier in the morning before the Mass, but that ritual was off limits to the public. Now the coffin was in its final resting place, and the priest was reciting the traditional words, *earth to earth, ashes to ashes, dust to dust*.

The priest next began to pray for those in attendance, the relatives and friends Will was leaving behind. Tom, with his head bowed and eyes closed, sensed that the people were staring at him. He tried to catch them at it, but when he looked up they would be looking down again. Tom wasn't wanted here. He was an outsider. Will's father Doug wasn't as reluctant as the others to be caught staring. Doug had made himself perfectly clear when Tom had called to ask him about funeral arrangements, and to offer his help. Doug said he didn't want Tom or his church to have anything to do with his son's funeral. Will's burial rites were going to be done in the traditional way, and then they would have a Mass for him, the way his mother would have wanted, and then he would be buried in the Catholic graveyard. Tom had considered being a coward and not coming, but he knew he had to be here no matter how much he was despised by Will's people. He owed it to Will, and he knew that God wanted him here. So here he was, his head bowed, listening to the priest conclude his prayers for those who had gathered to mourn.

There was silence for a few moments and then the

procession began to file by and throw dirt onto the coffin. Tom knew better than to try to join in the ritual. He didn't need any more trouble. Will's father was the last one in line. Doug paused, looked up at the sky, clenched his jaw, looked down at the coffin where his son's body lay, and then he let his handful of earth drop into the grave. He staggered as he turned to go over to talk to the priest. They shook hands, and then he said a few words to some of the elders, and then he came toward Tom. He looked like he had something to say. He stopped a few feet away and pointed his finger at him.

"You think you know, don't you?" he said. Doug's words were controlled, subdued, and intended for Tom's ears only. "…you think you know the way it's supposed to be. You think that if we, the pagan Indians, would just see it all your way, then there would be peace here in this valley. But it's never going to be that way. You think that you know the Creator and that we don't. You think a lot of things, and most of them aren't good for you or anybody else. Will's dead, and you think we are the ones who killed him. You think our Indian ways are responsible for his death. But you might want to take a look at your own ways and why you came here in the first place, and then decide if you just might be the one who put my son in that coffin."

Tom had nothing to say. He had nothing to offer the grieving father in front of him. He might have said that Will was in a much better place now, but that was too trite for words. He might have said that Jesus is the Creator, but what good would that have done? There was no sense in standing up to him and being a bold witness to the faith and telling him that the way to salvation was through Jesus Christ, and that if he didn't know Jesus then he didn't know the Creator either. But what good would that have done? Besides, Tom was feeling a little weak in the knees right now.

Receiving no response from Tom and wanting none, Doug brushed by him. He took a few steps, and then he stopped and turned around again.

"One more thing," Doug said, his eyes filling with tears now. "You might not understand it, but I'm proud of my boy. He had more guts than you'll ever have."

His message delivered, Doug stomped down the hill to his car.

Tom did understand. Will was a son to be proud of, and Tom knew he had played a part in his death. But was there anything else he could have done? He and Doug at least had that in common. There was nothing else either of them could have done. Or was there? Their beliefs had collided in Will, and that collision had caused too much pain for Will to survive. No, it was impossible for Will to have survived. Then Tom began to weep for Doug and for himself and for the loss of Will, and then he could feel an ache rising from deep within, and he fell to his knees, holding his stomach and groaning for those in the Cowichan Valley who were lost and suffering and didn't know where to turn to find relief for the pain. But then he realized that he wasn't the source of the ache; it wasn't his heart that was breaking. He was feeling God's heart. And in his distress he knew that what he was experiencing was only a brief infinitesimal hint of God's incredible love for those he created. Then the words began to come together in Tom's mind, and in a hushed firm voice he released them toward heaven.

"Forgive me, Jesus, for my failure to represent you...for standing in the way...and not revealing to the people your loving heart for them. I know now I can't do it...only you can. Please forgive me, Lord...and I ask you to fill me now with your love, so that I might minister your heart to those you lead me to in this life...one person at a time."

Tom ended his prayer, the ache having left as suddenly as it came. He stood and wiped his face on his sleeve, took one final look at Will's grave and then followed the last few dispersing mourners down the hill.

The wind had begun to blow in light gusts, and in defiance of the sun, a few stray clouds began to shower down their rain. In the north, toward the mountains, half a rainbow formed.

CHAPTER THIRTY-TWO

Tom stood on the Rowing Club porch in the soft twilight, the pink and blue hues of the August sky blending with the ocean. The warm humid air was paralyzed and forced to swallow the acrid smoke rising from the Maple Bay Inn alumni. They had returned twenty years after the crime to search for one another among the crowd of middle-aged bodies. He knew the reunion would be remembered as a heavy trip, a far-out time that was had by all. No matter how the event might unfold, its reviews had already been written in their minds. But as for him, he felt as straight as straight could be, so straight that he decided instead to feel superior, in order to compensate for his alienation from the group.

He turned his back on Maple Bay and returned to join the main party in the rented reception room, smiling his way through the wisps of blue and finding an opening at the crowded bar. He ordered another ginger ale and looked around at his fellow Maple Bay Inn graduates. A few of the more forward thinking revelers had arrived well-primed for the commemoration. Most of the rest were trying to catch up, knocking back the reduced-rate drinks as fast as they could. Tom figured they were hoping the alcohol would lessen their anxiety and jog memories of their youth. Another popular anesthetic was being administered in a discreet corner, where newly-discovered old friends were lighting up in remembrance of former times and passing a joint around, heads in turn toking and the other heads checking for approaching danger, like hyenas sharing a carcass, their sixties paranoia intact after all these years.

Too bad about the Inn burning down back in '77. He'd heard that said a few times, but he wondered how many of those present had ever been in the place and how many had just come for tonight's party? It was hard to tell. And why was he here, and how many of his former peers knew what he did for a living? He sensed that the word had gotten around, because a few former acquaintances managed to muster a quizzical stare for old times' sake, in harmony with the good-natured mood of the evening. In normal circumstances the typical response to his occupation from the stoned multitude was silent scorn.

Tom moved away from the bar with his drink and found a corner. He stood smiling, just one of the crowd. He saw the lone Indian, Sam Williams, conversing with Bert Landry, the local hardware store owner, formerly a Maple Bay Inn speed-freak, who straightened up in time to inherit the family business. His former passion was to drop Acid and play air guitar, impersonating Jimmy Hendricks. The only hint of Bert's rebellious past was the part running straight down the middle of his short, feathery, canary hair. Sam and Bert seemed an odd couple standing there. Sam had never been impressed with the middle-class establishment, which Bert now represented. A question occurred to Tom now, one that he'd never given much thought to back then. Why had Sam been the only Cowichan native to frequent the Maple Bay Bar? Racism wasn't an issue among the local peace-love-dove hippies then. Or was it? He considered giving Sam his regards, but then the image of Will appeared in his mind, and he decided he had no desire to share reminiscences right now. Will's death had been ruled accidental. That's what the coroner's report said. But that ruling was only relevant in the natural realm. There was another realm, the most important one. In that realm, the spiritual one, a seed had been planted, a seed of martyrdom. Because of Will's sacrifice, there would be a time of reaping among the native people in the Cowichan

Valley. But Tom wasn't going to stay around and be one of the reapers. He'd suffered enough here, and besides, he had a destiny to fulfill on the mission field. Out of the frying pan and into the fire.

The aroma of steak wafted through the door from the barbecue pit outside. They would be eating together, too. And why not? Why not enjoy the time? But there was something else, something missing. What was it? What was it that he had come for? It wasn't to preach the gospel. He knew that for sure, unless of course someone brought the subject up, but in this crowd that wasn't likely. He made his way outside where the anti-bug torches were already lit and heaps of steak and chicken were accumulating on racks beside the barbeque pit. Standing in relief against the muggy summer dusk were clustered animated bodies, conversing, nudging, sipping and grinning. Why had he come? What was it he was searching for here? There had to be something.

He wandered past the partying heads and onto the hard dirt path that led down to the ocean. Maybe he would remember what he was looking for there. He descended to the beach and walked along the shore until he found a place where he'd been many times before. He knelt down in the sand, and then he sat, leaning back against a bleached log. And he remembered. There they were, the two of them, together, walking along the beach at night, and wading into the phosphorescent ocean and laughing, and then they…. No, there was no sense going any further with that. He scooped a handful of sand and pebbles and threw them into the dark water, their spraying entry flashing back at his memory. Why had he come? There had to be a reason. And then he saw another image, this one of himself back then, primed with stimulants, ready for action, and confident. And then he knew why he had come. He was searching for his youth. That was it. But young Tom hadn't come to the reunion. And he knew that none of the others had their young selves show up either, no matter how hard they tried to resurrect their vibrant, young lives. He felt sorry for how most of them had ended up, and for himself. No, his youth hadn't come to the reunion. And Ruby hadn't come either. But he was here. And then he realized that instead of trying to show God's love for his peers, he had fallen again into his old habit of judging others. Who gave him the right to do that? Who was he to measure the success or failure of others? Besides, success in the world meant nothing to him now. To be approved in God's eyes was the only thing that mattered. His ministry in the Cowichan Valley was a failure in the world's eyes, but the seed of Will's martyrdom had been planted, and some day there would be a harvest. Of course that meant God would have to intervene to rescue His church. If He didn't, the Cowichan Valley church was sunk. And it was the same for the rest of the church in North America. If He didn't intervene, they were all sunk. But then if God were to come in power the way He did in the first century, then the people of God would be reborn and once again the church would be the alternative to the world's system. What a shock to the system that would be. Then the truth would be spoken, and persecution and sacrifice and martyrdom would be in fashion again. God's power had to be released through His church, or all was lost.

But whatever the outcome might be in affluent North America, he would have a new start now, far from here, far from this place. It would have been a different reunion if only Ruby had been able to come. But why think about that? Oh, sure, he wasn't fooling himself. He really did know. He did. Down deep he knew. He knew she couldn't come. It was impossible for her to come. And no matter how hard he hoped for her to come, she would never come again, and appear there, in white, black hair shining, the gray highlights stunning once more. He could almost see her, walking barefoot in the sand, coming toward him, his bride coming to the reunion. But she couldn't come. He knew the only way for them to reunite now was for him to go there. He stared across the water and imagined himself swimming to the mission field. It would be a long swim. Perhaps he would start tonight. He then dismissed the thought as unworthy of a man of the cloth. He couldn't go there to see her yet. He wasn't a coward. The world wasn't that tough. It wasn't his time to go. He wasn't defeated. There was more work to do, and Ruby would be proud of him for carrying on the fight. He could make it. Sure, he could make it. God was going to see him through. He was heading for a new beginning on the mission field.

He looked up at the clear night sky, searching. The moon and stars were shining, but to him they were meaningless. All he could see was darkness. And then choking out in spasms to the calm, dark waters of Maple Bay, those painful words came again, the ones he repeated every night now.

"Please God, why after all these years…after all these years? I still need her. Please, she can't be gone. No, she can't be gone. I need her, please. Oh, God, why now, after all these years?"

CHAPTER THIRTY–THREE

Jesse Thornton, married man, sat upright in front of his screen. A routine editorial. One per week, a simple task for a professional like him. They were less strident these days, the female influence no doubt. And there would be no more investigative features unmasking Indian practices either. He had mellowed. She was delightful, his Isabel. His heart was melting. He was in love. They had a hot honeymoon in Hawaii. Not his first choice. The daughter stayed with grandma. Now he had a mortgage on a three-bedroom split-level. His cholesterol was a trifle high. But he wasn't jogging. Only the odd beer. He was making a big effort to clean up his eating habits. It was the least he could do. He had to live for three now, but not for four. Mother-in-law stayed down on the farm, grinding her teeth. He had stolen her girls, and her free labor. Couldn't be helped. His irresistible charm had spirited Isabel away. Yes, he was a rare person, through no fault of his own.

But mother-in-law did manage frequent visits. Dropping in, she called it, every chance she got. He called it intruding, but he never said that out loud. He knew for the sake of future peace he would have to engage the woman in a heart-to-heart talk soon, though he feared that in any such conversation they would fall one heart short. And the daughter, well, she wasn't unkind, only sullen. She would get over it. And Isabel wasn't exactly taking their side against his, only to the degree necessary to keep the peace. He felt assured of that. And he was certain now she was not an airhead, far from it. He had no worries there.

But he was finding the goodness routine a little hard to

take. There he was, Jesse Thornton, being a good man. There were certain things he knew he wasn't supposed to do now. He had to behave, to be on guard. After all, the daughter was there. It was like knowing there were friends and relatives hiding in the next room, lurking in the dark for the most awkward moment to burst forth and shriek, *Surprise, Happy Birthday.* He had to be careful of what he said. But, oh, dear Isabel. She was worth it, wasn't she?

But now for his editorial. Exhaust emissions. That was a good one. Not as controversial here as on the Mainland, but it was an issue nevertheless. He needed a new angle. Exhaust? That reminded him. A few puffs would help him think. Just one cigarette, what was the harm in that? He coughed into his fist. No. He'd quit for five months now. No sense giving up at this point. Back to the exhaust emissions. His poor old Valiant was gone for good. Now that had been a first-rate polluter. It was sacrificed on the altar of marriage. Salesman Sig had talked him into a family-man's vehicle, a minivan. It was new and clean and lacked character. It needed a few dents and a lot more miles before it would measure up to his old Valiant. But Isabel preferred the van. Much more practical, enough room for everyone. And she was right of course. She had a good head on her shoulders. She knew her mind, and that was a good thing.

He decided the subject of exhaust emissions was too nostalgic. Government corruption was always an option. The real polluters. The pollution of government flowed from the capitol building in the form of.... No, he had to get serious. What about democracy? Now there was a great and noble concept. Democracy had been polluted by greed, the tyranny of the bottom line. No, that was a cliché. He was becoming annoyed at his stuttering keyboard. And the room was too hot, and Isabel would be home right now. The daughter was at grandma's. Lunchtime and Isabel, a wonderful idea. Get cozy this afternoon. But she wasn't as agreeable now, not like on the honeymoon, although at his age that might be in his favor. Yes, he would go home and see. There, the decision was taken.

On his way outside he speculated again on possible futures for a man like himself. He might specialize, become a syndicated columnist. He was no Robert McNeil, but sometimes he was struck by his own words. Jesse Thornton, man-about-town, young wife, an up-and-comer. Was that the expression? No, yes, something like that. A man of integrity. Although, he hadn't pushed too hard to have his feature on the Longhouse go to print. Who needed to read about all that spirit dancing nonsense? Tom and his demons, who needed it? The publisher, when he caught wind of the story, was against it anyway. He suggested to Jesse the best course of action was to leave the subject alone, meaning if Jesse wanted to keep his job he would be wise to forget the whole thing. Meddling publisher. But why make waves? There was no point, there was nothing else to be done. Tom said it himself. The native people themselves were the ones who had to stop it. What could anyone do? Culture wasn't against the law. They could kill each other if they wanted to. Entirely their right. Their inherent right. No, there was no sense stirring the pot. A simple accidental death report on page three. Young man dies in Longhouse. He had the police report to back him up. But poor Tom, with dear Ruby gone. He'd lost everything. He wouldn't marry him and Isabel in the end either, and so something else had to be done. Elder Baker was willing but didn't have a license. Justice of the peace, finally. Tom stayed stubborn to the end, standing on his principles. His Christian conscience intact. But look where principles had gotten him. South America. And his dear Isabel hadn't yet gotten over Tom's decision not to marry them. She felt rejected by him and her church and had lost interest in attending. It was a pity, but sleeping-in on Sundays with Isabel was a welcome result.

Yes, it was lunchtime, and Isabel was at home, and he knew she would be happy when he surprised her. He looked up at that big, bright spotlight shining down on the Cowichan Valley, but more importantly that clown up there was shining it down on him. He jumped into his minivan, started the engine, and wheeled his silver rocket out and around and away toward his Isabel, at home in their split-level just outside of town. Yes, for him, Jesse Thornton, editor of The Cowichan Leader, he was finally a winner, and life would never get any better than it was right now.

From the top of the mountain the view had not changed. The river flowed into the sea, the forest stood guard, the people in the many houses carried on with their lives, and the summer sun warmed the land of *Qu'wut'sun*. There were no banners down below that announced *Racism Simmering Here*. Will Joseph was gone now, a casualty of the battle, and Ruby Pollard was gone too, a victim of the sickness in the earth. Tom Pollard continued on his journey, but now he was lost and alone in his darkest valley. From the top of the mountain it was easy to see that all the people down there lived together in the same place. And when you came down from the mountain and lived with the people for a while you soon knew that the sickness lived on. And so did the questions. Whose land was it? Were forgiveness and healing possible? And where was the Creator in all this? There had to be answers.

The End

ABOUT THE AUTHOR

Rick Dewhurst earned his B.A. in English literature from the University of Victoria, with training in journalism. He worked as a newspaper sports editor before answering the call to start City Gate Church, where he has served as pastor since 1995. Rick enjoys a good game of Nine-ball. His first novel, Bye Bye Bertie, introduced readers to the offbeat PI Joe LaFlam. Rick lives in Duncan, British Columbia, with his wife Jane. They have three adult children.